Swept Away

———

A Novel of Life and Love during the American Civil War

By Tom Molnar

ISBN 978-1-734-35930-5

Apple Valley Press

Chapter One

Short background to the story: two years before

It was a cold and gusty night for April, 1859. Jenny didn't sleep well, up listening to the wind howling through the trees. Eyes closed, she heard her father's voice. "Jenny, you have to get up for school!"

She liked school. Usually she looked forward to going. Especially since her one room school teacher assigned her a seat next to Daniel. Since then, she always looked forward to going.

She quickly got dressed, and looked outside. Snow! Snow in April! Only an inch or so, not enough that everyone would stay home. She made herself breakfast, as she usually did, for her father and brothers were always up and already doing farm chores.

Her father stepped in for a moment to say, "Jenny, dress warm. That wind today will blow right through you if you're not prepared."

She looked up and saw him already going back out the door. "I will, Daddy."

Finished now with her quick breakfast, she waited, peering out the small window at the door. Soon, along came Sarah, her best friend, bending against the wind. Quickly putting on her warm coat and heavy scarf, she walked out.

"What a day!" she said to her, after swinging back the yard gate to join Sarah.

"Yeah. On a day like today, wish we didn't have to go."

They continued together on the snow swept road toward the one room school house. Normally, they had plenty to say to each other, but today they kept their heads down and leaned forward against the wind. By the time they got there, both girls were tired and cold.

Opening the door, they found most of the class already there. They weren't in their seats yet, and everyone was standing around talking about everything, especially the nasty weather. The room was actually hot. Miss Evans had a big fire going in the potbelly stove. She rang the bell, and the students settled into their assigned seats. The younger ones, those five and older, sat on the floor in front.

Jenny too, took her seat on the benches along the back walls where all the older students sat. Daniel sat down next to her, said "Hi," and immediately began talking to Samantha, the girl on his right. Jenny looked at her. She was older by two or three years, and she was always well dressed. She even had a house slave who attended to her hair. No one would say that the girl wasn't attractive.

4

She glanced at Daniel. Full head of dark hair that curled up around his ears, the dark stubble that adorned the side of his face, dark eyes that somehow always surprised her whenever he looked her way, and an infectious smile that most always seemed to her to have a bit of playfulness. Jenny regretted it was Samantha who got most of his attention.

Jenny turned her head around to be able to listen to Miss Evans, who was now addressing the class. As she looked at her, she began to feel dizzy, her breathing was shallow, and her view of the teacher seemed to be fading in and out. The heat of the potbelly stove began to seem oppressive. She closed her eyes, and then she was gone.

She didn't know how long she was out, but when she opened her eyes, it was Daniel whom she saw first. He hovered over her, a look of concern on his face. She heard him tell the others, "Move back, let her breathe." She looked deep into his eyes and smiled weakly up at him.

"Jenny, are you OK?" he asked.

Still lying on the floor, she looked to her right and left and saw Miss Evans and all the students peering down at her. "I guess so," she answered.

"Let me help you up," he said. With his one hand at her back and the other holding her arm, she stood up. Then, she immediately sat down on the bench. Everyone still kept looking at her curiously so she said, "I think I'm going to be alright now."

Miss Evans came, and standing over her, said, "Are you sure, Jenny? I can get someone from nearby to drive you back home."

"Thank you, Miss Evans. I think I'm better now. If I could just have a big drink of cool water."

Daniel was quick to bring the bucket of water and the cup from which all the students drank. "Here, Jenny," he said.

She drank from the cup attached by a thin rope to the handle of the bucket. Then she dipped it in for another drink. Handing it back to Daniel she said to him and to Miss Evans, "Thank you. I feel better already."

School continued that day as usual, and after she ate the lunch she had brought from home, she felt almost as good as ever.

That was two years ago. Since that day, Jenny and Daniel had become friends. She knew he cared about her and was glad that she didn't have any more fainting spells. School was over for them both, but they would meet, sometimes when he was on his way in his horse drawn buggy, or occasionally in town. Oh, she had become good at hiding her true feelings for him. But she could dream. After all, only three things stood in her way. She was seventeen going on eighteen and he was three years older. The American civil war was beginning. Worst of all, someone else was first in his mind. Jenny felt sure he was making the wrong choice. Somehow, she was going to prove it to him. He liked her, she knew that. The thing is, he still thought of her as a girl, and she had become a woman. A woman who would do almost anything to make him hers.

Chapter Two

At last, she was finished with her chores. Her menfolk, her two brothers and her father, were fed. Even their slave Marcus had eaten, and she had cleaned up the dishes. Now she could visit Sarah, her closest friend.

"Going to Sarah's" she yelled to her dad as she unlatched the fence gate. Jenny made a pretty sight as she walked along the road. Hair of a definitely reddish hue, height maybe five foot three, if she stood straight and tall, blue eyes tinged with gray, a wasp waist, and hips that seemed to her a little too wide. Walking the short mile to her house, she rued that she had been eager to take up all the work of her deceased mother. She had fairly pushed out Marcus, their slave. At an early age, she wanted to prove she was capable. Well, she was capable all right, but now she realized it was all just so much work.

She smiled as she walked along the road, keeping out of the wagon ruts. Sarah was so much like her, a year older, both had two brothers. Just one big difference, Sarah had a mom. Not only was it great to have a mother, it was a lot easier.

"Hi, Mrs. Foster," she said after knocking and entering.

"Well, hello, Jenny. I think Sarah's out back watering the garden."

Jenny went through the back door, and immediately waved with a smile to her friend.

Sarah set down the watering can and came up to her. A pretty girl, light brown hair, a cute figure. Jenny liked that she seemed to be almost always in good spirits. "Hi, Jenny. Glad they let you escape for a while. So happy you came over."

"Yeah, wish there was more time. Heard about Anna Marie's wedding. You're going, aren't you?"

The two girls sat down on the two benches, angled on both sides of the back door. "I wouldn't miss it. She's not all that much older than us, and getting married already. I hope you're going too."

Jenny leaned back on the bench. She was already a bit tired from all the work she had done that day. "Yes, I want to go. Just can't stand to wear the same dress. I mean, it's the only good dress I own, but you and everyone else has seen me wearing it at least a hundred times."

"Oh, silly," she answered, reaching forward to pat her knee. "Who cares what you wear. It's you we like, not the dress."

"I'm embarrassed. It's not like we're poor. I'm sure if I had a mother she would understand and probably even make me one. But my dad, I just don't think he gets it."

"I know what you mean. Men are just dense about those things. All they think about is the farm, the animals, and getting what they want, like maybe a new buggy or horse."

8

Jenny looked down, dejected. "You're right," she spoke. "Maybe if I talk to him, he would let me buy some fabric. I could make the dress myself. After all, I make their clothes."

Sarah suddenly looked bright eyed. "I know. Your eighteenth birthday is coming up, right?"

Jenny nodded yes.

"Well, your dad might not have any idea of what to get you. Just tell him to let you buy some pretty cloth for a dress. Surely he would let you do that and then he wouldn't have to wonder what to get you."

"If he remembered at all. Yes, that might work," she said, beginning to smile. She moved next to Sarah and gave her a hug. "Sarah, you have the best ideas!"

"I work at it," she answered with a grin.

There were other things they talked about that evening, before Jenny walked home in darkness. One was what everyone talked about—the breakup of the Union. Already, five southern states had seceded. The talk was, there would be war. What worried both Jenny and Sarah was that both of their older brothers were of fighting age. The chance that they could be killed was already on their minds.

Jenny had a tough life. At least she thought so. Her mother died early and she was left with a father, two older brothers, and a slave. She didn't like the slave, at first. He was a young skinny kid when he came, she remembered. Her father bought him at a good price. The thing is, Marcus had learned cooking from his mother, and his job was to cook their meals and teach her how to do it. Well, she didn't like that at all when she was young. Having to take directions from a Negro. But now, things were different. She was almost eighteen, and did all the cooking now while Marcus helped her father and brothers on the farm.

Daniel was the one who really bothered her. The boy she had a crush on since they met at the one room schoolhouse. The one whose arms she woke up in when she fainted. She should not have fallen for him. After all, he was almost three years older. That was then, at the one room schoolhouse.

They were both finished with school now, and yet he would still make her heart beat faster whenever he was near. What really irritated her was when she would see him passing by on his horse and buggy on his way to court Samantha. He would wave if he saw her. Probably didn't even know, thought Jenny, that he was breaking her heart. She wanted that boy.

She rang the dinner bell, and soon her menfolk would come in. All except Marcus. He knew it was his turn to come in after the others were finished.

"Sure smells good, honey," said her father. Amos was his name, a lean man with graying hair, light stubble on his face and a good natured manner.

"I'm starved," spoke her older brother, Jeb, setting himself down at the table. He was the largest of them, his tawny blonde hair tumbling out his hat, and his light skin already showing some tanning, though it was only April.

Last in was her younger brother, known as "Slim," though his real name was David. Secretly, Jenny liked him the better of the two, though she would never admit it. He listened to her sometimes, like an older brother, though he was only a year and a half her senior.

"Hand me your plate, Daddy."

She filled each of their plates and one for herself and sat down. Her father led grace.

Then the talk began as usual. The talk she was long since tired of hearing. The talk of the North and South, of the slaves, of the abolitionists, of what it means to be white and what it might mean to be black. To her mind, things seemed to be heating up between the North and South, but so far, everything seemed to be speculation. She hurried her meal, left them talking, and walked outside.

Then she saw Daniel, driving his parents' horse and buggy. She thought she knew where he was going. She hailed him with a big wave, hoping he would stop. Moving toward the road, away from the house, she was glad he waited for her.

"Howdy, Jenny," he said, turning to look at her while still holding onto the reins.

"Yeah, hi, Daniel," she spoke, walking quickly to get close to where he waited. She didn't know exactly what to say, she just wanted to see him.

"How have ya been?" she asked, coming up to the side of the buggy. She tried not to gaze too longingly at his trim shape, his kindly eyes and smile. She noted that with his brown waistcoat and white shirt he was more dressed up than usual.

"Fine," he answered. "Guess you know where I'm heading."

"Not sure, Daniel. If it were later, I'd say to Samantha's."

"You guessed it. Her folks are having me over early, for dinner. Think maybe they've accepted me."

"Gosh darn, Daniel. Just about everybody accepts you just fine."

Daniel bent down from his perch on the buggy till his head was only inches from hers. "Well, Jenny, I think this kind of acceptance is special. I'm inclined to one day make Samantha an offer, if you know what I mean."

Jenny's heart sank at his words, though she tried not to show it. "Really! That'd be pretty quick, Daniel. I mean you and she are barely twenty-one."

Daniel looked ahead into the distance, seeming to consider her words. Then, looking right at her again, he said, "Guess that's how love is, Jenny. It just comes over you and you think, 'Let's get on with it.' Someday, you'll know what I mean."

Jenny was glad Daniel stopped to talk with her, but this conversation was dragging her down. She sought to find something easier to talk about. "Would you stay here in the county, Daniel?"

"Sure would. My Pa's got a lot of uncleared land I could work on, and there's some acreage still unclaimed nearby. I got some plans in my head about how I could get it all fixed up and someday maybe even become a bit prosperous."

Jenny smiled as he talked about the future. She knew he always had ideas in his head, and she thought that someday he would be quite successful. She only wished she could be part of his plans.

"Lucky girl," she said, smiling up at him and trying not to show even a trace of the jealously in her heart.

"I hope," he answered. "You know, nothing is signed, sealed and delivered just yet." He seemed ready to move on. Then, a thought came to him. "Are you going to the Anna Marie's wedding, Jenny?"

"I'd like to," she answered, hesitating and deciding not to say more.

"Surely you'll want to be there. I think everyone who was at the school has been invited. With his and her relatives there as well, should be a big to do. You should definitely come."

Jenny looked up at him, still thinking of her lack of a nice dress to wear. Of course, she wouldn't tell him that. "I'll think about it, Daniel."

Daniel looked down at her and said, "I'd be glad to take you to the wedding, Jenny. It's right on my way."

"Jenny smiled back at him, but then had a second thought. "But I thought you would be taking Samantha."

"Sure am. She's my girl, I reckon. But I don't think anyone would mind if I also give you a ride."

"You sure about that?"

"Of course. Why don't we just put it down that I'll pick you up Saturday after next, about four?"

Still thinking about her lack of a nice dress, she answered, "That's real nice of you, Daniel. OK. I'll plan on it."

She backed away as he flipped the reins, and waved to his departing buggy. Turning, she slowly walked back to the house, deep in thought. Thoughts of Samantha and of herself. And, about whatever she was she going to wear for the occasion. She knew Samantha would be decked out. The girl was rich compared to her, and her family owned four slaves. One of them Marcus was seeing late at night. Jenny wondered if Samantha knew about that.

What was she going to wear? She didn't have many clothes. Her everyday things, for summer and for winter, and of course her Sunday go to church clothes. Not having a mother and growing up with her father and two brothers, clothes for a girl seemed like an afterthought for them. She knew how to sew, of course, but needed some nice fabric. But even if she could get some cloth, would she have time to make a dress?

She thought back of how she wanted to be an adult. To take on all the jobs of a woman. She had actually regretted that Marcus was doing them for her. Marcus, the slave, who seemed to know how to do everything. Now, with him working out in the field, she had to do it all.

She walked slowly back to the house. She decided that she would do it. All her chores plus make a dress. She just couldn't stand to be seen in her church dress again. Everyone probably already knew it was her only good one. She decided if she couldn't have another dress she just wouldn't go. She walked resolutely to the porch, knowing she would have to face her dad.

She stood there, thinking, before going in. How could she best ask him what she needed to ask? If he had any sentiments for the nicer things in life when he was young, and her mother was still alive, he seemed to lack them now. The man was matter of fact to a fault, used to dealing mainly with his sons and Marcus. He wasn't mean at all, just might not appreciate how important having a new dress was to a girl. She had to find a way to make him see.

She opened the door and walked inside. There he was, seated in the sitting room, reading a paper. A man who was fairly tall and lanky, with medium length soft brown hair that was now becoming gray. Fortunately, there was no one else there.

"Hi, Daddy."

"Jenny," he said, looking up from his paper. "Was that Daniel in his buggy stopping in front?"

"Yes, Daddy. Seeing me, he stopped to say hello. He's on his way to Samantha's house."

14

"Must like the girl. See him many evenings coming this way."

Jenny hated to say he was "courting" the girl. Instead she said, "Yeah, he's sweet on her."

"Well, she comes from a good family and a boy could do worse."

"Daddy, I need to talk to you about something."

"Talk. I'm listening."

"By the way, did you happen to pick up a letter for me when you went to the post office the other day?"

"Damn. I did. Sorry, honey." He immediately got up from his chair to go to his bedroom. "Here it is. I've been just so disgusted about all the news of the southern states seceding from the Union. It could even be war."

"Thank you, Daddy." She took the unopened letter from him.

"Sit down, Daddy. I need to ask you something."

He sat back down on the rocker, and asked, "Surely, this isn't something I need to be sitting for, is it honey?"

"This letter I'm pretty sure is for a wedding I'm invited to."

"Really? Who? he asked, suddenly interested.

"Anna Marie Simmons."

"Yeah. I remember. She was in school with you, though at least two or three years older."

"Father, I want to go."

"Of course you can, honey."

"But I have nothing to wear."

15

"Darling, you have a very pretty Sunday church dress."

Jenny looked away from her father. She wiped her eyes, trying mightily to suppress a tear from running down her cheek. Turning back to him she said, "Father, everyone has seen me in that dress a thousand times. I need something different." She was ready to tell him what Sarah had said. That it could be a birthday gift.

Her father seemed affected. He had probably noticed that his daughter was close to tears. "Does it mean that much to you, Jenny?"

"Yes, Daddy, it really does. Everyone will be wearing something grand."

"Everyone?" he got up, and put an arm around her. "If memory is correct, you're almost eighteen. Right?"

"Yes, Daddy." Jenny thought to herself, *He really remembered.*

"Well eighteen is an important time for a girl. When a girl surely becomes a woman."

Jenny was liking what her father was saying, except she felt she was already a woman.

"I want you to go out and buy the nicest fabric you want, and make that dress for yourself. Furthermore, we should have a party for you. A kind of coming out party."

"Oh, father," she said, going to him and wrapping her arms around him. "I love you."

Her father hugged her as well. "You know, he said when they parted, a nostalgic look in his eye, "your mother was sixteen when I first noticed her. Of course, we didn't get married till years later. Still, I remember her then. She looked so pretty. . ."

16

"He trailed off, then looked at her. "Wait," he said. He went back into his bedroom, and came back holding a gold piece.

Jenny looked at what he held in his hand as he held it toward her. "Daddy!" she exclaimed. "For me?"

"Yes, darling, all for you. Bout time I gave you something, for all you do. Besides, you're my daughter, my only girl. You go to town and buy the material you've been wanting and with what's left over get anything else you want. I'll have Marcus take you." "Oh, Daddy," she said, standing up on her tiptoes to plant a kiss on his cheek.

"Oh, one other thing. Check at the post office, and be sure to stop and pick up a paper for me while you're there."

She left the sitting room excited. It had been a long time since she had been in town. To see all the shops and stores was exciting. Especially with money in her pocket to spend. Just one thought bothered her. She really would prefer going with someone else besides Marcus. To be driven around by a black man, a slave, was not so uncommon, but she would rather go with a friend. Suddenly, an idea came to her. Sarah. Maybe Sarah would be able to go with her. Surely, if so, her dad would allow it. She knew he didn't want her to take the long trip alone, but with Sarah, maybe it would be all right.

She went back to where her father was still reading in the sitting room. "Daddy," she said, in her sweetest voice. "Would it be alright if instead of Marcus, Sarah and I go into town together?" There, she had said it, and she waited, hoping he would say yes.

"Well, I don't know, Jenny," he said slowly, getting up from his chair. "Not that the roads are dangerous, but if anything should happen to the rig, Marcus would be better able to take care of it."

Jenny was already keen on going with her friend, and she tried to think of what she could tell her father to help him change his mind. "But Daddy, the weather is already getting nice outside, and someone would be coming along sooner or later who could help." Then another idea came to her. "Maybe Sarah's father would let us take theirs. It's almost new, so nothing could go wrong with it." She looked up appealingly into his eyes.

"Oh, Jenny. You have such a way about you when you really want something. Reminds me a little of your mother. If you can go together in their newer one, it will be OK with me. Providing that you leave early enough and be sure to get back before dark."

Jenny stood up tall enough to kiss her father on the cheek and then whirled out of the room, not before saying "Thank you father." She was elated. Now, if only Sarah could go, and, in their new carriage.

Chapter Three

That night, she had that dream again. This time, she was at a party. Daniel was holding her tight, and bending, he kissed her softly on the lips. Eagerly, she rose to her full height, kissing him back. He drew back, looking at her with a question in his eyes. "Yes," she said, looking up into his dark eyes. "I'm the only girl for you."

Jenny roused herself from slumber, aided by the crowing of the rooster. Realizing quickly it was only a dream, she looked forward to the next day. Fortunately, it was Friday. Right after breakfast she walked over to Sarah's house. She told her what her father had said. Sarah really liked the idea of the two of them going into town together. She hoped her father would let her go. She had experience driving many times with her dad, and had made short trips on her own. However, she had never driven quite as far as the town.

While Jenny was still there, she went outside to ask her father, telling him that Jenny would accompany her. Jenny watched from a distance at them talking. Sarah's father turned to look towards her, seemed to think a minute, and said yes.

Now to tell her father they were going. When she did, he told her not to let Sarah pick up anyone along the road, and to be sure to get home before dark. Jenny was so happy; she stood tall and quickly kissed him on the cheek. Her father looked at her and then said, "You be careful, now, Jenny."

The next day, Sarah came by to pick her up. The girls were in high spirits. Though they had both gone into town many times before, it was always in the company of a parent, almost always their fathers. To be able to go on their own, to stop at wherever they wanted was exhilarating.

"Trot, Betsy," said Sarah to the horse, as soon as they were out of sight of their homes. Jenny too enjoyed the speed, until the buggy lurched as they dipped into a rut in the road.

"Not quite so fast, Sarah," said Jenny, putting a hand on her arm. "I would sure hate to wreck this beautiful buggy." "You're right. Didn't see that dip in the road until we were on it. My Pa would have a fit if I damaged his prized possession."

Almost an hour later, they arrived on the outskirts of town. As they passed by, it was interesting to see all the houses spaced rather close together. They saw people out in their yards, working in their gardens, hanging up laundry, and children playing. Those who looked up, they waved to, and were pleased when they waved back to them. It was so wonderful to be out and about on such a glorious spring day.

Pulling into town, they saw all the shops and people. Jenny momentarily remembered what her father had said about staying away from the tavern and the big white house on the corner where there were women of ill repute. But, she was free to do just about everything else. "I want to see it all," she said to Sarah, excitement in her voice.

"Me, too." Sarah guided the buggy toward one of the many hitching posts. She tied Betsy to it, and the two girls joined all the other people on the streets.

Both girls were most interested in Simon's general store, but wanted to save that for last. Jenny looked at the people as they walked. Country sort, like her and Sarah, wearing homespun clothes, men of fashion with their their stovepipe hats, some with full beards and others with curled up mustaches.

They mostly looked at the women. Some were all fancy with full crinolines that swayed as they walked, and attractive cardigans over tightly laced up corsets that gave them the popular narrow waist and full bosom. But most women were like themselves, wearing ordinary clothing with buttons up to the neck, dress cinched at the waist, coming modestly down to the ankles with sleeves tighter at the wrists so that work could be done, and an open jacket or shawl that could be brought together if the weather turned colder. Everyone, even children, wore hats of every imaginable sort. A fashionable hat was a woman's pride and joy, after her long hair, which was usually covered except at home and for special occasions.

Together, they walked down the bustling street, looking at the people and all the shop signs. At the end of the block they saw the church with its white steeple ascending into the sky. Just now, they were passing the barber shop, where through the large window they could see a man lathered up for a shave.

Then, behind them, they heard a fiddler starting up, and immediately he began playing a sprightly song. "Oh, let's be sure to listen to him on our way back," said Jenny. "And, don't let me forget, my dad wants me to bring him a newspaper. He's so interested in all the stuff going on in the country."

21

"I sure hope we don't go to war," answered Sarah. "Look! There's the apothecary shop. Ma sometimes gets medicine from there like when I was sick and Pa took fever. Let's go inside."

The store was empty except for one customer, but from behind the counter spoke a neatly dressed man with vest and white shirt and bow tie. "Hello, girls. Can I help you with something?"

"We're just looking," they both said, almost in unison. They stared at all the bottles, large and small, filled with different herbs, roots, medicines and powders.

"Well, if you're of a mind to part with a bit of money, I've just gotten in some bottles of Smith's Tonic, shipped direct from New York, that cures just about everything. Dyspepsia, indigestion, constipation, headache, eruptions of the skin, and malaria. Not to mention that taking a teaspoon daily enriches the blood and strengthens the muscles. Handy to have a bottle around the house when anyone is ailing."

"No thank you, Mr. Peters," said Jenny. She had seen his name on a placard on the wall. "Got to use my money to buy some nice material for a dress."

"That's just fine, honey. You girls look around as much as you like. We got something here for just about any condition you can imagine. Some can make a complete cure in a matter of days. Others might take a little longer." Turning from them, he addressed his one customer. "Mrs. Flinch, have you settled on which of those you would like? The one in your hand, I must say, is particularly good for rheumatism."

The girls walked out of the store, going right past the tavern, which, judging from the number of horses hitched there, seemed to have plenty of business even at midday. From it came the delicious odor of meat grilling, reminding them that soon they should stop for lunch. Then, they continued on, going past artisans—the blacksmith, cooper, and wagon maker/wheelwright. Not so many folks were there, but Jenny knew if one needed a new pot, horseshoes, or even a new buggy, this was where to find those things.

"That's the big two story white house my dad told me to stay away from," said Jenny, pointing it out.

"Why?" asked Sarah.

"There's bad women there, and men who pay them."

"Oh. Oh, I know what you mean. Let's go back. This part of town is boring. There's a lot more on the other side up a ways. Besides, I like the sound of that fiddler's music."

They passed quickly a boot and shoemaker shop with a small shoe cobbler right next door, and a large vegetable and fruit stand, though this early in the spring not a whole lot was available. With the most exciting part yet ahead, they joined the crowd that had formed listening to the fiddler, who not only played but sang with very good voice.

He had just finished, "My Old Kentucky Home," and people moved to put pennies in his box. "Thank you, thank you," he said, making a bow to the crowd. "What would you lovely folks like to hear next?"

Jenny hardly heard what was requested, for Sarah gave her a quick nudge and whispered, "Look who's here in town today."

Jenny followed her glance toward Rex, the banker's son. He was on the other side of the circle around the fiddler, and unfortunately, he had spotted them.

"Here he comes," whispered Sarah, excitedly.

A city boy, the son of a banker, everyone knew Rex had a way with girls. He liked to give them a ride in his swift, well-outfitted coach. Rich, because of his father, dark, gleaming hair, handsome in the finest made garments, even when wearing ordinary street clothes, and a smile that seemed to light up, especially around nubile young women. Everyone knew of him, and rumors flew that more than one girl had her heart broken. Of course, living outside town, Jenny didn't get all the news about Rex.

Quickly, he circumnavigated the crowd, and appeared at their side. "My pleasure to meet you in town, ladies. What beauty comes from the country. Let it be my honor to show you around."

Rex seemed to speak to them both, but it was Sarah who Jenny knew was attracted to him. She answered. "I don't know, Rex. Wish we had more time, but we need to make some purchases and then head right back."

"Too bad," he answered. "The fiddler, Jake here, is real good. Surely you could stay awhile to listen."

"Of course, we could," said Sarah, looking at Rex and then back at Jenny to make sure it was all right with her.

Jenny noticed that Rex seemed to draw even closer to her friend. The fiddler started up again, and Jenny recognized the song instantly. It was the beautiful "Lorena," a sad love song written a few years before. She listened intently, to the mellow voice of the singer, oblivious to Sarah and Rex.

When he finished she turned to Sarah. "Beautiful."

Sarah was paying more attention to Rex at her side, who was speaking softly to her in words Jenny couldn't make out. She wondered; would her friend be the next one to fall for the youthful Romeo?

People moved forward to put pennies in his hat, and the fiddler began again, another song she knew. It was "De Camp Town Races," such a lively melody. She always loved that one. She and others began joining in, and some, like her, swayed to the music.

The fiddler was good, with a mellow voice. The next song, Jenny also knew well, but she began to think of the time, especially as she still hadn't made her all important purchases. Between songs, Sarah was still talking with Rex. Jenny smiled. The way she was acting, Jenny knew she was taken with him.

"I'm going to the general store, Sarah. You coming?"

"I'll come soon. Want to listen to the music for awhile."

"OK. If I don't find what I want there, I'll go to the fabric store."

She left them, regretting a little that Sarah wasn't coming with her, at least not right away. A girl needed a second opinion when buying material for a dress. Nevertheless, as she walked away, she was excited to be going toward it, especially as she had money. She was going to go to the general store first, as other girls had told her the fabric store was considerably more expensive.

She stepped inside, after waiting a moment for two ladies who were just leaving. Immediately, her nose was accosted by all the heady smells. That of coffee, cooking spices, leather, pickling brine, and of course, people. The store was filled with merchandise from top to bottom, and some things even hung from the ceiling.

A number of people attended to one side of it or the other, but near the big pickle barrel, she was particularly aware of how eight or nine gentlemen were loudly arguing. Toward one side, she saw the post office department, where a man and a lady waited. She would go there later, but now she went directly to where large bolts of fabric, collars, ribbon and other sewing materials took up a fair part of one room.

She stood there, not knowing where to start, and placed her hand on a colorful fabric to feel its texture. Suddenly, she couldn't see. From behind, hands closed over her eyes and remained there, even when she turned her head. Finally, she recognized the laughter.

"Daniel! I know it's you. Unhand me." He did, and she turned to see him smiling at her. She blushed lightly, like she often did when he was near.

"Hi, darling," he said in his oh so charming way. "Fancy meeting you here."

"I could say the same for you, Mr. Daniel Jenkins. You and your shenanigans. You had me in a fright, you know."

"Aw, I was jest playing with you, Jenny. Taint often a feller sees the second prettiest girl in the county standing right in front of him."

Jenny knew who the first prettiest was, but she nevertheless appreciated the compliment. Especially coming from Daniel.

"Are you buying?" he asked, noticing where her hand still rested on a bolt of fabric.

"Yes. Daddy gave me some money and I'm going to make myself a new dress. Hopefully in time for Anna Marie's wedding."

"That's right pretty cloth there, Jenny. I could just see you wearing it."

"You like it?" She pulled on the bolt and held some of it up in front of her.

"Sure do. Think the color sets off your eyes."

She looked up at him and smiled broadly. "Daniel, you say the nicest things."

"When you smile like that, I think you could brighten a dark day."

"Oh, my!"

"You here all by yourself?" he asked.

"No, I'm with Sarah. We came in her father's new buggy. She was staying a bit to hear the man with the guitar singing."

"Good. Glad you didn't come alone. Well, I gotta go. Just came in to get some tobacco for pa and shoes for my horse, Mabel. They should be done with her by now. Say, tell Sarah if she would like to join us to the party, it's no problem. There will be room for me, Samantha, you, and Sarah too."

"I would like that we all go together. I'll tell Sarah. I think she would like both of us going together with you."

Jenny smiled as he left. She fingered the smooth, medium blue fabric and in her mind recalculated how much she would need and the cost per yard. Happily, she realized she would have money left over. Enough, she thought, to buy a contrasting shawl with a loop button for over her shoulders. Sarah! Where was she? Jenny wanted a second opinion.

At last, Sarah came into the store. The smile on her face told Jenny that all had gone well with her and Rex. In fact, she was gushing.

"I like him, Jenny," she said as she came to the cloth department.

"That boy has a history, you know," Jenny answered.

"I know. Jilted girls always tell stories."

"Fair warning, Sarah. If you take up with him, you could be next."

Sarah, looked closely at her, and then looked away into space. Turning back to Jenny, she, said, "Jenny we are the best of friends. Really, I just don't think that is going to happen."

Jenny smiled, hoping for the best. "Take a look at this material, Sarah. I like the color. What do you think of the weave and texture for a nice dress."

Sarah took the material in her hand, looking at it. "Oh yes, that medium blue is fetching. And, I like the weave. Just think it may need something extra to set it off."

"Yes, I thought so too." Jenny left her, and turned the corner to the more expensive fabrics. In her mind's eye she kept the blue, looking for something for contrast. Her eye was attracted to one of pure white wool. She could already imagine how it would set off the dress. "What do you think of this, Sarah? She held it up for her to see.

From twenty feet away, Sarah looked at it. Then she rounded the corner holding the bolts of fabric. "Jenny," she said, "I like it. Love the weave, and it will definitely enhance the blue."

"Plus, for a short jacket, it would offer some warmth. Now, I just have to figure out if I can afford it."

"Are you going to have time to make both the dress and the jacket before the wedding?"

"I hope so," she answered, with a bit of a worried look.

The girls waited in the short line to pay and to have Jenny's goods wrapped. Though she also bought a colorful deep pink ribbon to accent the jacket, she was glad to have some extra money to buy hard candy for her brothers and father. For him, she also got one good-sized piece of chocolate.

After checking for mail, her next stop before heading back was to get a newspaper. They stepped outside, and immediately saw a crowd gathering at the newspaper printing store. In loud voice, the editor's son's strident voice shouted the news. "Rebels attack Fort Sumter. Read all about it. Get your paper while there's still some left."

Jenny took one look at Sarah, said, "hold these," and ran to where the man was collecting money and handing out papers. She pushed to the front, and handing him her money, was pleased to get one of the last papers left. She knew how disappointed her father would be if she returned home without one.

On the long ride home, there was much to talk about. The possibility of a civil war was only one of them. More interesting for Sarah was how she was getting on with Rex. As she talked, Jenny feared she was rapidly becoming infatuated with him. Knowing something of his checkered relationships with girls, Jenny held her tongue, but didn't want her best friend to be hurt. As Sarah finished, she only said, "Sarah, you know there have been a number of girls who have really liked him."

"Oh, I know that, Jenny. I mean a boy like him, what girl wouldn't think he's special? I'm not going to throw myself at him, even though he is both handsome and rich with his father's money. I'm just going to see what happens. But exciting? Yes, I am truly excited. He wants to go to the wedding!"

"Really? Anna Marie's wedding?"

"Yes. He's going to pick me up in his fancy carriage. Won't I be the talk of the event, walking in with him?"

"Oh, Sarah. I just hope you don't fall head over heels and then be disappointed."

"Look who's talking. I know how you like Daniel, and he's already taken. What could be more disappointing? You should find someone else."

Jenny had to admit she had a point. She was so happy to have met him in the store and the fact that he was willing to pick her up to go to the wedding meant something. Still, as much as she liked him, she knew his heart was set on someone else. It hurt, but there was nothing she could do about it. In a way, Sarah was right. She was the one who was being a fool. Yet, there was no one else she would rather have.

* * *

When Sarah dropped her off at home, it was already almost dark. She walked right in, and seeing her father sitting in the drawing room, she immediately handed him the paper and the chocolate candy. He took one look at the headline and said,

"No! No! I can't believe they attacked Fort Sumter!" Jumping up from his chair, he held the paper up saying, "Jenny, do you know what this means?" Jenny was just setting her own purchases on the table and looked up at him. Before she could answer, he told her, "This means war! The federals are not going to give up their fortress without fighting back. This might even lead to a war between the states!"

Her father was talking loudly, and at the sound of his excited voice, both boys came into the sitting room.

"Dad! Dad! What's the matter?" asked Jeb, Jenny's older brother.

He held the paper up, showing the huge headlines spread over the top of the first page. "See that? They are shelling Fort Sumter! This is going to be war, boys!"

"Surely what's happening on the coast of South Carolina isn't going to affect us, is it Dad?"

"I hope not, but we could all get pulled into it. There's a lot of our own representatives that have been thinking of siding with South Carolina, Georgia, Florida and the rest. You boys know what I think of Mr. Lincoln. This might be all he needs to send troops into the South. There's going to trouble, boys. Mark my words."

Jenny listened with alarm to everything her father was saying. Her thoughts went to her brothers, and she needed an answer to one question. "Dad," she broke in. "You surely don't think Jeb and David will have to fight." She looked at them as they turned to her. She loved them both.

"I sure hope not, Jenny. Don't think David would have to, with his bad leg."

Her one question answered, Jenny went to the kitchen where leftovers from the meal awaited her. She ate silently, half listening to her father and brothers who continued to talk about the subject. Finished, with the little that she wanted, she cleaned up a bit in the kitchen, gathered her dressmaking purchases, and went upstairs to her room.

So much had happened on this day, she didn't know if she would be able to sleep. Besides, she still heard her father and brothers talking downstairs. She rued that they could talk for the longest time about something like that. She heard Marcus's name mentioned. Now, they were talking about their slave. Through her closed door, did she catch that one of her brothers was actually worried about him? If so, she could hardly believe it. She had known Marcus since she was nine. Learned to cook mostly from him.

31

They finally stopped talking, and Jenny was able to get to sleep. But not for long. The exciting activities of the day, seeing Daniel, getting her dress fabric, and finally the shelling of Fort Sumter conspired to cause her to awaken. She heard a quiet sound outside. Footsteps. She left her bed, moved the lace curtain and looked out. It was Marcus. Apparently, he was just coming back. Jenny knew where he was coming from. But so late? It made her wonder.

She put on her warm, full length robe, went down the stairs and tiptoed outside. Marcus was just across the small yard. "Marcus," she said in a voice low enough to not be heard inside. "Are you just now coming in?'

"Yes, Miss Jenny," he whispered, using the Miss appellation her father had told him to use now that she was older.

Jenny felt she had no right to ask, but her curiosity was getting the best of her. "What are you doing out so late?"

"Visiting, Miss Jenny."

"That girl. Angela, I believe is her name."

"Yes, Miss Jenny."

"Oh, Marcus, you don't always have to be so formal with me. I mean, at least when my father is not around."

"Yes, Miss Jenny."

Jenny felt she was getting nowhere. She was also beginning to feel that what Marcus was doing with his girlfriend was none of her business. "Hope you had a nice time."

"We did, Jenny. You know I really like her and she likes me back. I can tell you something else if you promise not to tell anyone."

Jenny wondered what it could be that he would tell her. "Yes, I think you know I can keep a secret."

In a soft voice, barely audible, he said. "She's teaching me to read." His hand was on the door of his little one room slave cottage.

"Really? I'm glad. Good night," she said, quietly opening the door to her own house. Walking up the stairs to her room, she thought about Marcus. Already, she had heard talk that if war came the North might try to free the slaves. If it happened, Marcus might be much better off if he knew how to read. Jenny had heard that some slaveholders didn't want their people to learn how to read or write. So much to think about, she realized, as she removed her robe and slipped under the blankets. Too much for one night.

She so liked Daniel. Was she wasting her feelings on a man who couldn't see that it was her whom he should take as a life partner? She thought back to the chance meeting with him at the general store. She couldn't forget what he said: "The second prettiest girl in the county." Jenny cared little of whether she was pretty or not. She just wanted Daniel.

Of course, she was right. She did have a hard time falling asleep.

Chapter Four

The reverberations of the attack on Fort Sumter continued. Both of her brothers and her father were talking about it nonstop. Did it mean war? Jenny didn't know. Fortunately, Anna Marie's wedding and the festivities afterward would go on. Jenny looked forward to it. She hoped fervently that there would be no altercation there. Already, she had seen how some were already committing to the North or the South.

At last, by working late several nights, by the light of two candles, she had successfully made herself a dress. She held it up to her body, seeing her reflection in the small mirror fastened to the wall. The soft blue was beautiful. Setting it down for a moment, she put the pure white wool jacket over her shoulders. She was pleased. The pink ribbons she had added around the neck and at the sleeves pulled everything together.

Tonight, Daniel would come for her. For a time, at least, she would have him to herself, until they arrived at Samantha's house.

Sarah, her best friend, was not coming with Daniel. She was actually going with Rex. A well off city boy, he wasn't really invited. But Jenny knew that he could be counted on to give Anna Marie a nice gift. As Sarah's friend, he would be welcome.

Already, she had finished making dinner. Her father, knowing how much the wedding and dance meant to her, had told Marcus to do the clean up after supper. So now, Jenny was free. She arranged her hair, added some color to her cheeks and lips, and even darkened her eyebrows. Now completely dressed, she looked at herself again in the small mirror. She was satisfied. She walked outside to wait for Daniel.

Somehow, Jenny was nervous, and she paced back and forth in her yard as she waited. She heard the wheels of a carriage coming around the bend in the road, and went to the gate. Someone she didn't know passing by. She went back to pacing in her yard. The sound of another came to her, and again she went to the gate. This time it was him.

He had been coming with some speed, but rapidly slowed his horse as he neared her house.

"Hi, Daniel," she said as he stopped by the fence. She noticed he had the extra board behind the front seat, and he had even added padding

"Wow! Don't you look beautiful!" He jumped down and offered her his hand to help her into the carriage.

He helped her up, and she immediately started to go to the bench behind him.

"No, Jenny. Sit in front with me."

"But isn't Samantha going to sit there with you?"

"Sure, but until then, I'd like to be with you."

"OK. Wow, look at you," she said, snuggling into the seat beside him. "I've never seen you look so dapper, Daniel." She eyed his stylish form fitting pants, his white shirt, tan vest and dark jacket.

"You like the outfit? I was in the store not long ago with Ma and she saw it. Readymade, she thought it would look good on me. Once tailored, it fit well. Seems a bit fancy to me."

"Oh, but I like it, Daniel. I bet Samantha will be impressed."

"Hope so. That's what Ma said too. Otherwise, I wouldn't wear it."

"Trust me. She's going to like it. Or I should say, she's going to like you wearing it."

In the short time that it took to get to Samantha's house, they talked about other things. To Jenny, it wasn't what they talked about at all. It was being next to Daniel, chatting about anything. He was so comfortable to talk to. Too soon, they arrived at her house.

Jenny took the back seat and watched as Daniel hugged Samantha and then helped her up. Samantha noticed not only Daniel's new outfit, but Jenny's new dress as well, complimenting them both. Then she settled in with Daniel. Jenny took in what Samantha was wearing. Her hair exquisitely done with loops bound by a glistening comb in back with a small bouquet of white flowers interwoven into the front. Her dress, a low cut lavender swirl, with puffed short sleeves. The couple talked back and forth, much as Jenny and he had done before. Jenny could only listen, feeling like a third unneeded wheel.

They arrived at Anna Marie's house, and entering through the open gate saw numerous carriages of all kinds parked around the perimeter of her large front yard, their horses tied to the heavy split-rail fence.

Daniel tied his horse to one of the remaining empty spaces, turned to look and waved to two girls behind them in another buggy. Then he assisted both Samantha and Jenny down.

Jenny looked at all the carriages and up at the house. She knew Anna Marie's family was well off, but until now had never seen their house. It was painted a cream color and featured tall columns supporting the spacious porch. Judging by its size, there would be plenty of room for guests. Jenny swallowed. She had never entered such an imposing house.

Daniel was such a gentleman. Arm in arm, he escorted both girls into the house. Jenny stood in awe in the parlor. Such a flurry of activity greeted them, with girls in lovely dresses and men in fine suits moving about seemingly at random. Were they late?

Apparently so, for the minister raised his voice above the crowd. "Ladies and gentlemen. Is there any reason why we cannot now get this young couple wed?"

A bevy of voices yelled out, "No," and various other things, giving their enthusiastic approval of the wedding going forth.

Somehow, the couple and their two bridesmaids and two groomsmen lined up on the far side of the spacious parlor. Jenny was enthralled at Anna Marie's wedding gown. All white, with a gossamer veil, and a flowing train. She had never seen Anna Marie look so lovely or seen, other than in pictures, such a beautiful wedding dress.

She stood entranced as the minister uttered the words of the ceremony, soon coming to the all important exchange of vows. "Do you, Nathaniel John Peters take Anna Marie Simmons to be your wife?"

"I do." He spoke loud and clear while gazing at Anna Marie, such that anyone would know there was no doubt in his mind.

The minister turned to Anna Marie, asking, "Do you, Anna Marie Simmons take Nathaniel John Peters to be your husband."

"I do."

Jenny noticed that she spoke so softly as to barely be heard. The minister looked at her, cocked his head, and said, "What darling? What did you say?"

Anna Marie looked at the minister and then at Nathaniel, and this time, in a loud voice with a big smile said "I do." Nate moved her veil aside with one hand and leaned forward to kiss her.

"Then, I do now pronounce you man and wife."

A hearty cheer arose from the crowd, many of whom, now that the ceremony was over, began dispersing to other less crowded parts of the house.

Jenny went to be with friends she knew from school. She noted that Anna Marie's family's slaves circulated around offering drinks both alcoholic and non as well as delicious looking pastries and other desserts. She accepted a drink of wine, feeling quite grown up, for she had never had more than a taste of what her father and older brothers on rare occasions drank.

The evening passed that way, convivially. Before long, a relative of Anna Marie's brought out his fiddle, and soon dancing ensued. Not long afterwards, Jenny noted there seemed to be a disturbance. The voices of some of the young men were getting louder and louder. Jenny was glad that Daniel was not among them. Finally, Anna Marie's father stepped in and told them that if they were going to be so loud they were going to have to go outside. Eight or nine of them did, but to Jenny it seemed that there they got even louder.

A shot was heard, and for a moment everyone inside hushed. Then expressions of "My God!" and cursing shattered the stillness as most of the remaining men rushed out both the back and front doors to see what was the matter.

Outside, a huddle of men stood over a youth on the ground, and in distance could be heard a horse and buggy rushing away. The men all looked disheveled, and a few had blood on their faces or on their knuckles.

"He just pulled out a gun and shot George," someone said.

"Why?" everyone asked. "Who did it? Why?"

"Is he. . ., is he dead?" asked Anna Marie's father.

"Think so, sir," said Henry, one of the groomsmen.

* * *

Jenny had stayed inside, with the rest of the women. The wedding party broke up almost immediately after the tragic shooting. On leaving, she had a glimpse of George, still lying on the ground. Daniel told them on the way home what happened. There was a heated argument. When the men went outside, it progressed to a fistfight. Jake, one of the smaller men, was getting beat up. He pulled a gun, quickly shooting his main tormentor. Then, almost before anyone realized what happened, he hopped into his buggy and drove off. "Why?" both girls asked Daniel.

"It's the North and South. That's the heart of it. Some think we should secede, and others think we should stay in the Union. It's all about states rights, slavery, and freedom to do what we want to do without interference from the government."

Daniel continued to explain, but Jenny had heard enough. She already knew the arguments, having heard it being bantered about by her brothers and father in their own sitting room. Something was terribly wrong, something she didn't really understand. Already men were fighting about it. The way things were going, she realized it could get much worse.

Daniel escorted Jenny to the door of her house. She whispered her goodbye, and on entering, she found everything to be quiet. She knew her father and brothers had already gone to bed. Walking softly to her room, she lit a candle and sat down on her bed. So much was going on in her mind. The image of George lying on the ground, his shirt oozing blood was almost too much for her to bear. Though not really a friend, she had known him, and knew him to be a decent young man.

She prepared for bed, exchanging her clothes for pajamas, and extinguished the candle. While lying in bed she prayed. For George, for her brothers, and for her country. There being nothing more she could do, she tried to sleep. Finally, it came, but an uneasy sleep, filled with disconcerting dreams.

* * *

Very early in the morning, before first light, there was a light tap on her partially ajar door. In a quiet voice she asked, "Who is it?"

"Jeb."

"Jeb, it's not even light outside. What is it?"

He entered her room. "Jenny, I'm leaving. Want someone in the family to know."

Jenny sat up in bed, rubbing her eyes to make sure it wasn't a dream. "I don't understand, Jeb. Why would you be leaving now?"

"Cause I'm going to fight. Lincoln needs soldiers to put down the rebellion. I'm telling you cause I don't think Dad or David would understand."

Jenny moved over on her bed. "Sit a moment with me, Jeb. You're going to fight against our own state? Against Virginia?"

"Jenny it's important to keep the states united. Don't know about you, but people like Marcus deserve to be free. I mean he works right alongside us and Dad, but he gets nothing out of it. Don't think it's right, Jenny."

She patted his arm and looked into his eyes. "Jeb, if you really have to go, I want you to be careful. Don't get yourself hurt."

"Ah, Jenny," he said, putting his arm around her. "It will be over before you know it. We jest got to show the southern states we're not going to stand for them attacking Fort Sumter and seceding from the Union. President Lincoln has called for men to be ready to fight for only ninety days. I'm going to sign up and do my part."

Jenny always felt small next to her biggest brother. She looked up into his eyes and turning, spontaneously wrapped her arms around him. She felt his arms go around her as well, and then he released her, his finger wiping a tear from her cheek.

"Gotta go. Before Dad wakes up and tries to stop me. I'll send you all a letter as soon as I know where I'll be. Tell Dad and my brother I love them." He rose from her bed, reached out a hand to tousle her hair, and then with a quick turn stepped out of the room.

She stood up, and went to the door. From his horse, he looked back at her and waved. She mouthed the words, "Goodbye" and waved, her hand moving only a little.

Even though it was still early, she knew she couldn't get back to sleep. She was too overwrought. Quietly, she went to the kitchen, started a fire in the stove, and heated up some oatmeal in a saucepan, adding a spoonful of sugar. She didn't look forward to being the one to tell her father that Jeb went to fight for the Union.

He entered the kitchen, rubbing his eyes. Seeing her he said, "Hi, honey. You're up early."

"Yeah. I could hardly sleep after what happened last night."

Her father looked at her, concerned. "What do you mean? Didn't you have a good time?"

Jenny looked at him, hardly knowing what to say. Finally, she blurted it out. "Dad, last night George was shot. He was killed."

"George. George." She could tell her father was recollecting. "You don't mean George Bairstall?"

"Yes, Daddy."

"Oh my God!" Taking a chair and moving it next to her he said, "Tell me what happened, Jenny."

She proceeded to tell him what she knew. He listened intently, and as she told the story, she knew that soon she would also have to tell him about Jeb leaving to join the Union. She didn't know which would shock him more.

As she finished telling about the shooting, her father just kept shaking his head, as if it was something he didn't want to believe. Then he stood up, leaving her to go toward the stove. "Things are going to get worse, Jenny. Mark my words; this is only the beginning."

David entered the kitchen. "Mornin,' Pa, Jenny. Don't often see you up this early," he added, looking at her.

"Mornin'."

"You OK?" he asked.

"Bad scene at the wedding," her father answered for her. Jenny was glad that her father began telling him about what happened last night. She regretted having to talk about it at all. Finishing her cereal, she wanted to leave the kitchen. Already, her father and brother were engaged in a lively conversation about what might happen next. Still needing to tell them about Jeb, she broke in.

"Daddy. David. Jeb left early this morning. He was heading north to join the Union."

They quickly turned around to face her. "What?"

Jenny suddenly had a lot of explaining to do. Both her father and brother asked her so many questions relating to what Jeb said to her. She could see they were vexed, both because he was going to join the Union, and because he could be killed in battle. Finally she told them, "Dad, David, I've told you all I know. I'm sorry he's gone too, but there's nothing anyone can do about it now."

A few days after the terrible wedding night, Jenny and her family got the news that Virginia had voted to secede from the Union. But what everyone noted, was that where they lived, in the western part of Virginia, their delegates had voted against secession. Already, there was talk of the west breaking off from Virginia and forming a second state.

While armies were being formed on both sides, Jenny prayed that somehow fighting could be averted and peace

43

could be restored. She didn't understand the deeply entrenched views that would fuel the war.

She looked forward to seeing Daniel, and without fail tried to be on the lookout for him when he would come by on the way to Samantha's house. As she thought to herself, theirs was a funny relationship. She secretly loved him and he apparently really liked her. But, she was always second best in his thoughts.

She heard his rig coming, and stepping out into the yard, walked closer to the front gate. She lifted a hand in greeting and he pulled on the reins. As he stopped, she swung open the gate and went to him.

"Hi, Jenny," he said, tipping his hat. "Sorry about the other night. Had no idea something like that would happen."

She stood there, one hand on the buggy seat, looking up at him. "Yeah, that was something I will never forget. Not your fault, Daniel. I don't think there was anything you could have done."

"True. I must say, you sure looked sweet in the outfit you made for yourself. I wasn't the only guy who noticed."

Jenny, looked down and away from Daniel. He had a way of saying things that made her heart melt. She was afraid that if she looked directly at him, he would see how much she was enamored of him. Not good, when someone else was first in his mind. Changing the subject, she told him about her older brother.

"Really, he joined the Union forces?"

"Yeah, slipped out real early. I think he knew Pa would be mad."

"This part of Virginia, a man could go either way. I'm hoping the whole thing blows over. Lincoln only called for a three month enlistment of 75,000 troops. Seems even the president doesn't think it will last very long."

"I hope so, Daniel. I'm worried about my brother. Hope he doesn't have to fight."

Daniel reached for her hand, squeezed it, and bending toward her said, "I hope not, Jenny."

"I'm glad you're not one of those rushing to enlist. If no one joined there wouldn't be any fighting."

Daniel smiled at her. "Jenny, you say the darndest things. Not that it isn't true. I better be going on to Samantha's. Glad I was able to see you, Jenny." He tipped his hat in her direction, flipped the reins and was gone. Jenny watched him drive off till he rounded the bend and disappeared from sight. She sighed, then went back toward the house.

Chapter Five

Weeks passed. It was Saturday evening. Chores done, supper made and pans and dishes cleaned up. Removing her apron and brushing her hair, Jenny looked forward to going to Sarah's house. There, they had fun. Saying goodbye to her Pa, she slipped out the front gate, and pranced merrily down the lane the short distance to her house.

Arriving quickly, she noticed a fancy carriage parked in front, and wondered who their company might be. She hoped she wouldn't be intruding. Coming up to the door, she knocked two times and went in without waiting to be let in. She was a regular there, so there was no need to be formal about it.

When she entered, she immediately saw who was visiting. Rex, the banker's son.

"Hi Jenny," said Sarah. Mr. and Mrs. Chandler, Sarah's parents, nodded their greeting to her as well. "You're just in time. Rex brought his fiddle, and we're going to sing along with him."

"Yes, join us, Jenny," said her mother. "You have such a lovely voice."

Jenny looked at Rex, who with his fiddle in one hand and his bow in the other was ready to play. He was impeccably dressed, dark, wavy hair, with a white, ruffled shirt, partially covered by a gray vest, dark pants, and shiny low cut shoes. He smiled at her, and asked them all, "Are we ready?"

Rex began playing, a song they all knew. As he played, he sang, in a deeper voice than Jenny had expected, and the four of them joined in.

(Stephen Foster song, 1848)

"I come from Alabama with my Banjo on my knee—

I'm goin' to Louisiana my true love for to see.

It rained all night the day I left, the weather it was dry;

The sun so hot I froze to death—Susanna don't you cry.

Chorus:

Oh! Susanna, do not cry for me;

I come from Alabama, with my banjo on my knee.

I had a dream the other night, when everything was still;

I thought I saw Susanna dear, a comin' down the hill.

The buckwheat cake was in her mouth, a tear was in her eye,

I says, "I've coming from the South"-Susanna don't you cry.

Chorus:

Oh! Susanna, do not cry for me;

I come from Alabama, with my Banjo on my knee."

They all enjoyed the music, and when they had finished the song, both Jenny and Sarah clapped. Rex was an excellent fiddler.

Jenny immediately had a song she would love Rex to play, but as she was a guest, she waited for someone in the family to make a suggestion. She was glad when Sarah asked, "Rex, do you know Jeannie? Jeannie with the light brown hair?"

"Sure do," he answered.

Jenny smiled. It was one of her favorite songs, and she knew every word by heart. A sad song, really. Rex brought the bow up to his fiddle, ready to start.

(Stephen Foster, 1854)

"I dream of Jeannie with the light brown hair

Borne, like a vapor, on the summer air

I see her tripping where the bright streams play

Happy as the daisies that dance on her way.

Many were the wild notes her merry voice would pour

Many were the blithe birds that warbled them o'er

Oh! I dream of Jeannie with the light brown hair

Floating like a vapor, on the soft, summer air.

I long for Jeannie with the day dawn smile

Radiant in gladness, warm with winning guile

I hear her melodies, like joys gone by

Sighing round my heart o'er the fond hopes that die.

Sighing like the night wind and sobbing like the rain

Wailing for the lost one that comes not again

Oh! I long for Jeannie and my heart bows low

Never more to find her where the bright waters flow."

Jenny wiped a tear from her eye. Somehow, the song was her own.

A loud explosion sounded in the distance. Then, another, and another.

"What could that be?" asked Jenny.

"It's war, that's what it is!" said Sarah's father.

"No! No! Pray it isn't so," said her mother.

Rex stood with his fiddle in one hand and the bow in the other. He turned to them saying, "I've got to rush back. Those cannon sound like they're coming from near town." He said a quick goodbye to them and rushed out to his carriage, and climbed aboard. With a flurry of hoof beats, he was soon out of sight.

After that, the get-together immediately broke up. Neither Jenny nor Rex thought of staying for the aromatic store bought tea and the sugary sweet teacakes. Jenny walked quickly back to her house, thinking all the while what war might mean for her and her family.

On opening the door, she found her father and brother, both of them standing, talking loudly.

"It's the Federals," said her brother. "They're taking it to us. Their overrunning this part of Virginia before we even have a chance to fight back."

"That's the problem," said her father. "People here don't know which way to go, to the North or South, and they're sending troops in to take away our freedom to choose."

"They really want to control the railroad, the Baltimore and Ohio. Then, they want to control us."

They stopped for a moment, noticing Jenny.

"You heard it, didn't you Jenny? The cannon firing in the distance?"

Jenny cocked her head. "Who wouldn't?"

"I just hope they don't come this way," said her brother.

Jenny's father put a hand on her brother's arm. "Just don't do anything foolish, son, like point a rifle at them. We have nothing they want here, unless they get so desperate they start plundering the farm."

"Just stand by and let them do what they want? Dad, I'm not a coward."

Jenny saw her father look at her brother in a surprisingly tender way. "Son, I know you're not a coward. Just don't do anything foolish to get yourself and maybe some others killed."

He stopped for a moment, as if thinking things through. Then he said, "That's probably the best course for all of here in Western Virginia. Think about it son, Jenny. We're practically surrounded by Union states. North of us is Pennsylvania and Maryland, and on the long border northwest we got Ohio. Then, there's Kentucky on our southwest.

"But father," said David, "We're part of Virginia and Richmond is the capital of the confederacy.

"Then where are they? We've heard many reports of Yankees entering our state, but so far no troops of those rebelling against the North. "Why? Cause they've got to come all the way across the mountains. All the Yanks have to do is cross the border."

"I don't like being pushed around by people who don't belong here. Dad, people will die if we don't do something!"

"They're going to die anyway, son. Keep neutral and at least there won't be as many dead in our part of the country. Remember, your brother went to fight for the North."

At those words, Jenny saw her brother close his eyes tightly, shaking his head.

"I know. I can hardly believe it. I get angry every time I think of it."

Jenny broke in. "Dad's right, David. Don't go. You can't go! Not with your bad leg. I know which way you're leaning. Please. Please. I can't stand to think of you fighting your own brother!"

David, whose hands had been clenched, relaxed them and looked at Jenny. Then he went to her and gave her a big brotherly hug.

Jenny felt the warmth of his body and arms, and looking up into his eyes, she said, "Promise?"

He withdrew, shaking his head. "I don't know, Jenny. Right now, I just don't know."

* * *

Jenny stayed close to the farm the next few days. She was afraid her younger brother would leave for the war, just as her older brother had done. Secretly, she hoped he wouldn't be accepted because of his foot. Meanwhile, reports kept coming in the news and even from passing travelers that Union troops were meeting little resistance and were taking over much of western Virginia. So far, she had not seen them.

Sarah had not visited her since that night when they heard the cannons booming. Finished now with the dishes, Jenny put on her bonnet and headed to her house. She wanted to find out more about Sarah and Rex.

"Hi Mrs. Chandler," she said on entering their house after a quick knock on the door.

"Jenny," she said, rising from her knitting to come to her, giving her a silent hug.

Jenny was not used to such warmth on the part of Mrs. Chandler. She looked at her closely, sensing something was amiss. "Are you OK, Mrs. Chandler?"

"No, I am not, Jenny. I am definitely not all right. It's our son, John. He's thinking he is going to join in the fighting. I am so afraid for him."

"David, too. David thinks he should enlist. I keep talking to him, telling him. . ."

"Him too!" she interrupted. "Will we have no young men left, Jenny?"

Jenny could see that Mrs. Chandler was upset. She tried to calm her, reiterating to her that she didn't want her brother to join and would try to talk to him.

"Jenny, you're a sensible girl. You talk to him good. I know young men get things in their heads, but surely he will listen to reason."

Jenny realized that Mrs. Chandler didn't know that her older brother had already joined, on the Union side. She hoped she wouldn't find out. "Where's Sarah?" she quietly asked.

"Out back," she answered, an odd look on her face.

Jenny exited the back door, and saw Sarah in the near field. She waved to her, and Sarah waved for her to come and join her. When she approached, she saw what she was doing. Picking strawberries.

Sarah set down her bucket, stepping up to hug her. "Did mom tell you? I mean about my brother?"

"Yeah. My brother too."

"Really? David?"

"I don't understand it, Sarah. I mean David has always been the gentle one, compared to my Pa and older brother. He's the one I can confide in. And now, he wants to go to war. War is terrible, Sarah. I once read a novel that described the violence and all the killed and wounded soldiers." Jenny began to break up, just talking about the subject. She stopped talking, hung her head, her hands hung uselessly at her sides.

Sarah put an arm around her. "Don't think about it, Jenny. Maybe things will somehow work out. Don't think about the worst that could happen. You will only get yourself depressed."

Jenny lifted her head and looked at her friend. She managed a smile. Finally, she said, "Let me help you with those strawberries."

They worked together, and later, when she left, Jenny went home with a small bucket of them. She looked forward to sharing them with her family in the morning. When she stepped in the front door it was late, and her father and brother had gone to bed.

She awoke the next day to find her menfolk gone, not surprising as they were early risers. She was glad they had seen the berries and had helped themselves to some of them. She made herself some oatmeal for breakfast, putting slices of fresh strawberries on top. After cleaning the dishes, her next job was to feed the chickens and gather eggs. She heard a carriage outside on the road, and was surprised when it stopped at their gate. Looking out, she realized it was Daniel. Quickly pulling off her apron and finding a brush to fluff up her hair, she rushed out.

Daniel had left his buggy. His hand was already opening the gate, and Jenny noted that his walk seemed different, less relaxed. She hoped that nothing was wrong. "Hi!" she said, as she came close to him.

"Jenny," he said, looking mighty serious. "Wanted to tell you I'm going off to fight."

"What?" she uttered.

"Can't take it anymore, Jenny. Those Federals invading our country and taking over everything. Do you know they are already in the next town over?"

"But Daniel," she said, trying to think quickly. "Don't you think this whole thing is going to blow over?"

Now she was standing next to him. She looked into his eyes and said, "Daniel, I'm scared for you. Please don't do it."

Daniel put an arm on her waist, saying, "Jenny, a man's gotta do what's right. I don't care nothin' about the slaves one way or another, but when Yankees invade your land, you have to stand up to them."

Jenny could see that Daniel was determined. She knew further words from her would not sway him. She feared the worst, and with tears in her eyes, she asked, "Is that what you came to tell me, Daniel Jenkins?"

"No need to get formal with me, Jenny. I'll do what I need to do for the South, and then when it's over I'll come back to see you. One thing I would like to ask of you.

She wiped away a tear. "What, Daniel?"

"Sure would love it if the second prettiest girl in the county would be willing to write to me. I'm sure to get lonely away from my folks, you, and Samantha."

There, he said it again. For her, he was number one, but for him, she was number two. She cared little if she was pretty or not. She only wanted to be first with him. "Sure, Daniel," she answered, after taking a deep breath. "I'll write to you. I just want you to be careful. Real careful."

"Thank you, Jenny. He put his arms around her, for a moment holding tight. She closed her eyes, reveling in his embrace. Too soon, he released her. She opened her eyes and boldly looked at him right on.

Jenny, don't look at me that way," he said. "I'll be coming back when the job is done." Already, he was walking away from her, looking back.

"You just make sure to take care of yourself, Mr. Daniel."

She stood watching him as he opened the gate, hopped into his buggy, and drove off. She knew exactly where he was going. To Samantha, in his mind "the prettiest girl in the county."

Walking back slowly to the house, she thought of what she needed to do that day. Mending socks and churning butter came first to her mind.

That night, as she prepared for bed, a horrifying thought came to her. Daniel was joining the Secessionists. Her brother, Jeb, had already joined the Northern cause, and her younger brother was strongly thinking about leaving too. Who would be left to do the work of the farm? And worse, might Jeb shoot and kill Daniel? Or would Daniel in the heat of battle be shooting at Jeb?

These thoughts were overwhelming to her. Tears came frequently as she tossed and turned in her bed. She tried reasoning with herself. She knew she was always one to fear the worst, particularly when worrying about those she loved. Maybe her worst fears wouldn't happen at all. She crossed herself, hoping and praying for the best. Finally, she fell into a restless sleep.

Chapter Six

Daniel was on the road, heading north. He rode with the best wishes of his parents, having said goodbye to them, his friends, and the two girls most important to him. He was well provisioned; really, his parents had outfitted him with more than he might need. Especially if the war was to be short, which everyone expected.

As he passed small town after small town, and directed his horse, Billy, toward the hills, he hoped to reach a larger town where they were recruiting for the South. His mind had long since been made up. It was the Yankees who were invading. He strongly felt it was his duty to stand up for his homeland.

He spent the night in an old, abandoned cabin, and with his head resting on an extra pair of pants, he slept just fine. Eating two larges slices of thick bread that his mother had baked, a large apple and water from his canteen, he was happy to ride on. At last he reached a city, and was glad to see recruiting posters and townspeople seemingly filled with excitement. He saw why. That very afternoon they were enlisting soldiers to fight the cause of the South.

Hitching Billy to a post, he entered a tavern with plans to have a drink and with hope of getting a slice of fresh pie. The place was smelly, with the aroma of unwashed men mingled with tobacco smoke and chew that dotted the walls near the two spittoons. Typical, he thought from his other times in a tavern. Drunken men are terribly inaccurate. His mother would have a fit to see such shabbiness in her house. But a bar was a man's place, only a certain kind of women entered one. Not much more could be expected.

"Hiyar, stranger," said the man behind the bar. "What can I get you?"

Daniel was feeling good. "whiskey," he said. "whiskey and water. Do you have pie?"

"Sure enough do. Berry and cherry."

"I'll take the cherry."

Daniel normally didn't frequent a tavern, but he was new in this town, and didn't know a soul. As he slowly drank his whiskey, taking forkfuls of the pie, he eyed some of the other men. Three of them sat around a table away from the bar in lively conversation. Of course, it was about the war. Daniel listened to them while downing his drink and pie. He was glad to hear their talk was all from the secessionist side of things. Then he heard the sound of musical instruments coming from outside. Not sure what might be going on, but curious, he paid the bartender and walked carefully down the two steps to the outside. The whiskey was generous, and he was beginning to feel its effect.

Across the way and down the street, he heard a band starting up. He walked over to a stage set up on the side of the street and watched as a crowd gathered. The music the band played was inspiring, jubilant, military songs. After they played for a while, two men took to the stage. One was obviously a war veteran, his military jacket decorated with medals. The other appeared dignified, wearing a long open coat, ruffled white shirt, and expensive looking boots. Daniel thought, *must be the town mayor.*

That man introduced the other, and as the crowd grew larger and larger, a roar of applause and cheering erupted.

"Ladies and gentlemen," he said, his voice deep and a bit harsh. "You folks know why I'm here. I ain't much of a talker, and I ain't here to lay flowery words on you. Y'all know what's going on just north of us. The Federals are attacking, taking over our land and killing our boys. You know we ain't going to take that lying down."

A huge cheer rose from the crowd, and Daniel enthusiastically joined in. He asked the girl standing next to him the man's name.

"Why that's Colonel James."

Daniel listened to the man's words.

"I'm not here cause I know how to talk. I'm here cause I know how to fight. That's what it's come down to. We got to fight to protect our homes, our people and our way of life. I'm just as aggravated as you are that it's come to this point. But we know the Yankees are already marching. We know they have already taken over territory in our state. We know they have already killed some of our own fine fighting men. What do we do? You know the answer to that. We're going to fight to protect ourselves and to drive them back home where they belong. We got men right here that are ready to join up to fight the enemy. Folks, let's give them a big round of applause."

Daniel was excited to hear the speech because the colonel said what needed to be said. He was glad to be among the dozens of men who ten at a time went up to the stage to be congratulated and applauded for doing their duty in this time of need. Later, he wrote to describe what happened. This is the letter he wrote to Jenny.

Dear Friend,

Bad news already. My horse, Billy, took lame when crossing a stream. Could still ride him, slowly, but guess I won't be in the cavalry now. I've been here now for ten days, and already I miss my folks, you, and of course, Samantha. This army life is so far not what I expected. Was holed up in a hotel for days and finally got military clothes and equipment. I gave the gun they gave me back, cause mine is better. Same caliber. They had a fine band playing spritely music in town the day I enlisted along with a lot of other men. Each one of us was called up on the stage, our names were announced, and we were congratulated. We shook hands with both the mayor and the colonel. On leaving the stage, we were further congratulated by a bevy of beautiful girls, who put garlands of flowers around our necks. Not as pretty, I should add, as you and Samantha. All to the sound of lively music played by the band.

Glad I'm not the only one from our area. Eli Simmons, Hank Peters, Henry Tucker and I are in the same company. Keith said he saw Caleb and John Sacker too. Think they are part of another company. Anyway, you'll be proud to know we are all here, preparing to fight the Yankees.

Right now, we're living out of tents, a mile or two from the city. They wake us up with a bugle every morning at the crack of dawn, and for almost two hours we're drilled before we get breakfast. It was right humorous how some of our company seemed to have two left feet, neither of them able to get the cadence of the drill sergeant. But doing it three times a day for what seems like hours has already got us whipped into shape. Haven't even fired a gun yet, but think that is coming soon. Sure to be a lot of drilling on that.

Can't say it's fun, but I suppose its life in the army. I'm getting to know Hank and Keith right well, don't know if you know those boys. They are a couple years older than me and a few older than you. Anyway, when we have some free time, we often talk about what we left behind. I hope not for long

Would really be most obliged to hear from you, and to know the latest goings on there. Just about any news from home is welcome news. Hope we can find the Yanks, fight them, and then be done with it. Once they find out we aren't going to be taken over so easily, this war may soon be over. Many of the boys are looking forward to fighting, and even killing the enemy. I look at it as a necessary evil, and don't look forward to shooting but will do my duty.

I hope this letter finds you in good health and would take it very kindly if you could write back soon at the address below.

Your friend,

Daniel

Jenny's father returned from town, handing her the letter. Jenny was surprised, seeing it was from Daniel. Not used to receiving letters at all, she held it tightly in her hands. She hadn't thought that Daniel would really write to her, especially so soon. She felt privileged to receive it, but already she was beginning to fear the worst. Putting it away in her room, she decided she would wait to read it until after supper when she could give it her full attention.

She set to work making preparations for their meal. She was so happy that David had not enlisted, at least not so far. True, he was another mouth to feed, but she wouldn't have had it any other way. Despite the hard work, she loved being able to take care of her menfolk, even including Marcus.

* * *

She went to the chicken coop, eyeing a nice plump one. The bird seemed to know her intentions, for it scooted around, with constant cackling, until she had it trapped in the corner. Grabbing it by the neck, she brought it out close to the chopping block. There, a rope dangled down from the tree, and she slipped it around the bird's legs. She pulled on the rope, the branch it was attached to bent down, and she picked up the hatchet that was on the tree stump used for this purpose. The bird's head was off in a second, and Jenny rushed away so she didn't get splattered. The headless bird's flapping wings made quite a racket until in death it settled down. Its blood still drained from the base of its neck.

It was one of the ordinary day to day things people had to do. That is, unless they had slaves or servants. Marcus used to do it for them, but since Jenny was older, he was needed more for the hard work on the farm. She knew he was out going down the corn rows pulling weeds. Just now, she saw him coming toward her.

"I'm looking forward to some of that later," he said. "That's iffen y'all save me some."

She looked up. "It's a big bird. Maybe you will get some. If nothing else, you'll get the neck."

"Muss say, I do like your cooking, Miss Jenny."

"Well, it's mostly what you learned me. I know it sure disappears from the table."

Marcus went back to his work and Jenny headed toward the house holding the bird by its feet. She held it away from her lest any remaining drops of blood stain her apron.

She laid the bird down by the wooden high backed bench her father had made and went inside to get the hot bucket of water she had warming on the stove. Holding the bucket by its two handles, she set it down, grabbed the chicken, and plopped it into the hot water. She waited only a short time for it to cool, and then quickly began plucking the feathers. Then all she had to do was open it up to pull out the insides, rinse it in the still hot water, and bring the bird in for cooking. She loved chicken just as much as anyone. To go along with it she got potatoes from the root cellar, some early onions from the garden, and fresh bread she had baked the day before. Churned butter was always favored to go with that.

For a change, the afternoon dinner was not contentious. Talk was talk, but no one raised their voice like they often did. Jenny ate her baked chicken, and when the men finished, she was glad there was a leg and neck left for Marcus. She reflected that Marcus often didn't eat quite as well as they did. Yet when he bagged a deer hunting, there was plenty for all to eat for days. She thought about that. She had heard that some of the states barred the colored from owning guns. Especially after the disastrous John Brown incident. But when she served desserts, like cherry or apple pie, the men liked it so much, often Marcus didn't get any. With Jeb gone, one less at the table, that might change.

Thanking her for the filling meal, her father and David got up to leave. They still had plenty of work to do on the farm before dark.

She set a plate for Marcus, rang the dinner bell, and waited till he came in. "You're in luck, Marcus. There's a leg to go with the neck."

"Thank you kindly, Miss Jenny," he said, looking at the remaining potatoes etc., before setting himself down at the table.

"You just help yourself to what's left. I'll be back later to clean up."

"Thank you, Miss."

63

Jenny walked back to her room. She was glad for some free time before chores would begin again in the morning. Sitting down on her bed, she eagerly opened the letter from Daniel, hoping there was no bad news.

Head down, she took in its contents. She read it again carefully, before setting it down. She knew most of the fellows he mentioned in the letter. She was glad in a way that they were joining the cause. Then she remembered that they might be fighting her brother.

Deep down, she felt they were doing the right thing. It was the Federals that were coming into her state and others, acting like they had a moral right to do what they did. She feared them. But how should she write back to Daniel?

She read through the letter one more time, deciding that he sounded homesick. He probably just wanted to hear some news about home. She thought, *what shall I tell him?* Finally, she got up off her bed to get paper and a pen. She sat down again and began writing. She wasn't quite sure how to write back to him, because despite her feelings for him, she knew he loved another.

Dear Friend,

Got your letter, and was glad to learn that you are in good health. I'm happy you were honored on stage for your nobility of being willing to fight for the South. Glad you didn't take up with any of those "beautiful" girls that put a wreath of flowers around your neck. As you know, you have a girl here waiting for you to come back.

Not sure about the others you name, but Hank must be the one who went to school with my brother, Jeb. He was at our house a time or two, but it's probably been years. Is he a good sized man, with sandy hair? A couple of the other names you mention also sound familiar, especially Caleb. Did he sing in the choir at church when he was younger?

As for what is going on around here, not much. Union soldiers come into town, make their purchases, and leave like anyone else. So far,

64

they haven't caused too much trouble. Sure glad they are not staying anywhere near our land. Pa says at least a regiment of them is camped somewhere on the other side of town.

Wish I could tell you a bunch of exciting things going on, but can't. I keep busy keeping up with the cooking, cleaning and taking care of the garden and more. You know all work will make a dull girl.

Did go into town with Pa the other day after supper. He needed to get a new bucket and supplies. We were in the general store for a while and I found they had a selection of those dime novels you hear about. Picked one out and Pa bought it for me. I often have a little time before bed, and must say it is fascinating reading. You may have heard of it. The title is "Malaeska, the Indian Wife of the White Hunter."

On Sunday they had a social after the morning service. Reverend Nichols and his wife provided fresh store tea and coffee and the ladies of the congregation brought chicken fixins, side dishes and desserts. Must say the tea cakes were scrumptious. My Pa and brother were both there, neither one is known to pass up a feast. And, of course, so was Samantha, looking so pretty in her pink crinoline. She really knows how to dress, and you would have loved how she had one of the slaves fix her hair.

Well, Daniel, guess that's some of the things going around here. You keep safe now and take care of yourself. It's starting to get pretty hot in the daytime, but I know it can be cold at night, especially when you're out in a tent.

Your friend,

Jenny

Jenny reread the letter. She saw her words, *"you have a girl waiting for you to come back."* She knew Daniel would read Samantha as that girl. But Jenny read it as herself. *Ah,* she thought, *life is so unfair.* Altogether, she felt she had said too much about the girl. One thing she did not mention to Daniel

65

was her thought that Samantha's bodice, beautiful as it was, with the lace trim and puffed sleeves, was cut a little low, especially for a church affair. Jenny had noticed more than one man eyeing her.

There was something else on her mind, troubling her. A thing she also didn't mention to Daniel. Her brother had joined the northern side. She didn't know how he was doing, as, so far, he had not written to her father or anyone. She hoped he was all right. What troubled her is that he could be in the army fighting the "rebels" as the paper called the secessionists. Her own brother could be killing people like Daniel.

A chilling thought came to her. Daniel would be on the other side killing "Yankees." He could even kill her own brother. Suddenly, the terrible complication of this war came to her, overwhelming her. Tears began flowing freely from her eyes and down her cheeks. She pulled out her handkerchief, wiping away the tears, barely able to keep herself from sobbing. She suddenly was able to stop, remembering what her father had told her, "Big girls don't cry."

Chapter Seven

Daniel knew something was up. Everyone knew it. But the generals all the way down to the lieutenants weren't saying anything to the men. The training was getting intensive. Five times a day now. Not only was it not easy, it was monotonous. After the last one, he sat on the ground by their tents eating with his friends, Hank and Eli. Eli was smaller than him, wiry, and seemed something of a thinker. He was the second fastest man in the company, a fact proven when the men held an impromptu race.

Next time, he would put his money on Eli. Hank was something of the opposite, a big, husky farm boy, strong as an ox, but a bit clumsy. Daniel was glad he had gotten to know them both. They were from the same part of western Virginia, and they even knew some of the same people he knew.

"I'm thinking we'll be marching soon," said Eli. "To battle," he added.

"Now what's making you say that, Eli? Just as I'm starting to enjoy all this drilling," said Hank.

Daniel saw Hank's smile. He knew he hated their five times a day routine.

"Just the way I notice them checking out the wagons and paying attention to the horses."

'Well, if we're ever going into battle, you'd think they would give us more practice with shooting. Not like everyone here is a crack shot," said Daniel.

"Yeah," agreed Hank. "Think I can count on two hands the times I've actually pulled the trigger and shot at something."

"They want to conserve ammunition," said Eli.

Just then, they heard the loud voice of Sergeant Evans. "Mail call!"

Those were about the only words he ever uttered that were always well received. The three of them jumped up immediately as the sergeant sounded out the names.

"Tom Clancy, Tyler Simmons, Billy Sacko, Emmet Stone . . ."

The list went on and both Daniel and Hank were happy to get mail. Eli turned away downcast after all the names were announced. Daniel knew he missed not getting a letter. Especially as they were lucky to get anything from home more often than once a week. He looked at the return address and was a bit surprised. A letter from Jenny, but still nothing from Samantha. Was the girl going to forget him the entire time while he served his country? When the war was over, hopefully in a month or two, he was going to have a talk with her.

The men went back to finishing their meal. Daniel tucked the letter into his pocket. He was going to wait until he could read his letter in private. He noted that Hank did the same. Suddenly, commands rang out throughout the company and regiment. "Fall in." "Hurry up soldier."

More instructions came when they were lined up in their places. "Boys we are getting out of here and likely won't come back. I'm giving you fifteen minutes to get your gear ready to march. Don't anyone from my company be late or you're going to be on my list. Do you understand?"

"Yes, sir," was the expected answer, and each man gave it.

"Fall out."

Everyone slung cartridge boxes over their shoulders and added the haversack and bedroll, then finally their canteen, before picking up their rifles. There was plenty of talk.

"Any idea where we might be going," Daniel asked his friends.

"We're going to do battle with the enemy," said Eli.

"Why do you think that?" asked Hank.

"Cause it's so sudden. You'd think we would leave in the morning, rather when the day's more than half over. The general knows something."

"Sure enough hope he does," said Hank.

"Haven't heard of any Yankee armies around here," added Daniel. "Think we're going to be in for a lot of marching."

Daniel was right. They marched and marched and marched, stopping only occasionally for five minute rests and for water. He had never hiked so hard in his life. Sweat dripped from his brow. No wonder, they had to be heading up and over the mountains. Glad he could handle it, for there were a few who had fallen out and were now clinging to the tops of loaded supply wagons at the rear.

Finally, as darkness was falling, the order was given to halt. Here, high in the mountains overlooking a valley far below, they would bivouac.

The order was given to "fall out," and the men looked around, trying to select the best place among the long grass and trees to choose where they would sleep the night. Campfires were permitted, and before long a number were started, some of the larger ones throwing long shadows of the men on nearby tree trunks.

Daniel and his friends, Keith, Eli, and John, decided they would make a shelter. Staking out a tree by laying their haversacks beside it, they tied two of the blankets together. Then they went into the nearby woods and found suitable limbs, after breaking off their branches, to place on opposite sides to hold up their homemade tent.

Keith had the idea they should slant it strongly in one direction. That way, he said, if there was rain, it would drain off. Good idea. Eli offered his blanket to tie with the other two, which they fixed on one side coming straight down to help keep out any rain on that side. *Wasn't the best*, thought Daniel, but would offer some protection from the elements.

Once that was done, they went to one of the larger campfires, and sitting on the ground, Indian style with their legs crossed underneath them, they watched four chickens being roasted. *Where did they get the birds? thought Daniel.*

Daniel was tired from the long, mostly uphill march. He knew that everyone was, and talk was sparse. The sun dipped below the horizon, and darkness closed in on them. Only the campfires brightened the gloom of night. Daniel and his friends looked hungrily at the fire, waiting for the birds to be fully cooked.

At last, they were lifted off the glowing embers, pulled off the spit, and though still hot, pulled apart by the seven men who had been watching it with anticipation. Daniel was happy to get a large thigh and leg, as well as the neck of one of the chickens. From his haversack he brought out a piece of corn bread along with some dried peas. With that and water, he ate, thankful to quench the hunger pangs that had been growing on the long march.

He and his friends ate companionably, until their appetites were sated. Talk went to what the morrow would bring. By all accounts, they were still a long way from where they expected to meet the Union army. At least one more day of long marching, everyone thought.

Gradually, the seven men around the still glowing embers left, to retire for the night. "Good night," Daniel's messmates said on leaving. Daniel had been waiting for such a time to read his letter from Jenny. He pulled it out of his pocket, edged closer to the fire, and in the dim light slowly began to read.

Dear Friend,

Got your letter, and was glad to learn that you are in good health. I'm happy you were honored on stage for your nobility of being willing to fight for the South. Glad you didn't take up with any of those "beautiful" girls that put a wreath of flowers on your neck. As you know, you have a girl here waiting for you to come back.

Daniel chuckled at what Jenny said about the "beautiful girls." He knew he had a girl waiting for him. But why didn't she write? He continued reading.

Not sure about the others you name, but Hank must be the one who went to school with my brother, Jeb. He was at our house a time or two, but it's probably been years. Is he a good sized man, with sandy hair? A couple of the other names you mention do sound familiar, especially Caleb. Did he sing in the choir at church when he was younger?

As for what is going on around here, not much. Union soldiers come into town, make their purchases, and leave like anyone else. So far,

71

they haven't caused too much trouble. Sure glad they are not staying anywhere near our land. Pa says at least a regiment of them is camped somewhere on the other side of town.

Yes, Daniel thought, Caleb *was* in the choir. He read the part about the Union soldiers with heightened interest. He felt bad that they were right there in town. At least from Jenny's letter they didn't seem to be causing trouble. He wished his own army could swoop down on them, driving them back to the North.

On consideration though, he knew the force near the town was small compared to what they expected to meet soon. He hoped with all his heart that a major victory would drive the Yankees back and settle the war quickly. He continued reading, coming to the part that interested him most—about Samantha.

On Sunday they had a social after the morning service. Reverend Nichols and his wife provided fresh store tea and coffee and the ladies of the congregation brought chicken fixins, side dishes and desserts. Must say the tea cakes were scrumptious. My Pa and brother were both there, neither one is known to pass up a feast. And, of course, so was Samantha, looking so pretty in her pink crinoline. She really knows how to dress, and you would have loved how she had one of the slaves fix her hair.

Even though he had eaten, Daniel salivated when thinking of all the delicious food at the church social. Hearing about Samantha, wearing one of her fascinating dresses with her hair done up, almost brought tears to his eyes.

How he would have liked to have been there, escorting her, talking to her, enjoying the occasion with her. Why didn't the girl write? Was he going to have to ask Jenny in a letter to tell her to write to him?

He tucked the letter back into his pocket and rising, started back to his friends' homemade tent. Ducking his head under the fabric, he realized they were already asleep. He took off his hat and boots and settled in. Wasn't by far the best of beds, but he was soon asleep.

* * *

March, march, march, march. For days now, it seems like it was all they did. Daniel and his companions discovered they could do more now than they had ever done before. Not easy, to walk over a mountain, but they had done it.

Finally, they were in the territory where they would meet the hated enemy of the north. In Eastern Virginia, a land that seceded from the Union, but where the invasion of Union troops had the entire South on edge. They must be defeated!

On this night, as they again roasted their meat on campfires, talk was incessant. Everyone knew that in one day or two they would face a large army of Yankees, bent on destroying the will of the South. They would not be successful. Every man in the confederate army knew that was true.

Yet, now that they were close to fighting, fear abounded. Each foot soldier, almost all of them totally unused to fighting, wondered how they would stand up to the stress of battle.

"Ok, boys," said Sergeant Evans. "Finish up and try to get some sleep. We've got a long march tomorrow to get us near the railroad that will take us to the enemy. You'll have to eat your rations on the way. Once there, we'll hop on a train that will take us to where we're going to meet those Yankees. We're going to give them hell, boys."

The word was passed down the line, and soon the whole camp was abuzz with excitement.

"So, we're actually going to use these heavy firearms we been lugging all over tarnation," said Hank, rubbing his forehead, which he often did.

"Bout time," answered Eli, already getting up from where they were sitting. Eli was the smallest of their mess group of four.

"Don't know about y'all, But I'm leery about shooting at men," said Keith. "I mean deer and rabbits and such is one thing, but killing a man?"

Daniel didn't say anything. He was taking everything in, and he tended to agree with Keith, a man about his size, with brown hair, who had come from the same county he had.

What Daniel wouldn't tell any of them, was that he was more than a little afraid of being shot. The Yankees might not be a match for southern boys, but he was sure they had been taught how to shoot a gun. Getting up from the log he had been sitting on, he said, "Well, boys, I'm going to turn in and try to get some shut eye. Sure won't be sleeping in tomorrow."

* * *

The trumpets sounded at first light, and wearily, everyone awakened. No time to eat, to do anything other than quickly take care of personal needs. Grabbing his haversack and rifle, Daniel and his friends got up as the company, the regiment, and the brigade lined up to march.

Again, they marched and marched and marched on another hot July day. Finally, toward six, they stopped, taking time to eat and rest. Then, they marched again.

Daniel marched alongside his friends, but no one had much energy for talking. Daniel thought to himself, *we're marching toward a battle, but once we get there will we have any energy left to fight?*

Finally, about midnight, the signal was given to stop, to fall out and get some rest. Tomorrow, they would continue toward the enemy.

No one had the energy to do anything other than to lay blankets on the ground and cover up. Daniel fell asleep immediately.

Morning came early, but at least now they were given time to eat.

"I thought we were going to be boarding a train," said Keith, in between chewing on his portion of salted pork.

Eli looked out at the landscape below. "Don't see any train station, or even any tracks in sight."

"That would be too easy," said Daniel. "Walk before riding."

"Sure hope we don't have to walk far," said Hank, who in between bites of his rations had taken off his boots and was massaging his feet.

"Like the idea," said Eli. "We'll just ride into battle on the train, all rested up and ready to fight them Yankees."

Daniel smiled. Though he knew it wouldn't be that easy, he liked the way Eli looked at things.

Too soon, they were off, marching again. Late in the morning, they arrived in Piedmont Station. All the cars were soon loaded with soldiers, but there was far too few train cars to hold even half the men. Daniel and his friends waved to those leaving for the battleground. They learned that it was only a thirty-five mile run to get to Manassas, and that later the train would return for them.

After what seemed like a long wait, the train came back. Daniel, his friends, and most of the brigade managed to squeeze on board. Excitement ran high, for they heard that they would disembark and then almost immediately be rushed into battle.

As Daniel and his companions rode along, they were amazed at the speed they were traveling along the countryside ripe with crops of wheat and corn. None had ever traveled on anything faster than a horse. Arriving now, close to the battleground, they looked at each other on hearing the boom of cannon and the rapid fire of hundreds of rifles. .

They chugged into the station, and immediately heard the sharp barks of sergeants and captains. On orders, they double-timed toward the sound of the pounding of the big guns and the clattering of the rifle fire. Already, they could see the smoke of gunpowder rising on the hill.

Suddenly, Daniel had an attack of fear. Were the captains marching them to their deaths? He moved along quickly with the others, glancing at his comrades to his left and behind. Was he the only one who was afraid?

They pushed on toward the summit of a hill where a good part of the confederate army stood just beneath the rise of the hill, firing over it toward the Yankees below. Through all the smoke and confusion, one man stood boldly tall on his horse directing the fighting men around him. Who was he? Did the man have no fear?

"Fire at will," was the order, and for a brief moment Daniel looked out at wounded soldiers crying out in pain, and then bent his head down to load his rifle. Setting the stock of his rifle on the ground between his feet, he pulled a cartridge from his cartridge box, tore off the paper with his teeth, and poured the powder down the barrel of the rifle. Then, placing the minie ball from the cartridge into the top of the gun, with his ramrod he jammed the bullet and its powder down the length of the barrel. He put on the percussion cap, cocked the gun, and standing tall and aiming, fired his first shot in the direction of gunshots and smoke on the other side of the hill.

He had no idea if his minie ball hit anything. Quickly, he bent down to load again. The process of loading had been drilled into every man and most of them were able to load and shoot three times a minute. As Daniel and his brigade kept up the firepower, he noticed that they seemed to be making a difference.

The fighting continued, with the incessant staccato reports of thousands of rifles, the rising clouds of smoke making it difficult to see the enemy. Daniel saw men fall around him, but in the excitement he paid little heed, for it seemed that even more of the enemy were lying on the ground. Then, came the order to fix bayonets, to charge up over the rim of the hill, and to scream at the top of their lungs to incite fear and confusion.

Of a sudden, more than a thousand men rose up screaming, cresting the rim of the hill and rushing down the other side with guns blazing. As he ran forward with the others toward the enemy, Daniel felt no fear though men were falling around him. They ran, reaching the bottom of the hill where they could see the enemy clearly beneath the smoke of their guns. It was a glorious sight to see for they were rushing away from the onslaught that bore down on them.

What started as an enemy retreat quickly turned into a rout, as scared men dropped their haversacks, their bed rolls and even their rifles, running as fast as their legs could carry them.

The rebel army continued after them, the whooping and hollering becoming even more pronounced as each man realized that they had the enemy on the run. The proud Yankees were hightailing it back in total disarray. The rout continued, and as the victorious confederates ran on, Daniel noticed that there were civilians in carriages also rushing back to Washington as fast as they could.

He suddenly realized that they had come to witness the expected easy defeat of the rebels. For them it must have been like watching a sporting event, and he surmised, that judging from the fancy carriages, they had probably brought picnic lunches and wine. Angrily he looked at them from across the stream, but he did not want to shoot them.

The order came to pull back. To halt, to return to their starting point. Why? thought Daniel. We have them on the run, why not continue?

He saw Eli among the hundred or more men walking back in no particular order. "We showed them, didn't we?" he said, putting an arm around him as they companionably trudged back up the hill.

"We did," answered Eli, "but at what cost?"

In the elation of winning the battle, Daniel had forgotten about all the fallen soldiers. Now, walking back up the hill, he knew exactly what Eli meant. Men were lying on the ground in all kinds of contorted positions, some alive, some begging for help or for water, others silent in sleep or death. He knelt on one knee to give a man a drink from his canteen, and in a moment, Eli knelt down to do the same.

Chapter Eight

Jenny heard the news. Who hadn't of the big victory for the south at Manassas? But she also heard reports of the terrible death toll and casualty counts. As word gradually filtered back through ongoing newspaper accounts, she was appalled at the travesty of war. What was even worse for her personally, and for many others, was that there were still no letters from the sons, friends, and husbands who had fought in the dreadful battle. Jenny had to wait, hope, and pray, like so many of her neighbors, that Daniel, her brother, and others she knew were safe.

At home, her father often rode into town to get one thing or another, but now, in these times, always to bring home the latest edition of the paper. Jenny would see him intently reading it, and then at the dinner table, or often while they worked outside, it was usually the main topic of conversation.

"Why didn't our boys pursue them after the battle back to Washington?" said her father, on learning the full story of the glorious southern victory at Manassas.

"Because of all the deaths, Pa. We must have lost hundreds of our own men, and many more wounded" answered her brother, David.

"God, I hope Jeb is all right. We still don't know his whereabouts, or if he was in the battle or not. I rue that he went to join the Yankees.

"I hope to God Daniel is all right too," said Jenny, who lifted her lowered head to speak.

Her father turned to her, and speaking with surprising tenderness, said, "I do too, honey." Turning back to his son, he continued. "The thing is, if our men had pursued them back to Washington, we could have ended the war right there. Now, the rash president Lincoln has issued a call for 500,000 more troops. It's crazy, that's what it is. Why can't they just leave us alone? Do they think the states have no rights whatever anymore?"

"Really, father?" asked her brother.

"Yes. Just read it in today's paper. 500,000 for a three year term of duty."

"Oh, my!" exhaled Jenny, shaking her head. "Surely no one thinks the war will go on for that long, do they, Pa?"

"With that man in the White House, who knows? That's why we should have pressed forward, commandeered the city, and make them sue for peace."

Jenny didn't listen anymore. Quickly finishing her meal, she left to go to her room. Sitting on her bed, she clasped her hands, bowed her head and said prayers for Daniel, Jeb, and for all those struck down in battle, "Rebels," as they were being called, as well as "Yankees." It shook her that so many men were dying. *God*, she thought, *can't you bring an end to this senseless killing?*

She started to read her new dime novel, but her mind was wandering so much she couldn't get into it. She went back to the kitchen to clean up the pans and dishes, and saw that Marcus was still there. Being a slave, he was always the last to eat.

She looked at him and he smiled, while he continued to eat. She considered if she had the audacity to ask him what suddenly came to her mind. Finally, looking straight at him, she did ask, not knowing at all how he would answer her question.

"Marcus, what do you think of all this battling and killing going on between the North and South?"

"Glad it ain't me, Miss Jenny. I sure enough hope Jeb be alright."

"Me too, Marcus," she answered, dropping her eyes as a tremor suddenly went through her body. She continued looking down, wondering if Marcus had heard of the northern talk of wanting to free the slaves. She let the idea drop, and began cleaning up the supper dishes.

Marcus got up from the table, saying, "Thank you, Miss Jenny."

She turned away from the sink basin to give him a quick smile, and continued with washing and putting away everything used for the meal.

There were other things she could have done that evening, but they could be put off. She wanted to see Sarah. Taking off her apron, she set it aside. Going to her room, she brushed her hair in front of her small mirror. Then, glad to be going out, if only to see a friend, she exited the gate and walked down the road.

On leaving the house, she felt better. She waved to old Mr. Peters who was driving his wagon, likely coming back from town. She noticed the birds chirping merrily in the trees. Thankfully, they knew nothing of death, war, and the sad state of the country. Taking a cue from them, she tried to forget her cares at least for a time.

She was glad when she knocked on the door, and opening it, immediately saw Sarah. Sarah came right up to her, her eyes brimming with excitement

"Jenny, did you hear the news?"

"What news?"

"Well, surely you know that the South won the big battle of Manassas.

"Yeah. Pa told me, and I've heard it from two others already."

"Did you know that Angela and her folks are having a party to celebrate the victory?"

"Really? Jenny's eyes grew wide at the news.

"And here's the best part." Jenny noticed that Sarah was fairly shaking in her excitement. "Rex is going to come by in his carriage to pick me up. You remember, the fancy one with the fringe on top?"

"Really? I envy you, Sarah."

The evening went quickly for Jenny, as she and Sarah spent the time talking about Rex, the upcoming event, and even a little about the war and how they hoped it would soon be over. However, the next day brought an unforeseen development.

Jenny awakened later than her menfolk, as she usually did. She heard commotion on the road outside their fence. Peering out through the curtains, she saw what was causing it. Troops of the enemy, marching in two long columns. She looked to the left and right and saw an unending line of soldiers in blue.

Afraid at first for them to see her, she wondered about her father and brother. Did they know, or were they too far back working the lower forty to see or hear them?

Then, she saw them open the gate. Ten, then twenty of them came into the front yard, talking loudly. They went to the pump, and began filling their canteens. *The nerve of them*, she thought. Still looking out the window, she saw her father coming, and immediately behind him David and Marcus.

He came right up to them, and she heard him say, "What do you think you're doing coming here uninvited on my property?"

The man who seemed to be in charge said, "We just came for water, sir. Surely you have no problem with soldiers filling their canteens."

Jenny watched her father carefully. She hoped he wouldn't say anything to rile them, even though she knew he hated the bluecoats invading the South.

"OK, go ahead. Would have been polite if you asked first."

Jenny saw a rough looking soldier come up face to face with her father. "Would you like us to politely ask before we take your pigs and cow too, old man?" He stuck his half-bearded face in front of her father's.

Swiftly, her father lashed out with a fist to the man's face, and he fell to the ground. He was up quickly, cursing and suddenly landed a roundhouse to her father's chin, knocking him down. Jenny ran to the door and rushed outside.

Her father got up slowly, rubbing his chin when she reached for him. She wrapped her arms around him, holding him tight, trying to keep him from doing something that would rile them further. She saw her brother look on angrily at the soldiers, his hands balled into fists.

Jenny heard their leader say, "Bart, you get away from these people. I want you off their property right now." Speaking to her father, who held his head sideways, still rubbing his chin, he said, "Sir, I'm sorry for what happened. We have no intention of stealing anything from you. Then, in a louder voice he said, "Men, hurry up and get your water. Then let's get off this man's property."

The soldiers did what he said, and Jenny took a long look at him. Dark brown hair, of average height, broad shoulders, with several days' growth of thick beard. When he happened to glance at her, she lowered her eyes immediately. She certainly did not want to be noticed by one of the enemy. Yet, she was thankful that he had acted in a civilized manner to avert what could have turned into a brawl or worse. She took another look at him as the soldiers were leaving and saw he was looking back at her. Was he smiling? The nerve of the man! Turning away quickly, she hurried into the house, trying hard not to think about him.

The danger was past, and Jenny, her father, and David were inside. Marcus must have gone to his cabin. Her father sat on a chair, his hand still under his chin. Jenny took a good look at his jaw. There was blood on the side of his mouth, and she toweled it off and quickly went to get some cream to put on it. Otherwise, she thought he was going to be OK. On taking a closer look, he did have a loose tooth. She hoped it would firm up in time.

"I wish our boys were here to defend us," he said, after Jenny was done attending to him. "They won a big battle east of us, but here in western Virginia, seems like they're leaving us to fend for ourselves."

84

"Pa, that's the way it is," said David. "Winning battles there will soon get us to Washington, and end this crazy war."

"I can't wait for it to be over and for Jeb to come home. I still can hardly believe he up and left us to join the Yankees."

Jenny also hoped that the war would soon be over. In the next several days she went about her chores, but always with the knowledge that thousands of Union soldiers were camped somewhere down the road. She saw a few of them when she went to town with her father and Marcus, who rode with them in the back of the wagon to help with the load of supplies they needed. She noted there was a marked change about town. People spoke in whispers in the general store and on the street. Few seemed to like it that the northerners had invaded and set up camp in the vicinity.

Her father got a newspaper as usual, and checked for mail. There was none. Jenny had hoped that by now there would be a letter from Daniel. Knowing that so many from both sides had died in the battle, she was worried for him. She made up her mind to write to him that very night.

Late that evening, after the sun had gone down, she retired to her bedroom, lit the wall sconce, got out her pen and paper and began to write.

Dear Friend,

We here have all heard about your wonderful victory. We were so happy. Pa said you should have gone on marching to Washington and end this war with a Southern victory. But that's just what he and some others are saying. Your generals probably know a lot more about it.

Daniel, I can't hide my fear any longer. We hear that so many were killed on both sides. I am so afraid for you. That we have not received any letter from you is just plain scary. I comfort myself thinking that there is a lot more to being a soldier than fighting and that you are busy and haven't had time to write. I pray that it is so.

Despite the wonderful news of your successful battle, the news here has not been good. We wish our soldiers were here to protect us from the enemy. Not sure if you know, but in the western part of Virginia, the Yankees have won some victories. In fact, right now there are a lot of them camped not far from us. People in town are mostly scared. They talk a lot in whispers, cause we can't do anything about them.

Yes, Daniel, we had a bad incident here just a few days ago. I was in the house when a whole troop of Yankees marched by on the road outside our front gate. There must have been two thousand or more. Then, some of them opened the gate and came into our yard. They didn't even stop at the house to ask, but just began helping themselves to the pump, filling their canteens.

That's when Pa, David and Marcus came back up from the lower forty. As you might imagine, there was some words spoken, and then Pa swung at one of them, knocking him down. I know, a real foolish thing for him to do, especially when there must have been twenty Yankees there. Well, the guy got up right away and swung at Pa, knocking him down. That's when I rushed out. Fortunately, the soldier in charge, a captain, sent the troublemaker away. He even apologized to my father for what happened.

So that's what we're living with around here. Sarah told me that Angela was going to have a party to celebrate your great victory, but I doubt if that's going to happen now with the soldiers staying on.

Don't know what else to write, Daniel. I just hope you are well. Would love to send you something through the mail, if you could tell me what you could use. Not sure if any food would keep during the summer, but maybe later, if you are still fighting for us when it gets colder. I sure hope you are home by then, safe and sound.

Your true and lasting friend, Jenny

Finished, she folded the letter and put it in an envelope. She thought about the last line she had written. How instead of "true and lasting friend" she wanted to write, Your true love, Jenny. Knowing, regretfully, that his girl was Samantha, she wrote what she did.

Chapter Nine

As Daniel and Eli made their way back to the standard of their regiment in the failing light, the true devastation of the battle hit home to them. So many men had fallen in contorted positions of death, and others wounded, crying for help. No wonder the generals chose not to pursue the enemy.

Another concern suddenly arose. Where were Hank, Keith, and John? Daniel hadn't seen them since they advanced against the enemy.

They heard the bugles sounding, calling them back. From the hill to the west, from down by the river, from everywhere, the Confederate soldiers began streaming back to their units. Those dead or casualties unable to walk were left where they lay, many crying for water or for help.

Daniel looked around as the army formed ranks. He saw men he had come with and fought with, and realized that some of the faces he had come to know were missing. The colonel's voice rang out steady and clear as raindrops began to fall.

"Men, we have defeated the enemy, but at great cost. You who were among the last to enter the battle have been assigned to carry out the work of removing the wounded, all those unable to walk of their own accord. Behind me are stretchers you are to use to bring the men here. Once they are here, we will put them in wagons and take them to the Pringle House, about three miles from here, which we are using for a hospital."

While standing in line, Daniel looked at Eli next to him, and then at the other men down the line. After walking past so many dead and wounded, the immensity of the task struck him. The Colonel continued, in loud voice.

"Remember, men. Our only concern is with the wounded. The hospital will not be a place to inter the dead. If a man seems sleeping, but you cannot quickly waken him, leave him. Tomorrow, in the light of day, we can better check on any that may still have a pulse. What we must do tonight is get those who can be helped to the hospital where they can be cared for. Do you understand?"

"Yes, sir!" came the reply of the men up and down the long double line, including Daniel and Eli.

Daniel looked at Eli. Together, they went to get one of the stretchers, which were nothing more than a heavy blanket with two poles running along the sides. They were among the first to go, and when they started down the hill of the battlefield, they quickly came to a man softly crying.

"We're here to take you to the hospital," said Daniel.

"Thank God," said the soldier, his voice weak and sounding cutoff. They turned him over in order to use his arms to lift him onto the stretcher, seeing then that his leg hung uselessly below the knee. The man's face agonized at their moving him, but aside from a groan, he did not cry out.

89

Daniel didn't know what to say to him. Not knowing how much blood he had lost or if he would live or die, he said nothing. They carried him back up the gentle hill, and saw that the ambulance wagon was ready. Two men were already there, lying on a bed of straw, and with the help of the driver, they hoisted him up to lay beside them. Then they went back for more.

Daniel and Eli didn't talk much at all during the hours spent bringing back the wounded. What could be said? Some men were so riddled with bullets, that when they rolled them over to see if they were alive it was no surprise that they were not.

With others, they had no doubt. They could tell by their cursing or by their audible praying that they were alive and had a chance of surviving. Some reached out to clutch their hands in thanks that they had come for them. Others were stoic, not saying a word and seeming to be in deep meditation. Still others were crying out in pain, or moaning low and incoherently. Daniel and Eli took them all if they showed any sign of life.

When their tour of duty was finally over, Daniel was tired beyond exhaustion. It was not easy work carrying bodies up the hill, and it was sad to see what enemy bullets had done to previously healthy soldiers. He and Eli ate the meal provided them in silence under the stars.

The next day, after reveille and breakfast, Daniel and his company were given a new assignment, burying the dead. To do the job they were armed with one shovel per each two men. Their instructions were to bury them. Nothing more. Probably nothing more could be expected due to the immensity of the task.

This time it was Daniel and Hank who paired up to work together. They, along with thirty-nine other pairs of soldiers set out toward Henry Hill. On reaching the top, in the morning light they saw the full extent of the dead. Some lying on their back, faces lit by the sun, others curled into fetal positions, head to knees, and a few whose leg or arms were in positions impossible for the living to assume. There were even a few whose body parts were separated from their torsos. In the bright morning sun, they stared at the fallen dead. It was a scene out of their worst nightmares. Other soldiers did the same, gawking at the unforgettable scene.

Daniel and Hank came to the first body. Hank reached down and pushed on his shoulder, turning him over. Dried blood came from his mouth, and a trail of it led down his neck. His face was ashen in death. Hank looked away, and noticed the movement of people far down and across the valley. He said dryly to Daniel, "Looks like we're not the only ones sent out to do this."

Daniel looked up from the dead soldier to where Hank still gazed. "Good. Must be people from the town. I'm glad. By now the Yanks have fled clear to Washington. We won't have to bury all their dead as well as our own."

"Even so," said Hank. "How are we ever going to bury so many?"

Eli came over to them. He introduced them to his partner, John. "I'm thinking," he said, "This is too many to bury in single graves. We'd be out here all day and night. Why don't we work together and lay two down together?"

"I like the idea," said Hank. "They fought together; don't think it would be a dishonor for them to lie together."

"Let's do it," said Daniel. With that, they went to get another body to lie beside the first. They looked down at him. He had been shot in the stomach and chest. His face was contorted. Daniel thought to himself, *hopefully, he didn't suffer long before dying.* "Anyone know either of them?" he asked.

91

They shook their heads no. "We should check their pockets and haversacks to see if they have anything on them to say who they were before we bury them."

The work of digging up the ground and burying the soldiers was arduous, and though the four men worked together, as the hours passed, they became more and more exhausted. They searched the pockets of the dead for identification, and if they had a haversack, they searched that as well, taking care to keep each man's belongings separate from others.

They found all manner of things, including letters, tintypes of wives, children, girlfriends, New Testaments, wallets, some with money and identification, pen knives, combs, other small personal items. These were the only things that remained of them, the only things that could be sent back to their loved ones. They decided that when they were finished, they would give them all to the lieutenant, who they thought would be the best one to return the remains to their families.

They stopped at bugle call. Time for supper. But not for much else. Except one very important thing. Mail call. The mail had caught up with them. Daniel waited like everyone else, hoping his name would be called. It was, and he went up to get it from the sergeant. It was from Jenny. He tucked it safely in his pocket and waited until the last name was called. Now back with his messmates, he shook his head, discouraged that he still had no letter from Samantha.

"You got a letter," said Hank. "You should be glad you got one."

Daniel didn't tell him he was disappointed that he didn't get one from Samantha. Seeing that Hank didn't get a letter this time, he said, "Not from the one I expected."

Right after supper and mail call, the company was sent out again. Still more men needed to be buried. It was mean work, not only because it was arduous, but to see the shattered bodies, some unrecognizable, was depressing to say the least. But they worked hard and quickly, not wanting to have to return tomorrow to complete the grisly job. Finally, as night fell, they buried the last man in sight. They hoped that the townspeople and the few slaves working with them had finished with the ones closer to the town.

Daniel and the others stumbled into their made up tents, too tired to do anything else but drop to the ground and sleep. As much as Daniel looked forward to reading Jenny's letter, nightfall and exhaustion kept him from it. Her letter, kept secure in his pocket, would have to wait till the morrow.

The new day brought a new assignment for Daniel. Sergeant Evans must have remembered that his horse had gone lame, and may have known that he had experience driving a wagon. Anyway, there were more men who were either sick or wounded, including the former driver, and Daniel was assigned to take them to the field hospital.

He chose Hank to accompany him, first of all because they were friends, and secondly because Hank was big, which would make lifting the wounded easier. Daniel thought about the letter still unopened in his pocket. He had heard that Union troops were active in western Virginia, but he hoped his family and hers were safe. Hopefully, he could read her letter that night, preferably alone by the campfire before going to sleep.

Daniel rigged up the horse to the wagon and went to the large tent they had erected to hold those needing to be transported to the hospital. He and Hank opened the flap and saw in the dim light at least a dozen men. A nurse, or civilian acting as one, met them inside. Introductions were made, her name was Cecilia, and she told them which of the men most needed hospital care.

They went to their beds, which were nothing more than blankets laid on top of hay. One by one, Daniel and Hank took them from the tent and laid them carefully in the wagon. Daniel already knew that the wagon would be bouncy on the road, but there was nothing more than hay to lay them on. Hank was strong, and Daniel let him take the heavier head side of the men until the wagon was filled with the wounded, laying in a row next to each other. Their moans on moving them made it clear that they were suffering. Daniel vowed to make the journey to the hospital as gentle as possible.

Fully loaded, with six men squeezed together side by side in the back they set off. They took the little traveled road toward the Pringle field hospital. Daniel tried to navigate the uneven road as gently as he could for the sake of the men. They traveled on the uneven surface made by previous wagons to the road and then continued on to the Pringle House.

At first glance, it was a beautiful mansion, but as they drew closer small tents appeared in disarray near the impressive structure. A few confederate soldiers moved purposefully and several carriages were parked on the macadam surface near the house. An old gentleman with white hair and rumpled clothes looked up at them as they drew near.

"You bringing more of them?" he asked.

"Yes, sir," Daniel answered.

"Pull around to the back. It'll be easier to get them in. Hope they're not too bad off."

They did that, and the old man followed, limping as he walked. "Right through that door," he said. "Just lay them down anywhere you can find. They'll get to them when they can."

On coming closer to the mansion, Daniel and Hank heard the moans and voices of those in pain. A confederate soldier came up to them and offered to help in removing the wounded from the wagon. They got the first man onto a stretcher and carried him in.

The floor was crowded with the wounded, some lying on pads, and some on the hard floor. There was nothing Daniel knew to say, with the scene in front of him, but he looked at Hank and shook his head, hardly believing what lay before him of wounded and dying confederates. Two nurses tended the sick. They were garbed in long, dark dresses with large white aprons. One looked up at them as they went about their grim business. The soldier helping them, whose name they learned was Todd, told them where to put those they were bringing in—on the right side where there was still room.

They returned for each of the other wounded soldiers, and as they were bringing the last one in, what looked like a human limb flew down from an upper window. Daniel stared at it, now lying on the ground in the bushes. Then he saw that there was a pile of many arms and legs there. He looked at Hank, whose eyes were also fixed on the heap of limbs sticking out from the bushes.

Hank shook his head. In a quiet voice he said, "Let's get out of here."

On the way back they talked about it, but it wasn't a subject that brought them any joy. They had not heard a scream before the limb was thrown out and that thought was their only comfort. They must have used chloroform or ether or even whiskey to deaden the feeling of the men before they amputated. Still, Daniel thought, *to go through the rest of one's life without an arm or leg. . .*

Unfortunately, their depressing job was not finished. Three more men had been found still clinging to life. Gently, they eased them into the wagon and slowly, so as not to jar them, made the return trip. This time, at the place where they had seen the limbs, two Negroes were there with a wagon. The old man was there also, and he looked up at them as they were slowly passing by going to the back entrance.

"Nasty work," he said. "Stead of pulling weeds, my slaves always seem to be called to do something else. "I hope to God all this killing is sending a message to Washington."

"Me too, sir," answered Daniel, respectfully. He realized the darkies were likely taking the remains for burial.

"Well, they've taken over my whole house to make a hospital. Me, my son and grandson are all living in a single bedroom upstairs." He shook his head with resignation. "Don't mind helping the cause though, especially as these are mostly our poor boys, trying to push them Yankees back." He turned toward one of the blacks. "Nate, you and Jim take those to where the fence runs by the woods. Bury them deep on the other side. Don't want any animals digging them up."

"Yes, sir," Nate answered.

Daniel and Hank took the short ride back to the base of operations. They arrived just in time for drill, the frequent object of derision. Hardly any soldier liked drilling. It was physical, repetitious, and the individual soldier stood under the perceptive eye of his sergeant and captain, who were always ready to seize on and sometimes ridicule any mistakes. Wasn't easy, there were so many commands to learn and execute in more or less precision fashion.

Daniel and Hank lined up with their platoon just in time to hear the first command. "About, face."

96

In a more benevolent mood, Daniel could see that understanding exactly what to do when facing an enemy was a good thing to know. However, he had arrived at the tail end of the battle of Manassas, and the sounds of rifles firing and cannon booming would very likely have drowned out any commands from his superiors.

Thinking back, as he mechanically marched in lockstep with his company and regiment, he remembered only the loud bugles sounding the charge or the retreat and the shouting voices of individual commanders. Particularly, Thomas Jackson, whose strong voice and mounted presence gave courage to all the stout defenders who strove to push back the Union invaders. Jackson earned a new name that day, "Stonewall Jackson," and had become a hero for his bold action under fire. His bravery may have won the day for the South.

Finally, after two hours of listening to commands and executing them, it was over. Time at last to eat, before settling into tents for some much needed rest. Daniel put a hand to his pocket to check that the letter from Jenny was still there. He was looking forward to opening it after supper. Then he could take time before the sun went down to read it in private. He looked forward to that.

Eli was making their supper tonight. Daniel, Hank, and Keith sat nearby, two of them on a log watching Eli tend the fire. Already the aroma, borne on wispy smoke, was attracting their attention. The Johnny cakes sizzled in the bacon grease in the pan while chunks of meat roasted on their bayonets over the fire.

"That's smelling awfully good," said Keith, lounging on the ground with his hat tipped to keep the setting sun out of his eyes. "How much longer?"

Eli looked up from watching the frying pan. "Why, you hungry or somthin'?"

"Sure am," spoke Daniel, eyeing the pan from where he sat on the log.

"Won't be long now, boys," Eli answered, turning over the Johnny cakes in the pan. He eyed the bayonet spits. "Meat might take a little longer but these will soon be ready."

"I'm famished," added Hank. "Don't we have coffee?"

"It's coming. Think it's ready now. Go ahead and pour it, but grab that towel. The kettle's going to be hot," said Eli.

"Aah, that's more like it," said Daniel, sipping his coffee.

Soon, they all had coffee and Johnny cakes, and before long the meat was ready. Settling back, they talked about the day and also about what they thought might be coming in the future. So far, there had been no talk or any reports of the Union army reorganizing and returning to attack their position. Eli speculated that the Confederate army would stay there, maybe for months, because the North would have to pass this way if they wanted to attack the capital in Richmond.

Daniel pulled his hat down over his eyes, partly to block the now setting sun, but also because he wanted to think. It came to him that if they did stay, and there were no forthcoming battles, he might be able to get a furlough. He desperately wanted to see Samantha. Jenny was also on his mind. Something about the girl tended to make him smile. He decided he would try to find a way to return home.

The men retired satisfied, after a good meal, and went to make adjustments to their tent. Two went inside, while

Hank stayed outside to reread the letter he had received at last mail call. Daniel came back to the now dying embers of the fire, and sitting on the log, pulled out Jenny's letter. At last, he could read it in quiet. He saw she had started it with, "Dear Friend." He smiled as he took it in both hands and began to read.

Dear Friend,

We all heard about your wonderful victory. We were so happy. Pa said you should have gone on to march to Washington and end this war with a Southern victory. But that's just what he and some others are saying. Your generals probably know a lot more about it.

He read the first few lines. *Yes,* he thought, *it was a great victory.* Jenny might not have known how many were killed and wounded. Still, her father was right. We should have chased them back and ended the war right then and there.

Daniel, I can't hide my fear any longer. We heard that soldiers were killed on both sides. I am so afraid for you. That we have not received any letter from you is just plain scary. I comfort myself thinking that there is a lot more to being a soldier than fighting, and that you are busy and haven't had time to write. I pray that is so.

Reading these lines, he realized she wouldn't have known that he was one of those called on to bury the dead and bring in the wounded. He needed to write to her.

Despite the wonderful news of your successful battle, the news here has not been good. We wish our soldiers were here, to protect us from the enemy. Not sure if you know, but in the western part of Virginia, the Yankees have won some victories. In fact, right now there are a lot of them camped not far from us. People in town are mostly scared. They talk in whispers, because we can't do anything about them.

Daniel was mad. He clenched his hand into a fist, the one not holding the letter. He thought, *we have held back the enemy here only to let them take over our home town. Poor Jenny, Samantha, and my own parents and the townspeople. Having to live in fear on their own land.*

Yes, Daniel, it happened just a few days ago. I was in the house when a whole troop of them marched by on the road by our front gate. There must have been a thousand or more. Then, some of them opened the gate and came into our yard. They didn't even stop at the house to ask, but just began helping themselves to the pump, filling their canteens.

That's when Pa, David and Marcus came back up from the lower forty. As you might imagine, there was some words spoken, and then Pa swung at one of them, knocking him down. I know, a real foolish thing for him to do, especially when there must have been twenty Yankees there. Well, the guy got up right away, swung at Pa and knocked him down. That's when I rushed out. Fortunately, the soldier in charge, a captain, sent the troublemaker away. He even apologized to my father for what happened.

Daniel didn't want to believe what he just read. He knew Jenny's father, a good, upstanding man. Yet knocked down by a Yankee soldier trespassing on his own land. *What has this country come to* he wondered.

So that's what we're living with around here. Sarah told me that Angela was going to have a party—to celebrate your great victory, but I doubt if that's going to happen now.

Don't know what else to write, Daniel. I just hope you are well. Would love to send you something through the mail, if you could tell me what you could use. Not sure if any food would keep during the summer, but maybe later, if you are still fighting for us when it gets colder. I sure hope you are home by then, safe and sound.

Your true and lasting friend,

Jenny

Daniel finished reading the letter and smiled at Jenny's last lines. She was a true friend. He hoped that there would be no further trouble there, and wished that the great army that he was a part of could go there and send those Yankees back north where they belong. Then he thought of Samantha. Why didn't she write? Surely it was common knowledge of their great victory. Even that didn't matter if she would only write. He was beginning to become concerned about her.

Slowly, thoughtfully, he folded the letter and put it back into his pocket. He would reread it, think about it, and then write back. He thought of Jenny and a smile came to his face. He was glad he knew her. There was something about that girl.

Chapter Ten

The army wasn't moving! Daniel was getting tired of the boring routine and constant drilling, several times a day. Seems Eli was right. Apparently, the whole army was staying in this strategic place to make sure the Yankees wouldn't attempt to come back this way to attack Richmond, the confederate capital. Daniel thought more and more of his folks back home, and the girl he left behind.

Finally, he received a letter from Samantha, and once again felt that all was all right between them. She had not forgotten him. Furthermore, she wrote that the Union army had moved on and the people in his hometown could live their lives free from fear.

Daniel wondered again about his army, thinking, *are we going to spend the whole winter here?* He wanted to go home. He wished the war was over. But, since that wasn't going to happen anytime soon, his second thought was to try to secure a furlough. Others had done it. Maybe he could get one as well. He so wanted to see Samantha and spend time with her just like before. He wanted to see Jenny also. He really appreciated that she was faithful in writing. Even more than his own mother had been. He was glad to learn from Jenny what was going on in the neighborhood and in town. Local news was always of interest to him.

* * *

Winter was coming. Already, most of the leaves had dropped from the trees and frosty weather greeted them in the morning. Ah, hot coffee with a warm breakfast was the best thing for that. Thankfully, his parents had sent him some warm clothes. And Jenny had sent him a warm hat. Wasn't like his military issue, but he wore it a lot—any time he didn't have to participate in the drills. The hat was so warm by comparison, he actually cherished it. And, of course, he remembered Jenny, the thoughtful girl who had sent it.

So, he thought, *what is the huge army doing just sitting here in one place? Ostensibly they were there to protect the enemy route to Richmond. But what army would set out in winter?* Daniel thought more and more that instead he should be home.

The next day, he and his friends began building a small log structure. One that was going to be their "winter quarters." Something to hopefully keep out the cold night air. A place that would actually have a fireplace. Now, amid all the talk and commotion of close quarter camp life, the sound of axes biting wood was steady.

"OK," said Eli, who had been bending over with an axe, hacking away to notch a log. "Here's another one ready."

103

Hank left from helping Daniel to position the previous log, and he and Eli carried the next one to the shelter which was rapidly taking shape. As they continued the next day with building, Daniel took some time to slip over to the Lieutenant's log house to put in his request for leave. On returning, he encouraged his friends to do the same. Later that same night, he wrote letters to Samantha, Jenny, and his parents

.

* * *

"OK, let's go," said Daniel as he and Hank grabbed their haversacks and bedrolls with their clothes inside. It was surprising how light they felt without having to also carry their rifles and cartridge boxes. Saying goodbye to their messmates, Eli, John, and Keith, they began walking out of the camp. It was still early in the morning. Already, they were passing soldiers in other battalions they didn't know.

"On furlough," said Hank to one soldier who looked inquisitively at him.

Daniel actually enjoyed the stares, though he felt sorry that more were not allowed leave time to return home. He suspected that his recent promotion to corporal had something to do with his luck in obtaining a pass. That pass was important. He held it safe in his underneath shirt pocket close to his heart. He wore an extra shirt now that cold weather had come to northern Virginia. On the pass were written the terms of his leave status: dates, a description of him, the Lieutenant's signature, and an official stamp.

The two men walked comfortably together through the camp, and when they reached the farthest point, they their passes out to show to the picket on duty. He looked at the passes, looked up at them, and said. "Wish I could go home too."

"Try," said Daniel. "They can only say no and they might say yes."

"I'll do that," he said, and waved them off.

From talking to others, Daniel and Hank had a fairly good idea of how to find their way to Manassas Junction, where they hoped to get on the train. Neither had much in the way of currency, but they knew that a law had been passed allowing confederate soldiers free rides on southern railroads.

After a long walk, they made it to Manassas Junction. No train awaited them, so they sat down on benches near the track, lifted off their backpacks and waited. Nearby were buggies and wagons of every sort, waiting either to pick up or drop off passengers and freight. Finally, they heard the horn sound, and soon the great train arrived, chugging into the station, followed by a huge plume of black smoke arising from its smokestack.

Even though stopped, the train engine continued to make noise which was accentuated by the shouts of conductors, baggage handlers, and men whose purpose was to unload cargo into their waiting wagons. Others were loading supplies into the train.

Daniel and Hank could see that the train wasn't going anywhere soon, and they watched with interest all the activity associated with the modern mechanical beast which was already changing old ways of delivering people and merchandise.

Other passengers were arriving. A woman with three small children, some ladies, and the two soldiers waited with the others until the "all aboard" words were sounded.

There was plenty of passenger space, so they sat down together on seats near the middle of a car where they expected to have a good look at the view as the train headed west.

"This is comfortable," said Hank, who sat down on the bench seat next to the window, with Daniel settling in next to him.

"Sure is," agreed Daniel, "but nothing like Pa's sitting room chair at home."

A few more soldiers got on as well as other passengers of all kinds: several businessmen wearing coats, vests and top hats, and a few middle aged women who seemed to be traveling together. The passenger compartment was only half filled and no one sat in the bench directly across from theirs. Daniel knew he didn't smell too fresh and neither did Hank. Maybe that was the reason. One more reason to get home, bathe, put on fresh laundered clothing and sit at the table with his Ma and Pa and little sister for some good home cooking. How he looked forward to that!

The train whistle blew, those saying goodbye along the track backed away, and with a mighty chug, chug, chug, the great train slowly started on its journey west.

The conductor soon came around asking for tickets or money. Daniel and Hank glanced at each other, and pulled out their furlough papers. The man looked rather closely at each, then looked at them, and said, "OK, soldiers. Enjoy the ride."

As the train picked up speed, Daniel gazed at the rapidly passing scene. He was going home. To his parents and to the two girls he most wanted to see. He smiled, and leaned across to punch Hank's shoulder. "See," he said, "We're respected. Our government in Richmond cares about us."

Hank turned to him and said, "I guess. Sure wish they could come up with some more appetizing food."

The 87-mile train ride was long, as the speed was scarcely over twenty miles an hour and it made several stops along the way. As it chugged into its final destination, Mount Jackson, dusk was falling, and the two soldiers wondered where they would spend the night. They each had half of a Union tent, acquired after the Yankee flight from Manassas, but the idea of spending a night in a tent while in a town seemed somehow silly. And, with darkness falling, it was much too late to set out on the long walk that would take them home.

The two stood not far from where they had left the train. "What do you think, Hank?" Daniel asked. "Should we see if someone will take us in or go to the hotel?"

Hank looked out on the town buildings, most within an easy walk from the station, and said, "I don't know. What does it cost to stay in a hotel?"

"Don't know for sure, but I'm thinking it's two or three dollars. And I've heard you get food and breakfast with that."

"Then it's worth it to me, brother," Hank answered. "Real food and sleeping on a real bed. Let's do it."

They walked into the hotel and approached the man at the counter.

"You two boys look like you could use a room," said the well suited middle aged man standing there. "For soldiers like you, fighting for our independence, I have a very nice room."

"Yes sir, and thank you," answered Daniel. "How much is a room?"

"Normally it's two bucks, but for you boys, I can do it for $1.50. You know, that includes a nice big breakfast in the morning."

Daniel looked at Hank whose face and nod showed he was definitely in agreement.

"We'll take it, sir," said Daniel.

The man got their names, wrote them down on the registrar, had them sign a paper and collected the money. While he was doing that, Hank noticed a sign showing they could get a hot bath for one dollar. As they had not bathed for a while, he was interested, but to him a dollar seemed like too much extra to pay. Especially as he would get a free bath at home.

A woman, whom they had not noticed lounging in a hotel chair behind them approached. She appeared to be of about thirty years of age with long black hair wearing a silky top which emphasized her breasts. "You boys are soldiers, aren't you?"

They turned to her, both answering, "Yes, ma'am."

"You deserve better, I mean fighting for our independence and all. I have a tub in my room already most filled with clean water. Come on over after you leave your things in your room and I'll add some hot water to make a nice bath for you. You don't have to pay the hotel's high prices. My room number is twenty-six."

They got the key to their room, noted there was a fairly large bed, big enough for two, a basin on a shelf with water, a washcloth, two towels and a small, high window overlooking the back. All quite cozy and as much as they hoped for.

"You want to go first for the bath," asked Hank. "She said room twenty-six."

"I'm a bit leery about it," said Daniel. "It could be just nice of her, but makes me wonder," he added, looking straight on at his friend.

"Leave your wallet here, and anything else of value," suggested Hank.

"OK," he answered, taking out his billfold and handing it to Hank. "Sure would like to get cleaned up without paying a fortune for it."

"Yell, if there's a problem. These walls are so thin, I'm sure I'd hear you."

Taking one of the two towels, Daniel went down the hall to room number twenty-six. Approaching the door, he heard soft singing, and as he came to it he smelled something sweet. He knocked lightly, and would have called her by name, but didn't know what it was.

"Coming," she said. He heard the door bolt being retracted.

Entering the room, Daniel saw the tub in the center, and looked at the woman, who looked at him in a funny way saying, "I added hot water, so you should find it comfortable."

Daniel looked around the room. It was softly lit with candles, and a red curtain on a large window was pulled tight. He felt a little funny, with the woman there, until she said, "This is a double room. I'll go into the other room, you make yourself comfortable in the water. There's soap on the edge of the tub. Oh, I see you brought a towel. I just appreciate what you boys are doing for us, keeping those Yankees away."

"Thank you, ma'am," he answered. "This is very nice of you." He waited until she disappeared into the other room and had closed the door. Then, he removed his outer and

109

inner garments and slipped into the water. What an experience! One he hadn't had for months. The tub was large enough that with his legs bent he could sink down to his chest in the warm water. Pure pleasure!

He would have liked to stay, but knowing that he was a guest and that Hank would come in after him, he got to work using the soap in his hair, making a lather, and then washing every part of himself. He was just about ready to emerge, a clean man, when the woman came back into the room. "This time, she was dressed in a far different way, if one could call it dressed at all.

"I've an extra treat for you, Johnny Reb."

Daniel looked at her. Her hair was down, and she wore only a short slip showing every part of her legs, with a neckline so low her ample breasts were almost fully exposed. She came closer to him, and then right up to the tub, and took a seat on its edge.

Daniel was glad his nether parts were safely covered by water, for the woman was definitely affecting him in a most personal way.

She leaned toward him. "Honey, I know you've been off fighting for us, missing all the things at home. I know a man needs a woman from time to time, don't you see. I can help you forget all those terrible things you've seen in battle."

Many things were going through Daniel's head as she sat there, waiting for his answer. He had never known a woman. This one was much too friendly and offering far too much to think that her offer had anything to do with appreciation. He felt sure she wanted money, though she had said nothing about it. On the other hand, she would be an easy way for him to experience the grand pleasure, with no further commitment or obligation. Only some money. But this woman was a stranger to him. Not one that he loved or cared about.

He looked up at the woman who now was looking down at him. She looked vulnerable, not hard and professional, at least not apparently so. Finally, he thought of what his father had told him about this kind of woman—that they often carried diseases that could have a lasting deleterious effect on him.

"Get off!" he said, in a loud voice. "Leave me to get dressed."

"You don't want me, Johnny Reb?" she said in a honey-sugared voice. She twisted on the edge of the tub, bringing her breasts closer to his face.

Daniel couldn't help but notice them, and in truth he would very much have liked to take them in his hands. But he didn't like that she refused even to acknowledge his words. "Do you not hear, woman? I came here at your kind offer of a bath. That's all."

Abruptly she got up, and standing a bit away from the tub said, "I was going to show you a real good time, soldier. Get up, get dressed, and get out of here!" She stomped out of the room, entered the adjoining one, and slammed the door shut.

Daniel stood up in the tub, dried off his upper body, then one leg and the other, and quickly got dressed, glad she didn't return. He left the large soap bar, but took a small one and returned to the room he and Hank shared.

"All done?" asked Hank, grabbing the other towel.

"She's offering more than a bath."

Hank stopped in mid-stride, turning back to him.

"What do you mean?"

111

"Well, she left the room while I bathed, but later came back wearing a skimpy slip that showed just about everything she had."

"Really? What did she say?"

Daniel proceeded to tell him everything that happened. He was amused that he was so curious, even having him describe her breasts. Hank sat down. Daniel knew he was aroused. Yet he also knew that he was of a religious nature, one who usually attended every one of the religious services that came around their camps.

"Guess I won't get my warm bath," he said, dejectedly.

Daniel went to him where he sat on the chair. "Hey, I took this small bar of soap. She won't miss it because she had a big one. You could use it and clean up with the pitcher of water on the counter."

"Yeah," he said. "Not a bath, but better than nothing."

While Hank was bathing himself with the soap and water, Daniel tucked himself in, glad to be sleeping on a real bed. He looked forward to a delicious breakfast in the morning and then to setting out on the long hike that would at last take them home.

Chapter Eleven

Jenny had long since cleaned up the dishes from breakfast and now was washing clothes this November day. She had on her coverall work apron which saved her clothes from getting wet and dirty, depending on what she was doing. Washing the family clothes was one of the tasks she hated to do because after a while the lye soap irritated her skin.

The day was sunny and breezy, and even though the temperature was probably only in the forties, she thought that given time things would dry. Finished with scrubbing the garments on the board, she already had transported them to the rinsing tub. There, after swirling them around, she wrung them out and went to hang them on the multiple clotheslines her Dad had erected near the kitchen door. As she was hanging them up, using clothespins, she heard the sound of a buggy and the front gate opening. Her father must have returned.

She was hoping to receive a letter from Daniel so went right back in to see him after hanging up the last of the clothes.

"Hi, Pa. How was your trip?"

"Well, I got what I needed and they took the peach preserves you made in trade for some of it. He laid his heavy armful of things on the table. They included soap, some ammunition, several huge pickles, coffee, suspenders, a lantern, and boots. "These boots are real comfortable," he said as he reached into his back pocket. "Here's a letter for you—from Daniel."

"Thank you, Daddy." She came to the table saying, "I'll put the kitchen things and the soap away."

"That's a good girl, Jenny. I'll get the rest later, but right now I'm just going to sit a spell and read the paper."

"I made some tea. You sit down and I'll bring you a cup."

Jenny was solicitous of her father. He had married a bit later in life and now she felt he was getting on in years. His hair was already mostly gray, and though he always worked a hard day on the farm, she knew it seemed to tire him out more lately. It was her wish that he would live to see and enjoy his grandchildren.

She turned away from him; he was already engrossed in reading his paper, and the thought of grandchildren suddenly made her think of Daniel. Of course, that wasn't very likely, knowing of his fondness for Samantha. Still, a girl could hope. She took the letter to her room. Toward evening, when she was done with her chores, she would savor every line he wrote to her. Her biggest hope was that he could get a furlough and come home. She so looked forward to seeing him.

114

Darkness came early this time of year, so she quickly made a light meal for her menfolk—her Pa, her brother, David, as well as for Marcus. David had since come in, wearing his brown cowhide winter coat with the liner inside. He took off his big brimmed brown hat, and noticeably limped to the sitting room, taking a chair to the side of her father. Jenny was secretly glad of his injury, the result of an accident with the tiller when he was young. Now, she wouldn't lose him to the Civil War. Her father and brother began talking about how they were going to try to trap the wily gray fox that one by one was killing the chickens.

"Supper's ready," she called out from the kitchen.

Jenny joined in their conversation a little, but not being all that hungry, soon left to go to her room, telling her pa she would come back later to clean up. Now she would have time to read Daniel's letter. She got it out of the top drawer and sat down on her bed.

My dear friend, Jenny,

Thank you for the warm socks you sent with your last letter. With the weather getting colder, they are helping to keep my feet warm.

We have been spending a lot of time at our camp near Manassas. Not moving, not fighting, just drilling several times a day, eating, sleeping and building our own winter quarters out of logs. That's what me, Hank, Eli, Keith and John have been spending our time doing. We're making a fireplace inside and hope to be warm when the real cold weather comes.

You might wonder what an army is doing just staying in one place. Well, they don't officially tell us anything, but some boys who seem to be in the know say we are staying here to make sure the Yankees don't come through this way on the way to our capital in Richmond. They tell me that it would be the natural way for them to come.

115

But I don't much guess any army is going to be moving troops in the winter. Already the roads are getting muddy with the rain, and when snow comes, it is only going to get worse.

So, here's the good news. I was finally able to get a furlough. Hank got one too. We will be leaving tomorrow on the train that will take us to Mount Jackson. From there we will have to walk many miles over some big hills, but I think in a couple days we can make it back.

You can imagine how I'm looking forward to coming home, to sleep under an actual roof, get washed up and put on clean clothes. Then I am looking forward to seeing you and Samantha and all the friends left who are not with the army. I would like to stop by to see you on the way to Samantha's. I'm hoping that since me and Hank will be home at Christmastime, someone will give a party where we can all have some fun. You can well imagine that Hank and I want to forget the war, at least for a time.

Looking forward to seeing you,

Your friend, Daniel

Jenny read the letter a second time and a tear caught in her eye. That's the way it always was for Daniel. He would stop to see her on his way to Samantha's. True, it was better than his not stopping at all. She should be thankful for that.

Though darkness had fallen, it still wasn't late in the day. She decided to put on her coat and walk over to Sarah's house. As she made her way there, she pulled her coat tighter around her for a stiff breeze made it feel colder than it was. She was glad when she saw the lamplight glowing as she arrived at her friend's house. She knocked quietly on the door, in case anyone was already in bed, and waited on the wood decked porch.

Sarah answered the door with a big smile when she saw her friend, opened it for her, and Jenny stepped inside.

116

"Shhh," she said, with her finger to her mouth. "My parents are already in their bedroom. Don't think they're sleeping yet, but you know."

Jenny saw that Sarah was already in her warm, corduroy robe, the pretty, brandy colored one. She looked toward the closed door "OK," she answered. "We can be quiet." She was very much aware that many farm families went to bed at sundown and got up early in the morning. She took off her coat, saying "Good to see you."

"Sure is. Now that it gets dark so early, doesn't leave much time to get everything done. How've you been?"

"Good. Since the Union soldiers have moved on, I feel safe walking after dark again. Got news today from Daniel. He and Hank Peters were able to get leave from the army. They should be coming home any day now."

"Terrific! Then they can come to Angela's party."

"Oh, the party is on again?"

"Yes, I just found out from Cole when he was passing through."

"Oh that will be nice," said Jenny, cocking her head and thinking. "Her parents have a big house. Wouldn't be surprised if she had a fiddler or two for dancing."

"You can count on her and her folks to do it up big. Not for sure of the date yet, but as close as it is to Christmas, they might have something Christmassy for a theme. Say, have you heard anything about your brother? Could he maybe get a furlough too?"

"No," Jenny answered quickly. "He doesn't write very often." Suddenly, the thought occurred to her that her brother, who joined the Yankees, could be a pariah in the mostly Confederate town. There could be trouble. "What about your brother? Any chance he also could get leave?"

117

"I'm hoping to beat all he does," Sarah answered, a bit of discontentment registering on her face. "I know he wants to come home, but I guess it's not that easy."

Jenny changed the subject to one she wondered about, especially since she hadn't seen Sarah for a week and a half. Casually, she asked, "Do you still see Rex?"

Sarah suddenly looked away, and softly said, "No, he hasn't been around. I've heard he has taken up with someone else."

Jenny noted her words were spoken with a certain finality. She knew of Rex's reputation, of being one to flit from girl to girl. Reaching out to put a hand on Sarah's arm, she said, "You just don't know about him, Sarah. When he's through sampling, he might settle down, but in the meantime someone just right for you could come along."

"Oh, I know, Jenny," Sarah said with resignation. "I guess every girl would like to get on with someone like him."

"Aah, yes," said Jenny, "An easy life with household slaves to do all the work. Wouldn't that be refined?"

Sarah sighed. "It could have been so."

"But, if you love someone, . . ." Jenny left her thought unfinished.

"Yes, if," said Sarah.

* * *

Both Daniel and Hank had a good night's sleep that night on the comfortable hotel bed.

In the morning, they put on their clothes and looked forward to the wonderful breakfast that the hotel offered,

118

included in their charge. Both men carried some food in their haversacks for the long journey over the mountains, but that was only sustenance food, fairly unappetizing, though enough to keep body and soul together. What they looked forward to, especially when the aroma drifted to their room, was real food. Wanting to get an early start on their long journey, they didn't delay on arising, and soon appeared in the dining room.

Though they were among the first there, the food was ready. Coffee, hotcakes with maple syrup, bacon, eggs, cut up potatoes and fresh bread with plenty of butter. Knowing they had a long journey ahead of them, they stuffed themselves.

Then they went back to their room, packed their limited belongings, and as the sun was beginning to make an appearance in the east, they began hiking out of town. Mount Jackson wasn't a large town, and as they took the upper trail, its houses soon grew smaller and smaller whenever they looked back. The sun's appearance was only brief, for soon it was obscured by gray skies.

Long before noon, they reached higher altitudes, and though they kept going, their breathing was heavy.

"We're going to need a break soon," said Hank, in a belabored voice, now ten paces behind Daniel.

"I was waiting for you to say something," Daniel replied, looking down from his spot a few feet above him.

"Could have mentioned it much sooner then." Hank joined him, looking down and breathing hard.

"This is tough, but let's wait till we come to a flat place where we can take a break and stop for a bite to eat."

"Agreed, if it doesn't take too long. Lead on."

Not long afterwards they reached a fairly level spot, stopped, took a drink from their canteens, and got out some cornbread from their haversacks. They were perched on a spot overlooking a river far below and what in the distance looked like miniature houses across the valley.

"Look at that view," said Hank, in an awe inspired voice.

"Pretty as a picture," agreed Daniel.

After resting, they took up again where they had left off, knowing that there were many miles to cover. Later, darkness began to fall, and with it the evening seemed to be growing cooler.

"This looks like a good place to stop for the night," said Hank. It's relatively flat, and we can get some shelter from the wind there by those shrubs."

Daniel looked up at the sky which now was clear. "There's a full moon rising, Hank. Should be enough to light our way. Why don't we continue as far as we're able to maybe get to the downward side. It will be easy going down, and if we can keep at it, we may be able to make it home by morning."

"Really? If you think we can do it I'll try to keep going. Bury me along the trail if I don't make it," he said, with something of a strained smile.

Daniel noted the smile and flashed Hank a big smile back. His friend was considerably bigger than himself, which made all the more weight to carry across the mountains. "OK, let's try. What keeps me going is thinking of a warm bed and family awaiting me. But if at any time you want to stop, we'll do that."

"OK." Standing up from where he had seated himself, he said with enthusiasm, "Let's go."

They continued for at least two hours, and then for some more, noting that now they were definitely going more downward than up. Daniel saw the winter constellation of Orion rising higher and higher in the sky, which meant it would soon be midnight. Though he didn't mention it, he was secretly glad that Hank had been willing, despite his weariness, to continue hiking. But now they were both exhausted.

A small town came into view below them, the moon cast shadows over the rooftops, and inside the windows they could see the soft glow of the fireplaces.

"Wish we could stay in one of those houses," said Hank, echoing exactly what Daniel was thinking.

"Too bad we didn't come on it earlier. At this hour of the night I don't think anyone would welcome us."

They walked along the edge of the village without seeing anyone stirring. As they were near leaving, they espied a shed, and coming closer to it they saw that it was closed by a stick of wood though a hasp on the door.

"What do you think?" asked Daniel. "This might be a place for us to stay."

"Depends what's inside there. It would stop the wind, and keep the frost off our tent."

They both came up to the shed, one standing on one side and the other on the opposite side of the door opening. Daniel pulled out the stick of wood, and they cautiously opened the door, first a little and then wide enough that they could see inside by the light of the moon. No animals rushed out, they were glad of that, and inside they saw some farm equipment, buckets, many loops of thick rope hanging on a post, and straw on the ground with enough room for two or more to sleep.

"Looks like a bed to me," said Hank.

"Much easier than setting up the tent," agreed Daniel

They began to bed down, taking off only their hats and boots, and Daniel tried to close the door so the shed would not appear to be open from the outside. Exhausted as they were from the long hike, both were soon sound asleep.

* * *

By the first light of morning, late, due to the season, three people, a woman and two men, made their way quietly toward the shed. The woman was unarmed, but both of the men carried loaded rifles. She showed them the door of the shed, minus the stick locking it, with the door slightly ajar. One of the men motioned her to go toward it, and to quickly grab the handle and open it. The men took positions directly in front, waiting until the door was opened with their rifles pointed inside.

Suddenly, the woman swung open the door, and both Daniel and Hank opened their eyes to the bright light of morning. They immediately saw two men pointed their weapons at them. One was large with a gray, prominent beard, and the other was thin and lanky, whose one arm seemed limp under his sleeve.

"Get up and raise your hands peaceably," said the one in a rough, uncompromising voice.

Knowing they were in the wrong, using another's shed without permission, both quickly did as he said, raising their hands high.

The slender, much younger man spoke with much more friendliness, and the woman too, who stood further away seemed suddenly much more at ease. "Secesh uniforms. What are you boys doing here?"

"On furlough, sir," said Daniel. "Got papers to prove it. Just wanted a place to rest overnight."

"Secesh are you?" said the other man. Then you're on our side. You don't have to go sneaking around. Just should've asked."

"We came in after midnight, sir" said Hank. "Didn't want to wake you folks up."

"Oh, hell, don't call me sir," said the older man, setting his gun down. I'm Willie, this here is my son, Jeremy, and that's my niece, Clementine." The men came forward to shake hands, and Clementine looked at them, seeming as if she wanted to say something but thus far not speaking at all.

Finally, she did speak in a voice loud enough to hear, but still not loud at all. "Come in and I'll make up a fresh breakfast. Got to be better than what the army gives you." Then speaking up she added, "You too, Willie, Jeremy. I'll make up some hotcakes, fry sausages and serve it with potatoes with butter on top. Oh, and of course, coffee."

Daniel said, "That's a lot of trouble for you, ma'am. We thank you kindly, but Hank and I got enough rations for the way home." In saying that he noticed what he could only interpret as a surly stare from Hank.

"Nonsense. It's only right for men like you who put your life on line to protect the South. Now don't go turning a good thing down cause of pride or somethin."

"Yes, ma'am," Hank was quick to reply. "We'd be more than happy to sit and dine with y'all." He glanced toward Daniel, wearing a smile.

They all went into the parlor of the house, where a little boy was quietly playing with some homemade wooden shapes. Willie stood over him for a moment, seeing what he was doing with the blocks. Then, he said to them, "You boys

123

take a seat. I want to see what Junior here is building." He bent down and sat on the floor next to the boy, then looked up at the others, a smile on his face. "He likes these wooden shapes I made for him."

Daniel learned from Jeremy that Willie was the boy's great-uncle, and he, Hank and Jeremy watched the two while making small talk and waiting on breakfast. Clementine came from the kitchen saying, "You men might want to wash up your hands cause breakfast is about ready."

They went outside to the well, pumped water into a bucket and washed. Willie carried Junior out with him, getting his hands wet in the water too. Then they tromped back inside where Clementine was waiting for them

"Jeremy would you pull up an extra chair?"

He did, and they sat down to a delicious home cooked breakfast.

Talk went to the war, not surprisingly. Daniel and Hank learned that Jeremy was one of the early casualties, losing his left hand to amputation. Clementine seemed not to want to talk, while the men carried on their conversation. Daniel noticed that she seemed to be becoming more and more agitated, putting her hands in her lap and her head seeming to twitch.

"I just miss him so much," she said, dropping her head as tears began flowing. "Who's going to help me raise Joseph?"

Willie, who was sitting next to her, reached for her hand, and in a low voice said, "Maybe he will yet come back to us, Clemmie."

"But I got no letter," she said in a loud voice. "It's been too long not to hear from him."

Daniel bowed his head. He hated to see her upset. He knew that sometimes letters were lost, and also knew that besides those killed, many were injured or had been brought down by infectious diseases. Yet some survived after weeks or even months of recuperation. "He ain't necessarily dead, ma'am," he said in the gentlest voice he had in him.

"Do you know somethin?" she asked, raising her head and looking directly at him.

He proceeded to tell her and the others what he knew, Hank and him having been assigned to take injured and sickly soldiers to the hospital. "They take care of them in a big house not far from the battlefield, and the ones who need longer care they send to hospitals in Richmond."

"God almighty! You would think they'd let a body know."

Willie spoke softly in her ear. "Have to be patient a while longer, Clemmie. He could be one of those Daniel is talking about."

She turned toward him, leaned her head on his shoulder, and with tears still falling said, "God, I hope so, Willie."

Chapter Twelve

Jenny got his letter, the one saying he was likely going to be coming home. Sometime early December. He didn't know exactly when. Jenny wished she knew, because she wanted to be able to fix her hair and wear something nice when he came. She was so looking forward to the day.

After a chilly morning, the afternoon of December seventh gradually became brighter as the clouds rolled away and the sun made its appearance. Meals were served earlier in wintertime, and Jenny was almost finished with cleaning the dishes when she heard the gentle gallop of a horse and buggy.

Leaving the kitchen and peering out through the sitting room window, she espied what appeared in the distance to be the man she was waiting for. Quickly, she went to her room, removed her apron, brushed her hair back, and pinched her cheeks to give them that ever popular rosy appearance, and put on her better shawl. Then, she went to the door, stepped out onto the little porch and waved as Daniel came to a stop in front.

She surveyed him as he tied his horse to the post, and went immediately to the gate.

"Golly, it is good to see you, Daniel," she said, eyeing him, taking in his demeanor, his white shirt, waist coat, jacket, dark pants and brown boots. As usual, he wore nothing on his head, his dark brown hair thick and swept by the wind.

"Glad to see you, as well," he said, drawing closer, and then, to her surprise, taking her in his arms.

Jenny was almost taken aback by that, but nestled happily in his arms the brief time that he held her.

"What is it with you?" he said. "How could you be even more beautiful than before?"

Jenny drank in his words, smiling. "You say the nicest things, Daniel. Would you like to come inside?"

"So much has happened. Let's talk. Just the two of us."

"Well, there's no one in the house now, but my Pa and brother will soon come in because the sun is already starting to go down."

"Ride with me in the buggy."

"I would love to."

Together, they walked out the gate, Daniel helped Jenny up, unhitched the horse, and set off. Daniel set the horse at a walk, and as there was a breeze, got out the blanket to put around her, and proceeded down the road.

"I really appreciate your keeping in touch with me, letting me know what's going on around here, and all your thoughtful gifts. The scarf, the warm socks, the mittens. You made them yourself, didn't you?"

Jenny loved hearing the sound of his voice, intermingled with the hoof beats and the rolling buggy wheels on the road. Content, she looked into his eyes, nodding yes.

"I'm damn lucky to know a girl like you. Some of the guys get hardly anything from home. It's like they're forgotten."

Jenny sat huddled next to him, almost a head shorter, as he sat erect, keeping his eyes mostly on the road ahead. "No one could forget you, Daniel," she murmured, mouth half covered with the blanket.

He turned to look at her, and smiled at how she seemed to be huddling from the cool breeze. "Yes," he said, "I'm damn lucky. My Mom, Dad, you, and Samantha back here looking out for me."

Jenny sat up and turned to face him directly. "Daniel, you're the one that is putting your life on the line protecting us. You and all the other men fighting for the South."

Daniel took his eyes off the road to look at her. "I'm glad you see it that way, Jenny."

They drove along quietly for a while, watching how the sun was gradually going down among white, puffy clouds. Daniel turned, leaving the main road to follow a little used trail through a canopy of trees.

"I've never been this way," said Jenny.

"Don't think many have. I followed the trail once out of curiosity just to see where it goes."

The two wheel wagon trail with vegetation in the middle curved deeper into the forest, and Jenny was beginning to wonder if the trip was safe. Then, she made

128

herself relax, believing that Daniel knew what he was doing. The trail led upwards, and before long, she began to see the light of a clearing. When they came to it Daniel had Bessie move forward until they could look down at a small lake below.

"Lovely," she said. "With the sun going down, lighting up the lake with color, this is a beautiful spot."

Daniel pointed into the distance. "See the trail leading around the left side of the lake? If you look, you can see the roof of the house where they live."

"Do you know anything about them?"

"Think they're brothers. An odd sort they are. I've seen them take their wagon into town to get supplies. Heavily bearded, with twice mended clothes. They look like folks you wouldn't want to talk to. When you get up close, they smell pretty bad."

"I guess it takes all kinds," she said, in her charitable nature.

"Yeah. Don't think they're at all dangerous. Just reclusive."

For a short time they were silent, and Jenny's thoughts went to what was often on her mind. She turned in her seat so that she could face Daniel directly. "Daniel, I've been wanting to ask you what it's like. What is war like?"

He turned to her, "It's terrible, Jenny, I mean the fighting part. Otherwise, it's mostly boring and sometimes tough."

"I'm so proud of you, Daniel."

"Well, I went in feeling proud, feeling real good about protecting the South from invasion, protecting our way of life. But now. . .," he hesitated.

Jenny saw his face kind of drop. She saw an expression she had never before seen on his face. An expression of pain. "It's OK, Daniel. You don't have to tell me."

Daniel seemed to regain his composure. He spoke, hesitantly at first and then in a normal voice. "I'll tell you how it was, Jenny. The fighting at Manassas had been going on since early in the morning. But our regiment was coming by train from Piedmont and arrived that afternoon. We were rushed toward the battle up on the hill. We saw a general on his horse standing tall, shouting above the noise to his troops not to fall back under the intense fire of the enemy. We were rushed into the battle ourselves, and from just under the top of the hill began firing at will into the enemy lines. The extra firepower of over a thousand new troops caved in their line, and suddenly they began drawing back. Their retreat turned into a rout and we chased them down the hill as they fled in panic."

"Ah, yes," she said. "Your valor and a victorious win for the South."

She saw him look away from her. When he turned toward her again, he said, in a very low voice, "I know, Jenny, that's how the papers describe it. But that's hardly the way it was. Nearly a thousand men died that day, and many of those that didn't were crying out in pain, moaning, begging for water. When our advance was called back and we returned up the hill, we couldn't help but see the ghastly mortal remains of those whose limbs, guts and even heads were blown away by bullets and cannon fire."

He turned to look at her directly, saying, "That's what war is really like, Jenny."

Jenny closed her eyes at the images he described, words failing her. She drew close to him, putting her arm around him. Both heads bowed, they said nothing. Then, she looked up. "Look at that beautiful sun starting to go down!" she exclaimed.

Daniel raised his head as well and looked out. "We're getting to the best part." They watched as the sun turned orange as it set lower and lower in the sky. White, billowing clouds caught the color, themselves becoming brilliant orange to fleecy white.

"Ah, it is truly beautiful," said Jenny, taking her blanket and nestling closer to Daniel.

"Ah yes," he said, turning to look at her. He took her hand as the sun slowly began to sink beneath the horizon, bands of streaming orange clouds illuminating the sky. They watched as it finished its descent, then stayed awhile longer in the twilight before he turned the buggy around and went back on the road toward her house.

By the time they returned, the sky had darkened and a few bright stars and a half moon appeared in the sky. Daniel got out, helped her down, and walked her to her front yard gate.

"Come in," she said quickly, not wanting him to leave." I'll quickly boil some tea and we have some delicious store bought candy."

He didn't answer but instead gathered her in his arms, and bending to her, kissed her.

Jenny reacted instinctively to his strong embrace and the feel of his lips on hers. She pressed her body on his, not wanting him to leave.

But, it was over all too soon as he stood up tall and straight.

"Are you sure you don't want to come in?" she asked. My pa and brother go to bed early cause they're early risers."

She saw him seem to look at her, as if he were considering the invitation. "No, can't stay as I'm going on to Samantha's."

Jenny's heart sank in her chest. She had thought that he had come only to see her. But no, this was only his usual stop along the way to **her** house. Quickly, she tried to compose herself, struggling to hide her feelings and to be civil. "But it's so late, Daniel," she said, those being the only words she could come up with.

"Oh, the horse knows the way I think, even in the dark and there's a half moon rising."

"But would she be expecting you so late?"

"She likes to sleep in, so I'm fairly sure she'll still be up reading by candlelight."

As it was obvious to Jenny that the man was ready to be on his way, she told him, "Thank you for coming by, Daniel. It was just lovely taking that ride with you and seeing the sun go down over the lake."

He was already stepping away, but turned to say, "You are really nice to be with, Jenny. You're special." With that, he was quickly at the gate, and opening it turned to wave goodbye to Jenny, whose feet hadn't moved at all since he walked away from her.

She felt rooted to the spot, watching as he stepped into the buggy, told the horse go forward, and drove away. *How could he do that?* she wondered. How could he be there with her, even talking of the things about the war he didn't want to talk about? She felt they had shared so much, how could he now simply drive off to see another woman? *Did he share his feelings that way with Samantha?* she wondered.

132

She walked slowly back to the front door of her house, and still thinking, opened it. The house was dark, save for a lone candle left burning by her father until she returned.

* * *

Jenny saw Daniel three more times in the short time he was on furlough. She never knew which day he would come, so she tried to always look her best. But it was always the same; he was stopping by on his way to Samantha's. What kind of a spell did that girl have on him?

In the meantime, her older brother also came home. How she and her family rejoiced to see him hale and hearty, still tanned from the sun, with some stories to tell. Jenny loved having him back, but she feared for when he would have to return. Then, there was something else she feared. Jeb had left to join the Union forces, while most of her town supported the South. She prayed there would be no animosity toward him.

A letter came in the mail. Addressed to the family, her father after glancing at it handed it to her. Jenny took it to her room. In fine lettering, there was much information included in the announcement, and she wanted to read it closely when she had more time. There was still some light left in the winter day by the time she had cleaned up after the meal. She rinsed her hands with water, drying them on her apron and went to her room to get the announcement. Standing by the light coming in from the window, she read it carefully.

"Music will be provided by Mr. Mandall at the piano with Mr. Taylor and his daughter Emily accompanying him on fiddle. The dance managers are: (She read the list of men who were to officiate and provide guidance to those participating.) The missive continued, "As a number of our brave fighting men are currently on furlough from the army,

133

we enjoin all present, especially the ladies, to honor them with our typical southern hospitality. We do not turn a gentleman down who asks for a dance unless previously spoken for or temporarily fatigued from dancing. Proper respect is to curtsy to him at the beginning of each dance and at the end.

Gentlemen, it is your right and obligation to offer your protection to the lady whose hand you hold at the dance. Proper respect is to bow to her before each dance and after. When the dance is over, escort her back to her chair.

We will not speak of dancing attire, as it should not be necessary, except to clarify that white gloves are the appropriate dress for both men and women for a formal dance."

Jenny read the rest of the announcement, and then sat down on her bed. It came to her that it might be the last time she would see Daniel before he had to go back. The thought came to her that it would be the best time to dress in such a way that he could not help but notice her. A smile came to her lips as her imagination took over.

That was Daniel's problem, she suddenly decided. He still thought of her as a girl. Well, she intended to show him, in a way that every man could understand, that she was a woman, one with her fair share of feminine curves. Now, how to do it. The first thing she thought of was her mother's corset. One she remembered helping her tie up in back. That would emphasize her figure. Then, she could easily make an alteration to her best dress. One to bring the neckline down lower. She smiled in anticipation. Daniel was going to know without a doubt that she was a grown up woman. She would leave no doubt in his mind.

The sky was darkening early, as it always did in winter. But it was not too late to visit Sarah. Like herself, she did not go to bed when the sun went down. Hurriedly, she put on her coat, and not telling anyone, was out the door, then quietly closing the front yard gate.

It took only a few minutes to reach her house, and looking up, she saw there was a light on in her room. Not sure if her parents had already gone to bed, she hesitated at the door, and then decided to try knocking quite softly.

Sarah came down from her room, opened the unlocked door, and ushered her in. She was wearing her night robe, but looked far from sleepy. "Jenny! Nice to see you. What's up!" She spoke softly, so as not to wake her parents.

Jenny kept her voice lowered as well, but that didn't detract from the eagerness in her voice. "Just got the ball announcement. So exciting. Did you get it too?"

"Oh, yes. Just this afternoon. I'm so glad. It's been so long since the town put one on. Everyone will be there."

"Including Daniel and some of the other men on furlough. I'm making plans about him."

"Plans? What do you mean?"

"Well, you know how I care about him. And that he thinks Samantha is the one for him."

"Yes, yes, I very much know that," she answered, seeming impatient to know the rest.

"Here's what I'm thinking. Daniel still thinks of me as that girl he helped when I fainted in school. His young friend, but not a full grown woman."

Sarah cocked her, head, looking at her friend from another angle. "You may be right. But what can you do about it?"

Jenny regarded Sarah in the last of twilight coming through the windows before answering. "Show him

135

something. Show him enough so he will have no doubt that I'm a fully filled out woman."

Sarah laughed, quickly holding her hands in front of her mouth so as not to waken her parents.

Jenny didn't know what to think of her friend's reaction, and stood looking at her.

"I love it!" she finally said. "You, who have always been so modest. And, maybe it will work. Who knows when it comes to men." She wrapped her arms around Jenny. "Let me help you with what you will wear. Oh, Jenny, this is delicious. When we are done, you are going to be turning heads. I'm so excited for you already."

They talked and talked some more. Later, Jenny left from Sarah's with a bounce in her step and a smile on her lips. She was going to do it. She was going to do what she needed to do to make him notice her.

Chapter Thirteen

It was the eve of the dance, held only a few days before Christmas. Jenny had been a little worried about the weather for it had been dark and cold, but now, as the day began to fade, streaks of sunlight lit up the sky.

Jenny was going alone. She had hoped her father would go and certainly her brother. But both said no, they would stay home. Jenny, concerned for her younger brother, that he would never meet anyone if he didn't socialize, had urged him more than once to go. But he in the end pointed to his leg, saying he wouldn't be very good on the dance floor.

So, she got herself ready to go, peeking in the mirror wearing the now lower cut dress, applying real rouge to her cheeks, and putting on her short cape, followed by her best winter shawl, and tucking her new white gloves into her handbag, she went to Sarah's. There, they would help each other put on the finishing touches before Rex came for them. Ready to leave now, she said goodbye to her father and brother and walked out, thinking as she walked, how fortunate Sarah was to have Rex take them both to the dance.

At Sarah's they helped each other tightly lace up their corsets, and both girls again peeked into the mirror to see the dramatic effect on their figures. Then, they spent some time styling each other's hair, striving for something just right for the occasion.

* * *

While the girls were getting themselves ready, Daniel was at his house choosing what he would wear. He was glad that both he and Hank were going. He looked forward to seeing friends he hadn't seen for a while, and he was proud that the town was having the dance to raise money to support the confederate cause. He also looked forward to seeing his girl, Samantha all decked out, as he knew she would be, and looking so pretty when she danced with him. Not that he would get to often. He knew the rules: be sociable, don't dance too often with any one person even if that person happened to be your spouse.

Since his return, besides seeing Samantha, he had enjoyed spending some time with Jenny. She was a great friend, and if he was honest with himself, he might realize there were some things he felt more comfortable talking about with her than with Samantha. One thing surprised him. She wasn't going with him to the dance, but with Rex and Sarah. He knew Rex. His handsome richness was not lost on girls. Somehow, he felt a little uneasy knowing Jenny would be with him, even though he knew he was not her date. Why did he feel that way about her? He guessed it was because she was like a younger sister to him, and he felt a need to protect her.

He was in his buggy now, taking the road to Samantha's, this time not stopping at Jenny's, though he did look toward her house while passing. When he picked up Samantha, he was immediately impressed by her appearance, both her lovely crimson gown and her hair in a fashionable bun with ringlets tumbling down such that when she turned quickly, they flew around her. Moving on, out of sight of her house, they exchanged a quick kiss before darting off with a gallop toward town.

When they reached the hall, before them was an impressive array of carriages of every type, from the humblest wagon to enclosed carriages pulled by two horses. Daniel was on the lookout for Hank, who was coming in from the other side of town.

"Hank!" he yelled on seeing him and the girl with him stepping down from their buggy.

"Daniel!"

Daniel quickly found a place to hitch his horse, he helped Samantha down, and the two couples moved toward each other.

"Hank, I would like to introduce Samantha Evans, the girl I've told you of often enough."

"Pleased to meet you," he replied, bowing slightly toward her.

"The pleasure is mine," answered Samantha with a genteel curtsy toward him. "I do hope Daniel hasn't mentioned any of my numerous faults." She glanced into Daniel's eyes.

Hank didn't respond to that but was quick to introduce his partner. "Let me introduce Miss Emily Barton, who has graciously agreed to allow me to escort her to tonight's dance."

Daniel made a slight bow in her direction, noted her amiable smile, her attractive honey colored hair, and how she was almost a foot shorter than Hank.

Introductions done, they walked two by two up the steps to the large door going into the hall.

The hall was abuzz with talking, and Daniel looked around at the dozens of candles lighting up the interior in soft, intimate lighting. Coat racks adorned one side of the room, the side without candles. In a corner of the other side, he saw a man seated at a piano with two girls on each side of him with their instruments.

One of the several dance managers stood up near him, and in loud voice announced, "Ladies and gentlemen, we are so glad you are here for a night of dancing and to support our troops. I am sorry that due to the size of crowd, there is insufficient seating for all, though certainly enough for all the ladies and perhaps enough for the older gentlemen as well. Before we begin, we would like to make sure that you all know the Gay Gordons. I'm sure many of you do, but may be out of practice. We will start tonight with that dance as it is a wonderful mixer. Then, we will continue with ball room dancing. Please remember ladies, as this is a social occasion, receive each gentleman who asks for a dance, unless your card is already filled. I know you are all anxious to begin, so let us proceed. First, those of you who are quite familiar with it please accompany us to the dance floor. Then, as you all pick up the steps, join in."

Daniel looked at Samantha, who nodded her head no. He was glad, for he would have said the same. He caught Hank's eye, and they both led the girls towards the chairs set around the dance floor. Standing next to them, they, like most people, watched and listened.

Daniel looked across the room. In the dim light of the candles, did he see Jenny? No, surely not, for that girl's dress was cut far too low. He had never seen her wearing anything like that. But wait, was that Rex standing between

140

Jenny and her friend Sarah? He couldn't be sure, but it sure looked like him.

Daniel suddenly realized he should have been watching the steps being led by the dance managers. More and more people were coming out on the floor ready to dance and he could no longer see across the room. Samantha put her hand on his, and he looked down at her. She was ready to dance. He lifted up his white gloved fingers, telling her he needed a bit more time to be ready. Then, he concentrated on the steps. He had danced it before, though probably more than a year ago. He smiled down at Samantha, took her hand, and she joined him to move to the floor. By this time, quite a few people were moving in rhythm to the piano, violin and fiddle.

The Gay Gordons wasn't a difficult dance at all, once you knew its few steps. For a social dance it was ideal, for couples holding hands formed a double line following the lead couple in front. The whole assembly formed a circle and each couple went four steps forward, four steps back, the woman then spun several times under the man's uplifted arm, and the man took the hand of the lady in front, while his partner took the hand of the gentleman in back.

The music was sprightly, though not too fast, and one by one, Daniel moved up the line. He saw Jenny coming ahead, spinning with her partner, and knew that soon he would be at her side. Two more minutes of dancing and he was there, taking her gloved hand in his. She smiled as he glanced at her face as they went forward, turned and went backward. Then, as she went under his arm, he had a full look at her beauty.

He had never seen so much of Jenny before, and his first impulse was to protect her from licentious eyes. Then she looked into his eyes and smiled again, as she dipped under his arm. He smiled back, hardly knowing what to think.

141

Too soon, he was dancing with the girl ahead, and Jenny was with the man behind. Daniel's need to keep himself attentive to the dance steps prevented him from dwelling on Jenny. When at last it was over, he escorted Samantha back to her seat, his mind still on the transformation he saw in Jenny.

"Darling, you dance beautifully," he said to Samantha, feeling the need to say something to her, especially as his thoughts were now on someone else.

"As do you, mon amour," she answered, using the French she had learned in school.

Daniel looked down at Samantha sitting and smiled. She was so pretty; he was fortunate she saw something in him. Still, looking across the floor, his thoughts went to Jenny, though it was hard to see her in the dim light of the wall candles. He made up his mind that he must dance with her alone.

Jenny was nervous. She had seen the way Daniel had looked at her, and she didn't know what to make of it. Yes, she wanted to show him her assets, but she was worried she might be going too far. She looked down at her uncovered front that showed more than just the tops of her breasts. She couldn't fathom what Daniel was thinking, but with some other men she had danced with in the Gay Gordons, she had no doubt what was on their mind. She was already getting more attention than she was used to.

A man she didn't know, with his hair slicked back and long sideburns came to her. He bowed slightly before where she sat on the chair and asked, "May I have the honor of the first waltz with you?"

Jenny looked at him. He seemed to have a gleam in his eye. She knew she must be polite. "Yes, Mr. . . ?

"So sorry, not to introduce myself. I am Theodore Turner, but friends call me Tad."

Tad was only one of many who swept her away in waltzes. Actually, she was beginning to grow tired of all the attention. What she really regretted, was when Daniel came to her, she had to turn him down for the next dance. Her card was already filled with that one and the next. It was hard for her to do, for he was the one she wanted to dance with the most.

Finally, his time came, and Jenny looked up into his eyes as he embraced her. The other men for her were only for dancing. With Daniel, she could relax and be herself.

Daniel looked into her eyes as they waited for the music to start. "You are so popular tonight," he said. He bowed toward her and she automatically curtsied to him.

"Too popular, all of a sudden," she sighed.

"A very beautiful dress," he noted, looking down at what showed of her bosom.

Jenny felt exposed, with his eyes on her, and she felt herself blushing.

"Very pretty," he added, still admiring her with a smile.

Jenny wondered. Was he talking about her breasts or her dress? "OK," she said, as the music finally started. "I've been wanting to dance with you, Daniel."

As the music continued, Jenny felt as if she could dance her whole life with him. She seemed to follow his lead automatically, as if they were one instead of two. Too soon, it was over, and she regretted that now she must dance with someone else. He bowed to her again and she curtsied, the custom they both knew, and he led her back to her chair, saying a quick word to Sarah at her side. "Daniel," she added quickly, as he started to leave, "I do hope you will stop again at the house before you have to leave. I want to give you something."

He came back to her, saying, "Jenny, I wouldn't miss saying goodbye to you before I have to go." Then he was gone, and already the next man on her list came before her.

She met Hank on one of the dances and learned he was Daniel's friend. That sparked her interest immediately. Actually, with all their talking, the dance was too short. She liked him and told him on leaving to be careful. "Take care of yourself, and try to find cover wherever you can if on the battlefield."

He smiled at her then, in a way that told her that she really didn't know what battle was like. Still, she added as they were parting, "And you help take care of Daniel too, and he you."

Hank broke into a great smile. "I will, Jenny," he said on leaving her.

Two dances later, it was Sarah who was dancing with Hank. He escorted her back to her chair, and in doing so winked to Jenny who also had returned to her chair. Jenny didn't know what the wink meant, but she kind of liked it. It was good knowing that Daniel had a fine friend, one who would be a good companion to him when they were fighting. 'Fighting,' suddenly the thought struck her. Both men could be gunned down. She put her hand over her mouth, not wanting to speak out loud her fear for them. She finally regained her composure, but it wasn't easy.

While Rex was dancing, for the first time neither Jenny nor Sarah had people scheduled to dance with them. They both welcomed the break. Then, they saw Rex out on the floor dancing with Samantha. When the dance was over, Rex took Samantha back to her chair next to Daniel. He

144

returned to them in seeming high spirits, saying to them, "Seems I've been missing something. Have to say, country girls are special."

Sarah looked directly at Jenny, and the two girls exchanged not only glances but thoughts. Was Rex suddenly interested in Samantha?

The dance continued like that, an evening that seemed to be enjoyed by all. Then, Jenny noticed several men to one side of the hall. They were talking among themselves rather loudly, and not happily. Two of the dance managers came up to them, more words were spoken, and one of the managers went to talk to the musicians. The music stopped, and the man stood ready to make an announcement.

"Ladies and gentlemen. It has been brought to our attention that some of our ladies are refusing to dance with certain gentlemen. It has been expressed to us that the reason seems to be based on a man's sympathies for the north or south. Ladies, this is a town ball, open to all people in our county and their friends. Please do not show discourtesy to anyone by refusing to dance with a gentleman. Let us all enjoy the dance, and refrain from bringing up discussions of a political nature."

The music resumed, and as far as Jenny could tell, things went peaceably after that. Nevertheless, Rex, she, and Sarah had much to talk about as Rex drove them both home.

Rex was a gentleman, not only taking her home, but also walking her past her gate and to her front door, before returning to his carriage to take Sarah home.

As she spun through the door, Jenny was already thinking of when she would see Daniel again, in only two days. Unfortunately, it would be the last time, for then he would have to return to the army.

145

* * *

She waited. It was late in the afternoon when they had finished supper and she had cleaned the dishes. For the occasion, she wore her finest dress, other than her Sunday best, with a pretty blue apron. She had fixed her hair attractively, so that her tresses cascaded down her neck and shoulders, and even added color to her cheeks. She felt it was important that Daniel see her at her best, for he might be gone for a long time. She hoped not. She hoped the war would soon be over.

Time passed slowly as she continued to wait for him. As darkness began to fall, she became worried. Did he forget her? Was he not going to stop at all? Standing at the door that she had cracked open, listening to the sound of his buggy, she heard her father tell her, "Good night, Jenny."

"Night, Daddy," she answered.

What am I doing here? she began to think, waiting for a man who obviously had forgotten her. She stayed a while longer at the door as darkness, illuminated only by the light of a rising moon gradually fell over the country. Then, she went slowly up to her room. Saddened, she lit a candle, deciding she would read a bit before going to bed. It might help to take her mind off of Daniel's not coming.

Did she hear something outside? She went to the window and looked out, but didn't see anything. Of course not, it was dark outside and the big tree's leafless branches cast moon shadows in the yard. Then she heard a light tapping at the front door. Cheered, she rushed down the stairs and quickly opened the door. "Daniel," she said, breathless with pent up excitement

"Sorry I'm late," he said. They made a big fuss over my leaving at Samantha's."

146

"Come in out of the cold," she said, opening the door wide for him. "Let me get a candle so I can see you."

He entered, and she quickly ran back upstairs to get the candle. She realized with joy that he was for once coming to see her last, rather than stopping by on his way to *her* house. She quickly came back down and set the light on a niche on the wall made for that purpose. She looked at him, feeling the chill outside air still radiating from his clothes. She took in his appearance completely, knowing she might not see him for a long time. His handsome tan greatcoat, his full head of wavy dark brown hair, tinged with shades of amber from the sun. But mostly, she took in his eyes and lips, now smiling at her.

"I'm so glad you came. You had me worried." She spoke softly so that she wouldn't wake her father or brother.

"Oh, you should know I wouldn't forget you. I want to remember you well all the time I'm away." He spoke softly too, looking into her eyes illuminated softly by the single candle.

Jenny's heart was beating faster than she ever would want him to know. The moment seemed almost intimate— the two of them talking softly with only the candle to throw light on their faces. She wanted only to look into his eyes. No that's not all she wanted, she truthfully told herself. Then remembering, she told him. "I've got something for you, Daniel. Wait. I'll get it for you."

Again, she was gone, though only to her room once more. He waited, and she quickly brought it to him, boxed, with a green ribbon around it.

"You shouldn't have, Jenny," he said taking the still unopened package.

"Go on, Daniel. Open it."

"Let's go outside where we don't have to be so quiet. Do you have a warm shawl you can put on?"

"Of course," she answered, thinking it a good idea.

They went outside on the porch where the light was actually brighter as the moon's rays slanted under the roof. To the left of them were two heavy chairs made of sawn lumber that her father had made, but they didn't sit down and stood facing each other.

"Chilly out here," she said, thinking of him on the long road back to his camp.

He stood looking at her in the moonlight, as if wanting to permanently remember her face.

"Go ahead, open it." He still held the flat box in his hands.

"OK." He began untying the ribbon and soon reached inside to draw out its contents. He held it up, smiling at her. "Jenny, this is so thoughtful of you."

"I hope you like the tan. I really wanted to get you something bright and colorful, but then thought it might make it too easy for the enemy to see and shoot at you."

"It's perfect," he said, putting the scarf around his neck. I will wear it with pride during the cold days of winter, especially knowing it came from you."

"It's made of wool, warmer and maybe easier to clean. I wanted to add some fringes to it, but thought that might be too fussy for a soldier."

"You do see guys wearing all kinds of things sent from home, but yes, glad you left off those fringes. I've got something for you, Jenny."

"Really? Daniel you didn't need to get me anything. I'm safe at home while you and the others are protecting the South."

He undid the top buttons of his coat, reached inside, pulled out a tintype, and handed it to her.

She took it gently in her hand, and looked at it in the moonlight. It was a picture of Daniel dressed in his military uniform. "Daniel," she said, "I can hardly believe you did this for me. This is so wonderful!" She held it in her hands close to her heart

"Let me see it again."

She held it out for him to see. Daniel bent down to look at the likeness of himself. "You think it's OK? That it really looks like me?"

"Oh, yes, so much so, and so handsome in your uniform. I will treasure this, Daniel, until you come home from this terrible war."

"I'm glad you like it. Wanted to get you something."

"This is the best thing you could have gotten me." She stood tall to give him a kiss on the cheek.

To Jenny, it seemed like he looked at her in a different way. Then, she felt him take her in his arms and give her a right proper kiss. The kind she had always hoped for. Automatically, her body leaned into his, and she kissed him back with a passion she didn't know she had. It was he who broke it off, and when he lifted his head he seemed to look at her in a new way, one she had not seen of him before.

He smiled. "That's how I will remember you, Jenny." He buttoned his coat, looked toward his buggy, and turning back to her, he took both of her hands in his, saying, "Pray for me, Jenny. And also for our cause. But if a higher calling

149

is meant for me, have no fear that I will always remember you."

Jenny's eyes were tearing, but she gripped his hands. "Yes, Daniel, I will pray for you, but don't even think of anything but returning."

He squeezed her hands, turned, and striding quickly went out the gate to his horse and buggy. She saw him wave to her by the light of the moon as he pulled away.

Chapter Fourteen

Early the next day, Daniel and Hank were on the road together. Daniel had given his last tintype of himself to his mother and father just before leaving. He was moved by how his mother held it to her heart, then wrapping her arms around him, telling him, "You be careful, son."

Both men had eaten a hearty breakfast to send them on their way, and had plenty of provisions supplied by their families for the trip. Their plan was to travel at good speed toward the summit of the mountain chain, and hopefully reach Clementine's house where they knew they would be welcome, and bed down for the night.

The going was rough, and in between their gasping for air in the rougher parts they talked about many things. Hank and Daniel had scarcely known each other before the war, having grown up on opposite sides of the town, but now they could talk about many things, both of the town and the war.

"I enjoyed the town dance," said Hank. "Got to meet a lot of interesting girls."

"For sure. Saw some of them wearing some pretty fancy outfits, including Samantha. Those girls do get themselves all prettied up."

"Samantha's one of the prettiest for sure, but there were a couple others that got my attention."

"Was one of them Sarah? I noticed you look pretty pleased with yourself when you were dancing with her."

Hank put his head down a little as if embarrassed. "Well, to be honest, I did like her a lot. But then I learned she was escorted by Rex, who I heard is a well-heeled town boy."

"That he is, a banker's son. I know Sarah. Think she's Jenny's best friend. Thing is, Rex has a reputation of getting girls real interested in him, and then leaving them for someone else. That's what I've heard, anyway."

"Speaking of Jenny. You know, I think she really cares for you."

"Yeah, we've been kind of close as friends. She's a special girl."

"Well, she seemed to be getting a lot of attention with that dress she was wearing."

"Never seen her wear anything like it before. I'm kind of like an older brother to her, and almost wanted to say something to her about it right there. I mean some guys were fairly gawking at her. Not much doubt what they were thinking."

"Know what you mean. She doesn't seem to be the provocative type. She seems too nice for that."

For a time, they stopped talking, but Daniel kept thinking about Jenny. He had seen her in a whole new way that night. As much as he felt protective of her, he couldn't help but be enticed by her body that her dress didn't cover. In fact, he had never before thought of her in the way he was thinking of her now. *Where is my mind going?* He asked himself. He should be thinking of Samantha in that way—the girl he was going to marry. Yet Jenny lay easy on his mind. Not only was she very much a woman, she was a friend. A good one. Maybe more than a friend.

They walked and walked and walked and walked. Uphill and down, but mostly ascending. At the end of the day, the sun again made a brief appearance, shining from the horizon and lighting up the landscape in a peculiarly beautiful orange way, before dropping down under the trees. They were almost there, at the little town they had stayed at before where Clementine, Willie and Jeremy had found them when they stayed overnight in their shed.

Approaching the house near dark, Daniel rapped lightly on the door. There was no answer. He knocked louder, and Clementine opened the door and looked at the two men on her porch. She hesitated at first, and then recognized them.

"Oh, you're the two soldiers who came by on your way home. Slept in the shed. Come on in. I can do better for you than that, though don't have much."

"Thank you, ma'am," they both answered, and Daniel added, "Any place to get out of the cold would be much appreciated." Daniel wanted to ask if she had heard any word of her husband, but didn't as he might well be dead.

They stepped inside, and felt the warmth radiating from the fireplace. Not sure where they should go within the house, they waited a moment.

"Sorry, I have only the one bedroom. My son and I sleep there, but there's plenty of room in the sitting room, if you would like to lay down your things there. My husband shot a big bear before he joined the army, so I'll get out the big bearskin and you can sleep on it. Myself, I go to bed pretty much when the sun goes down. Would you like some fresh tea? Sorry I don't have anything else to offer you, but in the morning I'll make you a good breakfast. Something to stick to your ribs, cause I know you still got a long way to go to get back to your camp."

Daniel looked around at the sitting room, set his knapsack down saying, "Ma'am, it's more than kind of you to put us up. We got food from home, so you don't need to go to the trouble of making a meal for us in the morning. We just appreciate your giving us a place where we can sleep to get out of the cold."

Clementine cocked her head, looking at him and said, "Now you don't think I would be that ungracious, do you? Here you are fighting for the South and me to send you off without breakfast? No, that's definitely not southern hospitality. You men bed down when you're ready, and I'll be up bright and early in the morning and make your breakfast. OK?"

Daniel and Hank both agreed. Clementine left out the back, saying she needed to get something from next door, and while she was gone, they arranged their gear and settled into the sitting room that was lit by a single candle in its sconce on the wall. It was sparsely furnished for a sitting room, with a small deacon's bench on one side, near it an upholstered armchair, and across, a simple wood spindle chair.

Clementine returned, entering the back door. She set what she had obtained down on the kitchen counter, and entering the sitting room, asked, "Sure you wouldn't like some tea before you lay down for the night?"

"No, thank you," both Daniel and Hank replied."

"Good night then," she said. "Extinguish the candle whenever you are ready to bed down. I'll probably be up before you in the morning."

They awoke to the delicious aroma of pork and boiled corn along with buckwheat cakes, flavored with honey. Daniel and Hank didn't stay too long, knowing that they had a long way to go. They heartily said their goodbyes, and started on their way. They reached the town of Mount Jackson late in the day, but had to wait until the following morning to board the train back to the camp.

Soon after they returned to their camp, the weather became terrible. Snow, ice, freezing rain and gale force winds had soldiers cursing their lot. Besides, with so many thousands of troops staying in one place, conditions became foul and the food sorely lacking in vegetables and fruit. Many men died from diseases carried by some of the soldiers and then transmitted to others. In fact, the number of deaths from sickness began to mount far higher than those caused by enemy bullets.

At last, by early March, the snow melted and the grass began to green from sunshine and the gradually rising temperatures. Now the army was finally on the move again. Daniel was glad to leave the confines of the camp, even though it meant sleeping in the cold night air in a tent. By now, his beard was full, and to some extent he had learned to protect himself as much as possible from the cold while sleeping in the tent with Hank. As the days' marches grew longer, no one needed to tell any of them that there was going to be a battle. *Better to fight the enemy and get it over with*, thought Daniel, thinking that after a major battle or two the war would end.

* * *

155

The winter had been bad for Jenny and her family as well. When the cold winds came, there was little she could do other than her usual chores and cooking dinner for the men. She was glad David had not tried to join the army, and she saw a lot of him on these cold days for there was little her father, David, and Marcus could do other than caring for the animals and sheltering them in the barn, out of the wind and the cold.

As for the war, though there was still much talk about it, it seemed to her that both the North and the South were sitting it out during the cold weather. That suddenly changed. She received a letter from Daniel saying he was leaving their camp and moving to the west. More than that he couldn't tell her. Reading his letter, Jenny realized that destinations and such would be secret information not shared with soldiers. Still, the thought that he was coming closer made her happy, until she realized he would be coming to fight the enemy, not to visit. But might she see him?

As the weather continued its gradual warming trend, talk turned to planting crops. Jenny was interested too, for soon she would be starting her garden. One that would supply their household with fresh vegetables.

Then word came that Yankee troops were on the move again and heading their way. She thought of what Daniel had told her in his very latest letter. The Confederate army was moving west. Would there be a clash? Would they be fighting each other? Her worries mounted as she thought of all the dead such a battle would leave in its wake. *Surely not!* She told herself. *Surely not.* But she was not so naive to believe that it couldn't happen. Her own brother and Daniel could be on a battlefield fighting each other.

Where was Jeb? She didn't know. She hadn't heard from him for a long time. He didn't write home very often. Would he be with those Union troops coming their way? She hoped if so he could at least stop by their house. But, on the other hand, she hoped he would not be with the advancing army. Not if they would be fighting against Daniel and the Confederate army. It was all so confusing and troubling to Jenny as she lay awake in her bed. Unbidden, tears came. Everything seemed to be happening, and there was nothing she could do about it. She could only tell herself to try to be strong.

* * *

More time had passed and now Jenny knew for sure they were coming. Coming from the west toward their town. A big Union army. In the afternoon, when Jenny was preparing their meal, she saw them. Marching past her house, the jingling of their equipment, the voices, the dust they were raising. What Jenny didn't know was that only part of the force was on the road going past her house. A much larger force was taking the north highway that also ran toward town. She stood as if entranced looking out the front window of her house at all the soldiers marching by.

Then to her surprise, a man opened her fence gate and casually walked toward her house. Unfortunately, Jenny knew he had seen her looking through the window. What was she to do? Her father, brother, and Marcus were in the lower field, probably not even aware of what was going on. As he came toward the house, she saw the decorations on his uniform and as he got close she recognized him. He was the Union Captain who had stopped before to get water. Was he going to ask this time before leading his men to the pump?

He lightly knocked on her front door. Had she not known for certain that he had seen her, she wouldn't have answered his knock. But she couldn't do that now. She opened the door and looked into his handsome, bearded face. He looked right at her, and she knew he remembered her from before.

"Miss," he said with a hint of a smile, "would it be OK for my men to get some water from your well?"

She looked at him as he waited for her answer. There was something about his eyes that she found unsettling. "Since you're asking, it's OK, I guess."

"Thank you, miss. We'll just fill up our canteens and then be on our way. Much obliged."

She should have let him go at that, but there was something about him that eased her fear. As he was turning to leave, she said to him, "Might you have heard anything of my brother, Jeb? Jeb Tilden? He joined the northern side last summer."

He turned back to face her. "Jeb Tilden. No, the name's not familiar, but then I'm lucky to know a couple hundred and there are thousands of us."

"Oh," she said, disappointment registering on her face.

"I'll ask around and if I learn anything, I can tell you if we come back this way."

Jenny felt she had asked too much, yet her brother's whereabouts was one big question on her mind. She looked into his eyes again and from out of her mouth came, "I'd be much obliged, sir."

He smiled, and leaving her porch he went back to his men on the road. Jenny stepped back into the house and closed the door. The thought came to her, *he is too much of a*

158

gentleman to be fighting in a war. Dismissing the thought, she set about doing what she needed to do to get supper ready. Before long, the men came and went, having filled their canteens. As the last were leaving out the gate, she saw him wave to her, and despite herself, she moved her own hand to say goodbye to him. *Strange,* she thought to herself. *Why do they fight? Why am I waving to an enemy soldier?*

Chapter Fifteen

Disaster. The army of Northern Virginia, Second Corps, that of General Thomas "Stonewall Jackson," as he has been known since Manassas, had lost its first battle. It happened at Kernstown. Daniel had lived through it, as had Hank. The loss was not surprising, given that the Confederate force of over 3000 had faced more than double the number of Union troops. However, surrounding them as the battle ended were the dead and wounded, some in agony, many begging for water. There was nothing they could do for them, for they had to retreat from a numerically superior force. The call for an organized retreat soon turned into a rout as the men in gray ran for their lives. It was General Jackson's first defeat.

They escaped, and Daniel hoped as they marched along, that the men left on the battlefield would be treated and cared for by the victorious Yankees. For days and weeks they marched, sometimes stopping to spend time in one place or another. Wherever they stopped, the drilling continued. Jackson's men licked their wounds, and each man was confident that their illustrious general would not go down in defeat again.

As the days turned into weeks, Daniel and his fighting friends from home began to realize they were moving gradually closer and closer to their hometown. It had been months since Daniel had been there, but the people there were never far from his mind.

As they drew closer, Daniel and his friends from home could hardly believe it. They were following a route south from northern Virginia that was taking them nearer each day. Word was that Union troops were actually coming from their town, and soon they might meet them in battle. Daniel was hopeful that Jackson's army, of which he was a part, would defeat the Yankees and then continue on to town. He could well imagine their entry as they pushed the union troops back to the North. People would be so proud.

May eighth, 1862

By dawn, Daniel and his regiment were already on their way. Every man knew that the Union forces were near. Excitement mounted. The Confederate advance crossed Shaw's Ridge, descended to the Cow Pasture River at Wilson's House, and ascended Bull Pasture Mountain. Brigadier General Edward Johnson, acting with General Jackson, led the advance to the base of Sitlington's Hill. Expecting a roadblock ahead, he diverged from the road into a steep narrow ravine that led to the top of the hill.

Then, General Jackson asked his staff to find a way to place artillery on the hill and to search for a way to flank the Union position to the north.

The Twelfth Georgia infantry, a part of his army, moved ahead and climbed the hill, equipped only with smoothbore muskets. Their ascent up Sitlington's hill wasn't

161

easy, for it was a steep climb made more difficult with their gear and rifles. Daniel, Hank, and the rest of their regiment also advanced, holding on to whatever they could to assist their climb. They made it, and the Confederate force spread out along the long, sinuous crest of the hill.

Daniel looked back. Would they be able to bring up artillery? There, atop the hill, the Confederate force waited, knowing the enemy was close at hand. As the sun rose higher in the sky, the crack of rifle fire rose from below from Union soldiers partially hidden in the small trees and underbrush near the base of the hill. The attack became more intense, and billows of smoke began to rise from below as Confederates and Union forces heatedly exchanged gunfire.

Daniel suddenly noticed that not only had the Yankees established a point of devastating artillery fire on a hill across the valley, but also more shots were coming from the side as Union forces attempted to flank their position. Then, he heard the welcome sound of the rebel yell as hundreds more of General Jackson's men arrived to push back the Union snipers and protect their flank.

For hours, Daniel and Hank fought alongside each other, their rifles becoming hot as they quickly fired and reloaded. Men cried out in pain or lurched back suddenly struck by enemy minie balls. But the cries of the wounded and dying were mostly drowned out by the constant crack of rifle fire and the booming of artillery. Then, as night began to fall, Daniel and the whole Confederate army were glad to see the Yanks melting into the distance, leaving the battlefield in defeat.

There was no cry of victory, however, as the weary soldiers assisted the wounded and collected the fallen. Those who were injured were taken to the McDowell Presbyterian Church, scarcely a mile away where they could be cared for.

The dead were gathered up and buried with the help of some of the townspeople.

As Daniel and his friends at last had time to sit down and eat from their rations, there was not much talk around the campfires. Daniel learned that the force they had faced had come from his home town, and were returning there with their wounded loaded into wagons. He feared for his family, for Samantha and Jenny, and as tired as he was, he would have liked to pursue and defeat them to prevent them from inflicting revenge on the community. He didn't think they would shoot civilians, but they could make it difficult for them and even steal their farm animals and supplies. With those worrisome thoughts on his mind, Daniel finally settled into sleep, to fight again another day.

On the next day, the Confederate army resumed marching after the Union army. Daniel wondered; *would they be able to catch up to them?* When at last there was a break, he and Eli and Hank conferred. Yes, it was true, though still distant, they were on the road that would take them home. *Home*, he thought as they soon resumed marching. There he would see Samantha, his parents, and Jenny. How he missed them. But would there be another battle with the Yankees before they reached the town?

* * *

Jenny, her family, and the townspeople heard of the confederate victory at the Battle of McDowell. The victory defeated the very same army that had been staying on the outskirts of town. The army with the Union Captain who not long ago had entered her yard for water.

Now, Jenny knew they were coming back, a defeated army bearing their wounded in their wagons. She was afraid, for a beaten army might take revenge on the townspeople. Then came word that the Union Army was being chased by the Confederate army, led by none other than General Thomas Jackson, "Stonewall Jackson," as he was lovingly hailed by all those who had heard of his exploits.

Surely, General Jackson would come to the rescue of the town. Her thoughts went to Daniel. Was he part of Jackson's army? Would she soon see him? Her heart lifted at the thought.

Over the next two days everyone waited, hoping that the Union army coming their way would be defeated, beaten back, and its fighting men captured before they reached the town. But something went wrong, or was their information about the pursuit of Jackson's army mistaken?

Her father told her things first, for now he went into town every day to get the latest on what was happening. Then today, he came home in a hurry, for Jenny could still see the dust on the road trailing behind him.

Quickly striding into the house, he told Jenny that as he was leaving, he saw the bedraggled Union army pulling into town with its long lines of marching soldiers and wagons laden with the wounded. He told her he had stayed long enough to see wounded soldiers being removed from the wagons and taken into both the Union Methodist Church and the county court house.

"Could you tell if there were very many of them?" asked Jenny.

"Seems so," he answered, from where he had gone in the kitchen to cut a slice of her fresh baked bread. "They were taking them in on stretchers, and judging from the number of wagons outside, they probably were going to be taking many more inside."

"That's so sad, Daddy."

164

"That's war, honey," he answered, coming back into the sitting room with a large piece of bread in his hands. "Be thankful its enemy soldiers and not ours."

Jenny stared at him. "How can you say that, Daddy? You know Jeb is fighting on their side."

"I know, darling. I think of him a lot. Just don't think he's with them or surely he would have stopped by the house before when they were camping near town." Standing next to her, he put a comforting hand on her shoulder.

She looked up at him, and managed a smile. Still, something was going on in her mind. Something she at the moment didn't want to tell her father.

The next day, when her father was going into town, she asked to go along.

"Not doing much, honey. Just getting a couple things from the store and of course the paper. Checking if there's any mail. Just hope the Union army doesn't make things difficult."

"Good," she answered. "I'm curious about them."

"Just don't get too close to any of them, Jenny. They are the enemy."

Despite what her father said, Jenny wanted to see what they were doing to take care of the wounded soldiers. Leaving her father at the store, telling him she would be right back, she walked the short distance down the street and went to the Union Church.

Uniformed soldiers and other people entered and left the building, paying her no mind, and she went through the door and looked inside. What she saw shocked her. In the large main worship space of the church, the pews were being used as beds, and on them wounded men in every imaginable position lay. She saw men bandaged on their heads, arms, torsos, and many whose red blood still seemed to be oozing from their wounds. Suddenly feeling nauseous, she lowered her head, covering her eyes with her hands. When she had courage to look again, she saw other men whose legs or arms were missing.

A woman came to her. She wore a white apron smeared with blood. "Honey, did you come to help?"

Jenny looked at her. The woman was probably in her mid-thirties, with kindly eyes, an efficient manner and a few strands of gray in her dark hair. Not knowing what to say, she stammered, and finally got out the words, "Do you need help?"

The woman held out her hand toward all those on the beds. "Yes we do. You see all these men here. There's just as many of them at the court house. If we had more to take care of them, to dress their wounds, to bring them food and water, to care for their needs, we could save more of them."

Jenny tore her eyes away from the soldiers to look into the woman's eyes. She saw sincerity and kindness there as well as determination.

"I don't know if I can," she answered truthfully. Not only did she not know if she could deal with so much blood and sickness, she didn't know if her father would let her.

"I know, honey. It's not easy. Some of these men will die. Others will go through life with a missing limb. But we are angels to them because we care. If you care, you can do it."

Jenny backed away from her. Then, surprising even herself, she said, "I will ask my father."

She walked out the door, not even looking back. Suddenly, the full terror of war came over her. All these lives traumatized by a war fought sometimes even by brother against brother. *Why? Why?* She asked herself as she walked back slowly to find her father.

She found him in front of the store, ready to leave. "Where were you?" he asked. "I've been waiting for you."

She waited until she got alongside him in the buggy. She looked at him, saw he was expecting her answer. "Daddy I went to the Union Church. Where the wounded soldiers have been taken."

"Jenny, you shouldn't have."

"It is so awful, Daddy." She turned away from him, bowing her head and tears began to fall.

He turned to her and put an arm around her shoulder. "I know, honey. That's why you shouldn't have gone there."

"Daddy they need help. All those men, and the woman told me just as many more have been taken to the court house. There are not enough nurses to take care of them."

Her father still had not told the horse to move. "Don't tell me, Jenny. Don't tell me you're thinking of doing it."

"I don't really want to, but anyone can see they need help."

"Jenny, these are Union soldiers."

"I know, Daddy. Jeb is a Union soldier too. If he was here or in some other place wounded, you would want someone caring for him too, wouldn't you?"

Her father turned away from her and looked straight ahead. Moments passed before he turned back to her. "I suppose I would, Jenny."

167

She smiled and turned to give him a big hug. Then she said, "I don't even know if I want to. I don't know if I have it in me to do it."

Her father flipped the reins, and started underway. As they rode along back to their home, he said to her. "Think about it, Jenny. Not everyone is cut out to do that kind of work. But if you decide to, we can spare you at home for a while. The spring crops are planted, and Marcus can take your place with the cooking and cleaning for a time. After all, someday you're going to leave us to get married and then we'll have to get by." He took one hand off the reins to give her a sideways hug.

Jenny hardly knew what to say. She put her hand on his arm, looked into his eyes and smiled at him. She loved her father.

* * *

By the next morning Jenny had worked it out with him. She would take the buggy in the morning, or wagon if he needed supplies too large for the carriage. She would go to care for the soldiers, and would pick up a paper and anything else her family needed while she was in town. That way she could go to help the wounded and return by dark. Her father still didn't want her to be out longer than the hours of daylight, but it was May and the sun was out early in the morning until late in the day.

She set out, with some misgivings about whether she would be able to deal with the wounds of the soldiers. Soon, she arrived in town, stopped to water and feed Brandy, her father's horse, and then went to the Union Church hospital, pulling around to the back side.

With some trepidation, and wearing her large apron, she pulled open the door. In the low light of the church she

168

saw the rows of beds and people moving about. No one seemed to notice her, and she thought that maybe she should walk back out and try going in the front door. Then, the lady she had talked to before, the one who asked her to help, saw her and quickly came toward her.

"So glad to see you came back," she said, with seemingly great affection. "I'm so sorry, I didn't even get your name when we talked before, or give you mine."

"I'm Jenny," she answered. "Jenny Tilden."

"And mine is Annabelle Winslow, though everyone just calls me Anna. Jenny, I'm so happy you came to help us. Let me show you around and you will quickly see what needs to be done. You will notice that we have mostly men in blue, though there are some Confederate wounded here as well. For us, it doesn't matter; they are men who need our help."

Jenny followed Anna along the rather narrow pathways between the beds. She saw the men, saw the bandages on their heads, arms, legs, and even saw men who were missing parts of their bodies. Most had their eyes closed, but some of them looked at her with interest or curiosity. Despite the evident pain on many of their faces, for the most part there was a friendliness in their eyes, and as Anna moved along in front of her, she felt that she wanted to do what she could to help these men.

There was no one she recognized, until she saw a man with closed eyes who somehow seemed familiar. She delayed a moment to look at him. His forehead was dressed with a large bandage, and though his legs were covered, she sensed by the unnatural bulge underneath there was also something wrong with his leg.

Anna asked, "Do you know him?"

Suddenly, Jenny remembered. "Yes. He was the Union Captain who stopped at our house for his men to fill their canteens."

"He's in a bad way, Jenny. His head wound will heal, but his calf was torn by a minie ball. They amputated many with his kind of injury"

Jenny looked back at the man as Anna led on. They reached the back part where medical supplies were kept. Through the doorway, Anna pointed out the pump. Adjacent to where the bandages, medications, etc. were stored was the kitchen. Jenny peeked in and saw two black women preparing a meal.

"I'm glad you got here early," said Anna. "When the cooks are ready, we'll wake up those who are sleeping, those not so sick that they can't eat on their own, and serve them breakfast. When that's done, we clean and redress their wounds, and give some who are in great pain paregoric to help them deal with it. There's more to our work, of course, much more, but we'll show you some of those things later." Anna introduced her to the other two nurses, Lydia, and Elizabeth, called Lizzy. Lydia was a tall and lanky woman, maybe in her late twenties, rather plain looking but with a warm smile. Lizzy was shorter than herself, warm blonde hair, youthful, with a bubbly personality. Jenny liked her immediately, but wondered how she could seem to be so cheery in a place like this. Already, at their first introduction, she felt she had made a friend.

Soon, it was time to wake the men up for breakfast. Jenny watched Lizzy do it before doing it herself. "Up and at em, men. Chow time. Wake up and savor what we have for you today. Don't be late for breakfast." Those were her words as she cheerily moved between the beds, giving each soldier a pat on the shoulder or back.

Jenny smiled and began going down another row of beds, cheerily announcing breakfast. No matter to her or Lizzy that some groaned and wakened less than cheerfully. She was getting the message across in a most optimistic way.

The men awakened, and Jenny and the other three nurses went back to where the cook was already ladling out food. She learned the breakfast was called "Indian mush." It consisted of corn made into a mush with salt and molasses added for extra flavor and nutrition. Not a lot of variety, but she found by trying some that it was tasty. Also, there was coffee, something the men enjoyed almost more than anything else. Especially as it was sweetened with honey or sugar.

Taking a number of bowls on a tray, she and the others set about bringing them to the men. There were some, she learned, who would have to be spoon fed, but they would be taken care of after the others. As she went down the line, passing out bowls, spoons and then coffee, she thought about the Union Captain. Now that everyone except the most seriously injured had been awakened, would she see his eyes open? And if she were the one to give him his breakfast, would he recognize her?

Not remembering just where he was in the hospital, Jenny passed out the last of her bowls and spoons and returned to get more. Going back to where she had left off, she saw him. His eyes were open and he was looking at her. As she came up to him with the bowl of Indian mush, she saw him smile, a pained smile but genuine. She gave him the bowl and asked, "Do you really remember me, captain, or do you smile at all the nurses?"

He twisted in the bed to look at her full in the face, grimacing with pain for a moment, before he said, "I remember. The farm house outside of town where my men and I stopped to get water from your well."

171

"Ah, your memory is quite good. Funny that a girl of the enemy has stayed in your mind."

"Enemy?" He laughed lightly. Then he began coughing and didn't seem to be able to stop. She set her tray down and grabbed his shoulders, trying to stop the cough. It lasted for over a minute, and then he was himself again, though obviously weakened.

"Enemy, you say, and you are taking care of us. No enemy, but an angel." He smiled as he said that.

Jenny stooped down to pick up her tray, and when she arose, she saw that he still was looking at her. She was a bit aggravated at him, and didn't know why. She turned away, feeling that somehow his eyes looked into her heart. But he was still the enemy, no matter that she felt called to help him and others. She moved on, to take care of other soldiers. Yet, she couldn't quite get the captain out of her mind.

Chapter Sixteen

Weeks passed, and every day Jenny rose early, took the buggy, and went to the hospital. Then, tired from all her work, she left just before the late June sun went down. She had seen a lot of pain and suffering, but now things were slowing down as soldiers either recovered or died. The Union Captain, Tom, had made a remarkable recovery, even though the head nurse at first thought he wouldn't live. He might never walk normally, but now he was up and helping with the soldiers who were still recovering.

Jenny had tried to talk to her father and brother about the travails of her work at the hospital, but they seemed not to want to hear it. Understandable, she thought, for much of what she had seen was difficult even for her. Besides, some Union soldiers stole some of their pigs, and it was only after a heated discussion that her father let her go back to nursing the sick.

As for Captain Thomas Langston, Captain Tom, as she had taken to calling him, she didn't know what to think. Was she, a Confederate girl, beginning to feel too close to him? Was she already regretting when he would leave? She didn't think he could return to the Federal army, for he would never be able to march long distances with his bad leg. With these thoughts in mind, she needed to talk to someone. Someone who would understand. On her return home that very night, she decided to write to Daniel.

My dear friend, she began.

Sorry I haven't written for a while. There's a reason, and I hope that you at least understand, because many around here don't. I've been working as a nurse at the Union Church that was turned into a hospital when the defeated Union troops came back into town. Yes, I've been bandaging and caring for them, plus two Confederate boys that somehow were brought back with them.

Hope you understand that I'm not trying to help the enemy, it's just that I can hardly stand by when they are suffering so much. My brother Jeb, you may remember, also joined the wrong side.

If you have ever visited a hospital and seen the suffering you would know what I mean. Some of them have had their leg or arm amputated and others just needed to have some care and tenderness before they died. It is so sad, Daniel.

I wrote two letters for dying soldiers to their parents, one a young boy of only seventeen, who somehow came to see me as his personal angel. I hoped so much that we could save him, but his injuries were too bad. As he lay dying, with me sitting by his side holding his hand, he asked me to write to his parents. I won't tell you what he had me write; it was so touching that tears are coming down my cheeks just thinking about it. We had to bury him with the others out back in the churchyard cemetery.

But we carry on. I worry so much about you. I know more battles are coming, and I pray that you won't be hurt like these men we are caring for. I don't know what I would do if that happened. We keep hoping that the war will finally be over and that you and all the others can return home to all those who care about you.

She hesitated, not knowing exactly what else she wanted to say. She hoped he would not be angry at her for helping Union soldiers. No matter, she had to tell him. She hoped he would understand, because it seemed so few people did. She also didn't want to tell him about the Yankees stealing most of her father's pigs. She knew that would only get him mad, and where he was there was nothing he could do about it anyway. She believed that soon the Union soldiers would be gone and leave them alone.

She also didn't want to tell him about Captain Thomas Langston. She herself didn't know what to think about the man. She had no attraction whatsoever to the Union cause, but she could not honestly say the same thing about him. But she believed he would soon leave, for the makeshift hospital would be closing and return to being a church. Then he would be gone, and she would probably never see him again.

She continued writing her letter:

I do see Sarah and sometimes Samantha, her mostly at church. We don't travel as much as before with the soldiers around, as everyone is kind of scared of them. There's a few who even show up at church. We try not to say anything against them, but I think everyone in town is anxious for them to leave.

I think of you with this cool spring weather and I hope you are keeping warm enough in the tents now that you have left your winter quarters. I know sometimes it still gets real cold at night. Everyone, including me will be so happy to see you again.

Sincerely, your friend,

Jenny

(Daniel answers her letter, telling her of his experience taking men to the hospital. They continue to correspond.)

175

A year passes

Things are changing. Their slave, Marcus, ran off after he found out about Lincoln's Emancipation Proclamation. Her father was mad about that, all the more so because he made off with his rifle. His leaving made that much more work for him and for David. Jenny hadn't heard anything about Marcus since he left, but she believed he was going to join up with the Union army because he wanted to free the slaves.

In other news, Jenny had recently met up again with Captain Thomas. "Tom," he said, "just call me Tom." He came back into her life, riding a horse. When the makeshift hospital was closing, he had been friendly to her, maybe too friendly. She shouldn't have let him kiss her when they parted. Once his leg was better, they had spent much time together tending to the wounded and had shared some sad as well as happy moments.

Now he was back, and she honestly didn't know what to think. He didn't live that far from her, in a Union county, only fourteen miles away on the other side of the ridge. Her heart was with Daniel, but the Union Captain was definitely starting to affect her thinking.

There was more news, too. Rex, the banker's son didn't have to fight on either side. His father's money bought him freedom from conscription. He had long ago left her best friend, Sarah. Of late, he had been taking up with Samantha, and to Jenny, it seemed as if Samantha was giving him encouragement.

She didn't write to Daniel about that. The thing is, if Daniel really loved her, it might break his heart. She would see how it played out between them before saying anything. In a way, Rex and Samantha could be a good match. Both

176

came from money. If so, maybe she could finally get Daniel to see that she herself was the right girl for him. But what of the Union Captain? Should she break off with him before things got too serious in his mind? Or in hers? Decisions, decisions. What should she do? She didn't want to end up a spinster. Yet she knew she was "particular." She wouldn't have just any man.

Whenever she went into town, Jenny saw that more of the young men had come back from the war. Too many were missing an arm or leg or had nasty wounds that you could see now that the weather was warming up and they were wearing lighter clothing. Some of the men seemed morose to her, others were cheerful despite their injuries. Just goes to show how one takes things. It probably helped that they were welcomed back and looked on as heroes by the townspeople for having fought for a noble cause.

Suddenly, she thought of Daniel, although he was never far from her mind. What if he came back missing an arm or a leg? How would she feel about him then? She shook her head, and couldn't quite hold back tears. She would still love him, she vowed. Far better than if he didn't come back at all. She decided she must write to him. Now that summer was coming, she knew there would be more battles. She hadn't heard from him for over a month, but partly it was her own fault for not writing to him recently. With all that was going on, her thoughts were in a jumble. Maybe by writing she could clear her mind as well as connect with Daniel.

Dear Daniel,

Sorry I haven't written in a while. My excuse is that with spring, I had to help a lot with the planting. Especially since Marcus ran off, I think to fight on the Union side, leaving me, Pa and David to do everything. I have had to work extra hard, but now that everything is planted I have time to breathe again.

I can see how Marcus wanted freedom. Might feel the same if I were a slave. Don't really have any bad feelings against him except he took Pa's rifle. That really made my father mad!

Now, with more time, I've have been meeting with the Ladies Aide Society at church. Don't know if you've heard of it. It supports the war effort mainly by providing lint to be used by the doctors and nurses to dress wounds. We scrape lint off linen and other fabrics and send it off. I know it sounds boring, and it is, but we talk about all kinds of things while we work and enjoy each other's company.

Met a woman not much older than me there whose husband's name you mentioned in one of your letters. His name is Eli and hers is Clara. We have become friends. She brings her three year old daughter Emily with her. Such a cute, thoughtful girl for three years old. Even though she is such a young age, Emily is no trouble, but sits at her mother's side on a blanket and plays with a doll or toy. I'm not the only woman there who loves her, and sometimes we stop and say or do something to make the girl laugh. She is so delightful.

Jenny wondered how to proceed with her letter. She certainly didn't want to tell Daniel about the Union Captain, and she wondered if she should say anything about Samantha. Nothing was for certain with her, and knowing of Rex and his way with girls, nothing could be certain with him either. Still, she knew things had been going on for a while between those two. In fact, their relationship was beginning to give her hope. She just didn't know if she should say anything to Daniel. She thought some more on it before continuing to write.

Sometimes Pa sends me in to town to get supplies, especially as he and David are extra busy without Marcus. I always enjoyed going there, but not so much now. Don't see a lot of young men, I guess they're all at war, except for some who have come back injured. It's so sad to

178

see what the war has done to them. I must say, some are cheerful, despite their loss. When I was caring for the men in the temporary hospital at the church, I saw many who were wounded that way, though they were mostly on the Union side.

Otherwise, things go on pretty much as usual, with the exception that everything is more expensive. Coffee and store tea are hard to get at all. One thing most of us have plenty of is eggs, thanks to our hens. Knowing that so many small children have been without their fathers for so long, we wanted to do something for them and their mothers.

Mrs. Schmidt suggested we could have an egg hunt as Easter would soon be upon us. She had known of the custom as a child when she lived in Germany. So, in the church hall fourteen of us met, each of us bringing hard boiled eggs and different kinds of natural dyes. We had a great time together decorating the eggs. So many different colors we used to decorate them!

The next day, being Easter, we all attended the special church service, and afterward the deacon announced that there would be an egg hunt for all children ten and under in the church yard. The children were given little baskets we had made out of reinforced paper, and on signal they went for the eggs. There was so much excitement as they chased around, looking for them in the high grass, around the flower beds, and even in the crooks of trees and shrubs. Good thing we had told the older children to share with those younger. Afterward, we enjoyed hot chocolate and cookies in the hall. The event was such a success that there's talk we might do it again next year.

Well, Daniel, that's pretty much of what I know of what's been going on around here. I keep praying that the war will finally be over and that you, Hank, and Eli and the other men will come back home safe and sound.

Miss seeing you, Your friend,

Jenny

Chapter Eighteen

June, 1863: Daniel was hopeful for the summer offensive. News had filtered down to the soldiers that General Lee was going north to take the fight to the North. The hope of Lee and every man in his battle worn army was that major victories there would finally put the confederate army in front of Washington itself and make the Yankees accept terms for peace. Surrounded by the confederate army, Daniel felt that Lincoln would have no choice but to sue for peace and end the war. Daniel knew that the enemy would not go down easily, but he put his faith in General Lee and the noble soldiers he fought with that they could defeat the enemy and at last end the war.

Daniel had seen a lot in two years of fighting. He had seen many men die, some of them friends, both from gunfire and from sickness. When he thought about it, he realized more had died from disease—dysentery, typhoid, pneumonia, malaria, and even measles. Two years of fighting, waiting, fighting, and living among men. He seldom saw women, and he sorely missed his mother, Samantha, and Jenny.

He did get letters from time to time, the only thing that helped him to keep in touch with that other world—the world where things were normal. The world where there were stores, churches, farm animals, and women and children. In sum, an ordinary world where all kinds of things were possible. Where love was possible even for a hardened soldier who had already seen far too much suffering and death.

He was so glad that Jenny had been a faithful letter writer. She, more than anyone else, kept him in touch with the world at home that he so eagerly looked forward to returning to. His mother and Samantha on occasion wrote too, but not nearly as often. One thing was beginning to bother him. Of late it seemed that Samantha's letters lacked feeling. Was she getting tired of waiting for him?

Of the upcoming military engagement, the intelligence coming down from sources connected to those who made such decisions was that the reinforced confederate army would soon meet a major Union offensive. Daniel's friend Eli, in particular, held that belief, and Eli was seldom wrong. No one officially told anyone less than a colonel that kind of military information. But soldiers had a way of finding out things, and while sometimes wrong, they were usually right. Daniel knew that the Yankees would not be beaten easily. Their army was larger than that of the South, but so often in the past a smaller southern army had whipped a larger northern one.

Everyone believed that General Robert E. Lee was a brilliant tactician whose army of tough southerners could beat an army of Yankees twice their size. Nevertheless, it was likely to be a major confrontation and Daniel knew that many men would die on both sides. He feared death, but he personally believed in the fight for states' rights and an end to Northern oppression. In his heart, he had to admit that he was so tired of the killing that even his own life didn't matter if only the war would end. Yet he so wanted to live. He wanted to know love, to raise a family and work hard so they had everything they needed and more.

As he lay inside the tent, it was something he thought about frequently, and he knew he was far from alone in those kinds of thoughts. His best friend, Hank, didn't have a girl to go back to, but from things he had said, Daniel had no doubt in his mind that he would find one. Maybe even someone he knew.

His other good friend, Eli, was married and had a three year old daughter. Like everyone else, he wanted the war to end so he could go back to his family. Eli tended to think of himself as bullet proof. Men had gone down around him, but he thought the minie balls missed him because he was so skinny. Skinny, yet wiry and strong. Daniel shook his head, done with thinking for the night. He pulled the blanket over himself, offered a silent prayer, and quickly fell asleep.

The nights were getting warmer in June of 1863 as General Robert E Lee's Army of North Virginia headed north. It was composed of roughly 70,000 men, and Daniel was proud to be in that number. Excitement grew as they crossed into Pennsylvania. The land looked so well maintained, with crops growing and wood fences that had never been stolen and used for army firewood. Daniel and all the soldiers were glad to see the order and beauty of a land that apparently had not been exposed to the effects of war.

They marched now under the leadership of Major General George Pickett. Since he had recently been assigned to their regiment and brigade, every soldier wanted to know what kind of man he was. Sitting around their evening campfire, Eli, as usual, had the information for his friends.

"Well, I'll say this for him, he was appointed to West Point by President Lincoln himself. Apparently, they were friends. But, he was dead last in his graduating class."

"Really," said Hank, raising his head as he munched on a large piece of pork. "We're being led by the last man in the whole class?"

"Swear its true," said Eli, eyeing Hank. "You can read it for yourself."

"He smells of perfume," said Daniel. "I caught a whiff when he was riding by."

"Yeah," said Eli. "Think he likes to be a pretty boy. Heard he's taken with a girl half his age who lives in Lynchburg."

"How old is he?" asked Daniel.

"Don't know exactly," answered Eli. "Somewhere in his thirties, I'd guess."

"I care less about all that," said Hank. "All I want to know is if he's a winner. Does he know how to lead us on to beat the Yankees?"

"Don't know about that," answered Eli. "All I've heard is that he's anxious to do battle with the Yanks here in Pennsylvania."

"Suits me. If we can beat their army here, won't be far for us to go to Washington and make them accept Confederate terms for peace. Then, maybe we can at last go home."

"Yeah," said Daniel, reaching out to grab Hank's hand. "Then, brother, you and me can take that long walk home over the mountains."

"I'll be right there with you boys," said Eli.

183

The army of Northern Virginia continued moving north. As they marched, the soldiers saw wagons laden with supplies and later learned they were obtained from Northerners. Hopefully, they were paid for. Having been sometimes short on rations, every man looked at those wagons and hoped that there was fresh beef or pork on them. Then, after marching for days, Pickett's brigade stopped while the rest of the army moved on.

"Why are we stopping now?" was the question of the hour. It was early afternoon, and everyone felt the warmth of the hot July day. To stop now when all reports were that the enemy was only a day's march away made no sense to anyone. Daniel and his friends wanted to go on to meet the Yankees in what they felt would be a glorious win for the South.

Daniel found the stay to be exasperating, particularly when they were able to hear the faint boom of cannon in the distance. True, there was almost no danger in fulfilling their assignment of protecting the supply wagons loaded with meat, poultry and grains. Yet Daniel and most of the troops wanted to be in on the glory of fighting the battle they thought would bring honor to the South and end the war. Fighting fever was in their blood.

Finally, the relief army arrived. Pickett's men were awakened by bugles very early the next day, long before sunrise. They learned that they were to move twenty-five miles toward Gettysburg, where the battle was already taking place. That morning and most of the day they marched in the sultry July heat.

Sometimes they passed small villages and homesteads, where curious Northerners watched their passing. Daniel noted that few of them seemed friendly, in fact he had the distinct impression many wished them dead. But that couldn't deter the mounting enthusiasm of the invading army, ready at last to claim victory. In fact, the whole army erupted into cheering as they marched, their spirits were so high. But as they came closer to the battleground, every soldier was amazed at the huge amount of firepower. Each advancing soldier wanted to know how the battle was going and who was winning.

"It's a bloody fight out there!" a returning soldier uttered.

"We lost a third of our company," another said, "but we gave it to 'em worse!"

Daniel was proud of those men who had stood up to the Yankees. He knew that before long he and his friends would be on the battlefield.

Already, the sun was beginning to go down, and word came they were to wait till tomorrow to get in on the fight. Meanwhile, before the light faded, they saw men carrying away the wounded to the field hospitals that were set up toward the rear.

The scene was downright discouraging, but as Daniel, Hank, Eli and John settled in for the night, making supper for themselves and putting up their tents, they began to realize that likely the morrow would be the decisive day for the South. Especially since their brigade was part of a newly arrived fighting force that would be attacking the Union front. Their excitement at being a part of the army that would at last overwhelm the Yankees was difficult to contain, and though Daniel and his friends knew they needed rest to be fresh for the morrow, sleep didn't come easy.

Awakened, by the sound of the morning bugle, Daniel and his friends were ready and anxious to receive their orders. None came, and they wondered at that, but resumed their normal morning activities which included making breakfast and heating coffee. As the day went on, Daniel and his friends became more and more nervous.

"What is going on?" thought Daniel out loud.

"It's the generals," said Eli. "For one reason or another they still can't make up their minds."

"Damn!" uttered Hank, expressing each of their feelings quite well.

Finally, sometime around noon, a huge line of confederate artillery was wheeled into place and at approximately one o'clock in the afternoon they exploded into action, shelling the hill almost a mile away where the Union troops were concentrated.

Pickett's army remained in safety behind Seminary Ridge, including Daniel, Hank, and Eli. As the shelling began, they covered their ears with their hands at the noise of the bombardment, now answered in kind by Union artillery. Every man stood at ready, waiting for orders to move, fearing the enemy shells that flew in front of them, and sometimes crashed among them. Fortunately, few caused casualties among the men on the ridge. Daniel wondered how anyone within range could survive the withering firepower spewing from the cannons.

The Confederate artillery fire continued, and surprisingly was no longer being answered by the enemy. Had they done their job of chasing them off the hill? Every soldier hoped so, for now orders were given to march down from the safety of the ridge and to line up for the dangerous march up the hill held by the enemy. Daniel and many other soldiers noted that their approach would take them almost three quarters of a mile over territory that was farmland, with hardly a tree or rock or anything that would offer them protection from enemy guns.

It was a glorious sight as the one and a half mile long line of Confederate soldiers marched forward toward Culp's Hill, where hopefully the shelling had already taken its toll on

186

the enemy. 15,000 men walked in unison toward the top. As Daniel marched with the others, glancing to his right and left at the lines of the Confederate army, his heart felt proud that he would be in the number of those who would dash the Union hope of victory over the South.

Then, as they came closer, enemy canons opened fire. Suddenly, hit by exploding shells, great gaps in the line appeared as up to ten men at a time were blown away. Daniel couldn't see well as the whole field was filling with drifting smoke. For a time there was disruption in the line of the Confederate advance, but the loud commands of the officers restored a semblance of order, and despite the continued shelling and now gunfire the men stayed the course. Then, the long line reached a fence that needed to be climbed over, making each man an easy shot for enemy guns.

Daniel hopped over as quickly as possible and so did Hank, but Eli fell, and as Daniel turned to look back at him, he saw he didn't get up. Things were now getting desperate as the cries of the wounded mingled with the immense noise of guns going off above them. Suddenly, Daniel was whirled around by a bullet that penetrated his side, and he fell head first to the ground. Then, he immediately felt a sharp pain in his foot. He saw Hank ahead, moving forward, and hoped that he would make it to the top and victory. In the confusion, the smoke, and the cries of battle, Daniel painfully crawled back to find Eli. He found him coughing, gasping for air. Eli saw Daniel moving toward him, and when he was close, he tried to speak despite his labored breathing. "Tell Clara I died bravely." Eli stopped, though wanting to say more, and Daniel saw that he could hardly catch his breath. "Tell her I will always love her." Eli fought for air. "Our little girl, Emily. . ." The sentence was left unfinished. Daniel put a hand on Eli's shoulder as he struggled to say more, but Eli shuddered, closed his eyes and lay still.

Daniel laid his head flat on the ground. Tears came, and for a moment he forgot the sharp pain in his side and his foot. Another battlefield death. But this one affected him more than all the others because Eli and he were from the same town and had been together the entire war. As for himself, he too was breathing hard, and though he felt pain in both his side and foot, he didn't dare rise to where the bullets were flying over him for he knew it unlikely that he could run or even walk. His left foot was not only painful but warm, and he thought that maybe his boot was filling with blood. Yet there was nothing he could do as the battle raged on except hope that it would end and help would come.

Chapter Nineteen

Two months later

"Ready," asked Daniel.

"Yeah. Just gotta grab this," said Hank bending down to lift up his extra sack.

"So, you boys are going to take the train south and then you have to walk over the mountains to get home?" said Emma, the woman who with her daughter had cared for them in her house.

Daniel looked at her, realizing he would more than likely see the woman for the last time. A kindly woman, with graying hair arranged in a bun with wisps that came down on her forehead and over her ears. She wore a medium blue dress largely covered by a white apron. "You have been so good to me, Mrs. Peters. Don't know if I would have made it without your care."

"You're a strong boy—man, I should say. I'm glad you got better, and to be honest, even though you're a southerner, I'm glad I was able to help."

"Well, have to leave," he said as he moved toward the door. He looked back at Mrs. Peters and then walking toward her, dropped his equipment and put his arms around her. "Thank you for everything."

Mrs. Peters seemed moved by his embrace, and when he stepped away she said, "You boys go back to your families, your girlfriends, and start a new life for yourselves away from all this fighting."

Daniel and Hank couldn't have agreed with her more. The fight between the North and the South would go on, but with the injuries they had both sustained, someone else would have to fight any remaining battles. Daniel regretted that the Battle of Gettysburg, with so much bloodshed on both sides, was not the final battle. In his mind, he didn't see how the South could carry on after such a devastating loss. Glad he was that he would no longer be a part of it. Glad he was to be going home.

Despite each of them sustaining a permanent injury, they left Mrs. Peters' house in high spirits. They had learned that the train left twice a day taking mostly injured soldiers to hospitals or toward their homes. The trip was short, and luckily without too long a wait they were able to board another train taking them to Mount Jackson. Since it was already late in the day, they decided to stay at the same hotel. This time, when they went inside, they didn't see the lady who had offered them a bath, and more. They got a room and asked about breakfast times. They knew they needed to get an early start if they were going to be able to make it to Clementine's house, where she would likely give them shelter.

In the morning, they were the first ones up to get breakfast, even taking some of it with them so they could leave all the more quickly. This time, they were sure of the way, and soon they were high enough in the mountains to look down on the city. Now, it was Hank who led them on.

Daniel spoke from several lengths behind him, "Can't keep up with you at this pace. How about stopping for awhile?"

"Sure. Want to stop here on the side of the hill or wait until we reach a place where it's level?

"A minute here, while I catch my breath, and then when we reach level ground."

Daniel stopped where he was, and Hank came back down to be beside his friend. He looked meaningfully at Daniel's boot, saying, "I don't know how you keep up at all."

"It is a problem. Know my days of running races are over."

After resting, they continued their journey, though they couldn't travel the distance in the time they hoped. Finally, they saw the little town perched on the hill and saw Clementine's house off to one side. They walked toward it, but on coming close saw that there was no light coming from inside.

"Hate to wake her and the child," said Daniel softly.

"I know, but don't think she would want us to sleep in the shed again."

They approached her door quietly, and Daniel decided to knock softly, hoping that if she was still awake she would hear and if not then they wouldn't bother her.

There was no answer to his first gentle rapping, so he tried again, slightly louder.

A light appeared from within the house, and they heard soft footsteps coming toward the door. Someone peeked out at them from behind a curtain, and then the door opened.

"You're back!" she said. "Oh, I heard of all the bloodshed at Gettysburg, but so glad you boys are OK. Come in. Come in!"

From behind her a deep voice asked, "Who is it coming here so late, Clemmie?"

Clementine made way for them to come in, saying to the man behind her, "It's those two confederate boys I told you about. The ones who told me you could have been sent away to a hospital while you recuperate. They're the ones who gave me hope for you."

As they entered the dimly lit room, brightened only by the light of the candlestick Clementine held in her hand, Daniel could make out a large, bushy haired man, bent a little over the cane he held in his right hand.

Clementine moved her candle in his direction, saying, "This is my long lost husband, Jesse. Jesse, this is Daniel and Hank who also have been fighting for our cause."

Jessie extended his hand and the men exchanged handshakes before Clementine said, "Coming in so late, you boys must be tired. You know I, that is, we don't have an extra bedroom, but we have extra blankets and as before we can offer you our sitting room for the night."

"Tired we are for sure," said Daniel, "and we sorely appreciate you all giving us a place to stay."

Hank looked at Jesse and added, "You sir, know what sleeping conditions are like in the army. This is far better."

"I know exactly what it is like, but don't dare call me sir. Even if I had been a captain, which I wasn't, in my house, everyone is equal."

"Pa and I will go back to our bedroom so you boys can settle in. Not long after the rooster crows, I'll be up and making you a breakfast. Sleep well."

Daniel and Hank murmured their thanks, and after arranging the blankets and removing their boots, quickly settled down to sleep. Dead tired, it wasn't long before the only sound that could be heard in the house was the deep breathing of slumber.

In the morning, after a delicious breakfast of bacon, grits, and muffins, and a fond farewell, Daniel and Hank were on their way early, anxious to begin their long trek home. This time, they wouldn't have to leave again.

Though they still had a long distance to travel, it was far easier going mostly downhill than mostly up.

"I was so glad for Clementine that Jesse finally came back to her. To me, she seemed a different woman," said Daniel.

"I know. With more than half his leg amputated, he was fortunate to survive. Not surprising that he had to spend so long in the hospital."

"He does seem to get around fairly well using the cane in his house and then the crutch he uses when outdoors. I think he doesn't want her to help him any more than necessary."

"Oh, yeah, Jesse's got his pride," said Hank. "He's a true blue southerner."

"Blue! You said the wrong word, Hank."

"Gosh-darn, you're right!" he answered. Then, both men could hardly stop their laughing at using blue for a southerner

They made it back home at last, though the journey took longer than it had previously. Daniel's parents hadn't yet received his most recent letter, so they were quite surprised that evening when he showed up at their door. He announced his coming, "Mom, Dad, Sissy, I'm home!"

His mom was the first to reach him. "Honey," she said, wrapping her arms around him. "I'm so glad you're back. You must be hungry, after walking all day."

Immediately his father came, shaking his hand while holding him with a strong arm around his back. "Son, welcome home."

His little sister was next, looking not at all little anymore. She wrapped her arms around him too, saying, "Daniel, I've missed you."

Daniel took a moment to look at all their smiling faces as they ushered him into the kitchen.

"You're in luck, son," said his mother. "We had a right good ham dinner earlier, and it won't take long at all for me to heat some of it up for you. You must be starved."

"Really, Ma, Hank and I had some leftovers Clementine gave us to eat along the way. I'm not real hungry. What I would really like is to get cleaned up and out of these clothes I've worn much too long."

Daniel noticed that his father had been looking at him. "Son," he said, "we knew you were wounded at Gettysburg and spent time recuperating at that lady's house. But you never told us about your injuries. I'm just looking at you now, and you look damn fine to me. Except I notice a limp. Are you fairly well healed up?"

Daniel looked at his father and saw in his eyes the concern and love the man had for him. "It's covered up by my boot, Dad. If I were all OK, I'd still be in the army somewhere fighting. I'm lucky, compared to many. Still, it's not something you're going to like to see."

* * *

The next day, having bathed, shaved, wearing fresh clothes, and having already eaten breakfast, Daniel set out in the buggy. He planned to get on with working on his father's farm, part of which he would inherit, but first there were two people in particular he needed to see. Samantha and Jenny.

September, a good time of year. Not as hot as July and August, but still warm enough with often delightful evenings and everything still green. Daniel was attracted to the countryside of his county, and it was with particular joy that he realized he might never have to leave again. Though he knew he would never be able to run again, there was nothing preventing him from pursuing his dream of having his own productive farm. Only one thing he lacked—a woman to share it with. One who would bless him with sons and maybe even daughters. He smiled as he thought of that. He was going to Samantha's house.

Of course, there was no way he could tell her he was coming. The telegraph lines didn't go out to the country, only to towns, and he knew from his parents that she also would not have received his latest letter.

Though he was keen on seeing Samantha, he also wanted to see Jenny. He hoped to see her afterwards. He was passing her house now, and noticed there was a paint horse tied to the rail of her front yard. He wondered who's that could be. He was not familiar with any horse with those

195

markings. Probably a friend of her father's or brother's he thought. He doubted that her older brother, Jeb, would be back from the war, unless he too was injured.

He passed by their farm, and saw that maybe things were not quite as manicured as before, but one crop had been harvested and another awaited the reaper. As he moved ahead, and moved closer to Samantha's house, his spirits lifted higher. Samantha might not have written as often as Jenny, but they were a pair. Or so he thought.

* * *

Daniel's heart was broken. He had been to Samantha's house, only to find Rex there. Of course, he had surprised them, for how could he have told her he was coming? But he was the one who was surprised. Oh, she was friendly, and Rex was too. Yet seeing how they looked at each other as they conversed with him told him more than he wanted to know. He learned they had been going together for a long time, nigh onto a year. So, Samantha was not one of Rex's temporary crushes. Daniel even caught from something they said that plans for marriage were forthcoming. Once he knew the situation without a doubt, he didn't stay overly long. He felt himself to be definitely a third wheel. Suddenly, his whole life plans were laid asunder.

Daniel was thoughtful, even morose, the entire trip home. He noticed Jenny's house as he went past, but he was too down in spirits to even think of stopping there. It was beginning to get dark when he arrived home. He had missed a meal but didn't feel like eating. He did see his parents, and said hello but had no desire to talk. Of course, they knew him well enough to sense immediately that something was wrong. "Samantha's no longer my girl," he told them, going immediately to his room and shutting the door. Sure, he heard them talking in hushed voices but he had no interest at all in what they might be saying. He just wanted to be left alone.

The next day, he ate breakfast quietly, and then went out to do some work he knew needed to be done on the farm. He surprised himself by actually keeping quite busy, even doing some things that took his mind for a time off of what he had just experienced. In a way, it pleased him that despite her, he could still do skilled work that required some thought.

As days went by, Daniel did a lot of thinking. Gradually, it came to him that maybe Samantha was not in all ways the best match for him. She was wealthy and having slaves made her life easier. In contrast, he was of moderate means, used to working with his father in order to make things better for themselves. His family did not depend on others to do the work for them--they did it themselves.

As much as he hated to think it, he began, grudgingly, to think that maybe Rex was possibly a better match for Samantha. He also grew up in luxury, bought by his father's money. Daniel suddenly stopped himself. This type of thinking was too hard for him to continue. He no longer had the girl that he thought he did, and surprisingly, no one else came to his mind.

* * *

Jenny was stressed. She knew now that Daniel was home yet he hadn't even stopped by to say hello. She knew, of course, about Samantha, how she seemed now to be caught up with Rex. She had known it for some time, but somehow never informed Daniel of it. He would find out for himself. Apparently he did find out. She knew he had been home from the army for days. Like Hank, he had suffered an injury, one so serious he was discharged.

Sarah was the one who had told her some of these things. When she went to her house the last time, she learned that Hank had been there to visit her. Sarah was not ready to talk very much about Hank; apparently his visit had been a surprise. But Sarah and she were too good of friends for Jenny not to know something of how it went. Sarah's too often smiles told her that. But what she really wanted to know was about Daniel, for she knew that Hank was his best friend.

When questioned, Sarah had told her, "Yes, they came back together, both with war injuries. Daniel's was to his foot, or leg. Hank was wearing a glove on his left hand. I didn't feel comfortable to talk about it, but it seemed that the glove was mostly empty. I was so sorry for him, but he didn't seem to think much of it. Said it got him out of the army and he was glad for that."

"Does Daniel know about Samantha?" Jenny had asked.

"I'm sure he does. Jenny, you know more than anyone that he would have gone to see her first. Probably immediately the day after he returned home."

Jenny thought about that and knew Sarah to be right. The two girls talked some more and then Jenny left to go home, thinking all the way back and even later of what could be the reason Daniel hadn't visited her? She couldn't figure it out. They had been friends for so long.

The next evening Captain Tom came to see her. A social visit. As much as she enjoyed their time spent together, the man just didn't excite her. Not like Daniel did. Still, she knew Daniel might not ever see in her what she saw in him. She saw Tom to be an honorable man, one who said what he meant and one who had no particular animosity toward anyone. He had fought against the South because he felt strongly about the Union. Besides, most people in his county were on the Union side. He felt the war had gone on far too long, and he longed for peace.

This time, she saw him coming in his buggy rather than just his horse. Outside the gate, he got down, opened the gate, and with his perpetual limp walked to her door. "Hi," he said, as she stepped onto the porch. "Thought you might like to go for a ride."

She looked him over. He was always neatly dressed, usually with his tan vest, a long sleeved button down shirt, with his full head of sandy hair blown by the wind.

"Oh, Tom," she said. "This evening is the one I go to the Ladies Aid Society. I hate that you have come all this way."

"Where is it, at the church?"

"Yes."

"I wouldn't mind giving you a ride. At least that way I could see you there and back and maybe a bit after."

Jenny considered. "That would be nice of you, Tom, but we ladies can take a long time. I mean we're scraping lint to help the wounded, and there's always plenty of talk too. Could be as long as two hours."

"That is a long time. Do you think they would mind if I took a look at what they're doing?"

Suddenly, Jenny's mind was racing. She had accepted Tom though he was from the Union side, but she didn't know how the women would feel. Especially someone who lost a husband or son in the war. Someone like her new friend, Clara. Poor Clara! Jenny had just learned from Sarah that her husband, Eli, had died at Gettysburg. She hesitated, "I, I don't know about that," she stuttered. "I know at least one of our women recently lost a man to Union fire."

"I understand. Still, after coming all the way here, I'd hate to drive back without hardly seeing you. I'll take you and just wait outside."

"You sure?" she asked, smiling at him.

"Why not? Got nothing better to do. Plus, it'd be just the two of us all the way there and back."

"OK. Wait for me here on the porch while I get my stuff ready. I'll only be a minute."

The ride to the church was uneventful. Jenny and Tom were used to talking about whatever they wanted, but they made a point with each other of saying almost nothing about the ongoing war.

"You're going to wait for me outside here?" she asked.

"Yeah, though I might ride off for a bit if I get bored. Won't be gone long in any case."

"Thanks," she said, waving him a goodbye as she entered the building.

Jenny entered, saw that some of her friends had already sat down in a circle and were starting the work. They exchanged greetings. She noted Clara was there with her daughter, Emily. She was seated quietly, and Jenny saw evidence of much crying etched on her sad face. She went to her and hugging her said, "Clara, I'm so sorry." Clara remained sitting, and looking up at her, said, "Thank you. Maybe I shouldn't have come here today; even my hands don't seem to want to do what they should."

"It's probably good for you to be around other people, Clara. People who care."

Martha came through the door and asked, "Whose is that nice looking gentleman waiting outside?"

Of course, Jenny had to answer to him, which only started a discussion among the ladies. Soon enough, they learned he was a former Union Captain, which brought some of them to saying some rather unkind things. Jenny was just about ready to give them a piece of her mind when suddenly Clara stood up and went to the door, leaving Emily playing on the blanket that was next to her. Jenny had no idea what she was going to do.

Concerned, she followed her, and from the doorway saw her standing in front of Tom. "Why do you kill?" she asked him, and then again, "Why do you kill? Why can't you people leave us alone?"

Jenny saw Tom looking at Clara, amazement in his eyes, not knowing what to say to the woman. Then, standing right in front of him, Clara raised her arms and brought her clenched fists down hard onto his shoulders. She did it a second time. "Answer me! Why? Why?"

Jenny ran out and quickly stepped between them. There was no doubt in her mind that Clara was overwrought. She gently put her hands on her shoulders and directed her back toward the church hall. Clara lowered her head and now seemed meek and willing to return with her. Jenny looked back to Tom and in a quiet voice said to him, "I'm sorry. Her husband was killed at Gettysburg. She just found out."

As she ushered her into the building, Clara was in tears. Clara said to her. "I'm sorry. I'm so sorry, Jenny. I don't know what got into me. Tell him. . ." Jenny could see she didn't know what to say. "Tell him whatever you want to. That I'm just a crazy woman who lost her husband. I didn't mean to take it out on him."

201

"It's going to be OK, Clara. I'll tell him. Don't worry about it. Tom is not the enemy. It's the whole system that's making one part of the nation fight against the other."

Jenny and Tom had a lot to talk about on the ride home and later. Once Jenny had told him of how Clara had just been informed of the death of her husband, he could understand how he would be the one to bear the brunt of her feelings. He didn't hold it against her. In fact, Jenny was glad to learn that he actually wondered if there was anything he could personally do to help her. She liked him all the more for that.

One thing impressed itself on her mind. No matter if the country wanted to fight on, she herself was no longer going to take sides, except if necessary to defend her family and those she loved. To Jenny, the killing somehow had to stop.

What was more on Jenny's mind than anything else was Daniel. She knew he had been home for almost two weeks and still had not come to see her. What was the matter with him? Or was it her? She knew where he lived. She didn't feel it quite right for her to go looking for him. But she was reaching the point that she would do it if she had to. She just couldn't wait much longer. If he was through with her, even as only a friend, she had to know.

Chapter Twenty

It was late in the evening on a Tuesday night. The sun hadn't yet set, but it was after the hour when she might expect a visitor. Especially as it was still the time of year when the sun went down fairly late in the day.

She was in her room reading by the light that still came through her window, when she heard a horse and buggy coming down their road, one that was little traveled toward nightfall. Then, she looked up and almost unbelieving, saw who it was. Daniel!

Quickly, she ran down the stairs and opened the front door. "Daniel!" she said.

He seemed a bit downcast as she saw him walking toward her, but lifted his head when she called out his name.

"Jenny," he said as he reached her.

Though dressed neatly, much the same as he usually was when he visited, wearing clothes that always seemed to fit him well, she saw a difference in him tonight.

"Sorry, coming so late. Had some chores to finish up. You OK with me stopping by now?"

Jenny looked into his eyes now that he was close. She sensed a sadness there, but answering, said, "Daniel, if I was awake, you could come at midnight."

"I guess maybe you heard about Samantha and me. It's over."

"Yes, I did hear something bout that, Daniel." Jenny didn't know if she should lie and say she was sorry about it or not. She ended up saying, "Guess being in the war it was a surprise for you."

"Sure was. It's tough, but you carry on. It's not exactly the end of the world. Knowing you, don't suppose you ever felt that way about someone."

Jenny had to turn away when Daniel said that. She put her head down, pretending to cough. Regaining her composure, she reached out to put a hand on his shoulder. "Girls feel things too, Daniel."

"Glad you understand, Jenny. I'm so used to coming this way on my way to Samantha's and stopping by to see you. Now, I won't be going to her house anymore. Still, I'd like to visit with you on occasion for old friendship's sake."

Jenny saw the sincerity in his eyes. It was one of the many things she liked about him. Still, when he mentioned "friendship" it hurt her. "Daniel, I like it when you come by," was all she could think of to say without saying much, much more.

Daniel eyed her, and smiled. He reached out his hands and took hers in his. For a moment, he held them tight. "Friends," he said, "the best of friends. What would you think if I came by Saturday afternoon and we go for a ride, just the two of us?"

Jenny wanted to say, "I would go anywhere with you, Daniel," but instead said, "I'd love to. I can pack a snack for us to eat while we're out."

"Great! I'm looking forward to it already."

"Me too!"

* * *

Jenny was suddenly beginning to feel herself popular. Tom was coming to see her, and now Daniel. Fortunately, it was a good time of the year. The crops had mostly been harvested. No more pulling weeds in the big field and less for her to bring in from her garden. Now, in addition to cooking, cleaning, washing and sewing she had only to do some canning to help carry them through the winter. But her evenings were mostly free, and that's when the men came. Already it was late in the afternoon, and she thought Tom might have started on his way to her house.

Jenny had been doing a lot of thinking since Daniel stopped by. She knew her heart still belonged to him, but if the man was so obtuse that he couldn't see it, maybe she should move on. Captain Tom was a likable gentleman, and even if he didn't make her heart flutter, he was still the marrying kind. A girl could do a lot worse. Maybe genuine love would come in time. That's what older women had told her. Especially her late Aunt Martha. "You marry, and then with children and all the work, you sit down one day and talk and realize you truly love him." Jenny always remembered those words.

The afternoon was mostly over as Jenny finished cleaning up in the kitchen. She removed her soiled apron, fixed her hair and rinsed her hands and face. Tom hadn't

205

come earlier in the week and Jenny hoped he wouldn't come today. That's because it was the late afternoon when the Ladies Aide Society met to help the troops. Mostly, scraping lint so it could be used in dressing wounds.

Ah, then she heard a horse trotting down the road. She looked out the window; it was he. Did he forget that this is the night she always went? The last time at the church hall must have been terrible for him, and Jenny knew it had been very unpleasant for her. Not only what happened with him and Clara but some of the things that escaped from the lips of more than one of the ladies. Things said against Tom because he had fought on the Union side.

She made her mind up right then and there that if Tom was indeed going to go with her again, she was going to have something to say to them.

"Hi!" she said as he came to the door. She stepped out onto the porch, and admired his clothes. The man was always well dressed, at least when he came to visit. "Did you forget this is the evening I go to the church hall?"

He put his hand to his head. "Oh, this is the night?"

"Yes. I'm sorry, your coming all this way."

"I knew it," he answered, dead serious this time.

"Then why did you come, Tom? I'm free most any other day."

"Cause I'd like to do it again."

"Why?" she asked, the question on her face as well as her lips.

"Are you ready to go? I'll tell you on the way. One thing," he lifted up the small bag he was holding. "Peach preserves. For you."

She looked into the bag. "That's so nice of you, Tom. Surely, you didn't can them yourself."

"True, it's from my mother. We have about a half dozen peach trees and she goes to work canning them about this time every year. Of course, she knows about you, and how special you are to me."

She took the bag, and in thanks, gave Tom a quick kiss on the cheek. She went inside to put them away and quickly was back on the porch with him. "Guess we should go now, if you really do want to come. You're going to have to tell me, cause I can't imagine why you would want to return there."

He did tell her, as the horse trotted along pulling them in his buggy. He said he was upset at how Clara had acted toward him. He talked to his mother about it, and she, though of Union sentiment, had no difficulty understanding how a woman who had just lost her husband could feel tremendous animosity for a former Union soldier. His mother inquired about the woman. Did she have anyone to help her now that her husband was gone?

Tom didn't know the answer to her question. He knew that she also was a farm girl, but if she had anyone else besides her husband to operate it, he didn't know.

"So," Jenny said, "I still don't know why you wanted to return."

"Well, my mother felt bad for her. I do too. Not knowing any way to help, she gave me four jars of the same peach preserves I gave you. To give to her."

"Really? I think you must have a very good mother."

"I shouldn't be the one to give them to her. I don't want to go inside that hall. I know, being from the Union side

I'm not welcome by her and probably others of the ladies. You give them to her for me."

Jenny considered. "Yes, that's probably the best thing to do. I'll tell her they came from your mother. Hopefully, that way she will accept them. Don't know exactly what her situation is on the farm. Think she has a brother nearby who helps. But anybody would appreciate fresh canned preserves."

"That's what I'm hoping, Jenny. This terrible war. Good men on both sides. I don't understand how we got into this."

Jenny put a hand on his knee as they approached the church. She looked at him, saying, "I don't think anyone understands, Tom." As they arrived near the door she got down. Looking up at him, still in the buggy, she added, "You staying around, same as before?"

"Might take a short ride; otherwise I'll be outside on the grounds. Hope all goes well inside."

Jenny thought about his last comment as she opened the door to go inside. He probably realized that she might take some flak for going out with a Union Captain. A former Union Captain. She set her mind on entering. She was going to say her piece to them. She would not listen to any more criticisms on whom she was traveling with.

After entering, she went to the large room, and was glad to see that most everyone had arrived. There was still a place next to Clara, just to the side of her daughter, Emily. She nodded to Clara, and said, "Emily, nice to see you. What are you playing with today?" Emily looked to her mother, who told her, "Tell Miss Jenny, Emily."

Jenny knew the girl didn't speak too well yet and was glad when she said, "A top. And I have yarn to play with."

Jenny looked at Clara, and they both were happy that Emily had said more than a couple words. Jenny remembered the preserves, which she had set down next to her. Taking the cloth bag, she moved them in front where Clara could see them. "Clara, these are for you. Tom's mother sent them."

Clara looked down at the bag, put her hand to move the cloth so she could see, and then looked with surprise at Jenny. "For me? His mother sent them for me after how I acted with him?"

Jenny saw the surprise in Clara's eyes, and how she seemed mystified. "I think she is a good hearted woman, Clara. Tom is too, or he wouldn't have brought them for you."

"Oh my Gosh! Is he out there? I can't believe how I acted with him. I am thoroughly ashamed of myself."

Jenny put a hand on her shoulder. "I think we understand how you felt. Not one of us always does what we're supposed to. It's OK, Clara."

Mrs. Peters called the session to order, and for a time all eyes and ears were on her. The work proceeded under her general direction, not that most everyone there needed guidance on what to do. No one had so far said anything against Tom, so Jenny held her tongue, refraining from saying what she had in her mind to say. She kept her eyes on her work, but sometimes glanced at Clara, noting that for some unknown reason she seemed agitated. At one point she asked her, "Are you alright, Clara."

Clara nodded, indicating that nothing was the matter. Then, suddenly she got up and went toward the back. Jenny heard the door swing open, and fearing for the worst, went to the window in the small entrance room and watched.

Tom was there near his buggy, and Clara slowly walked toward him, as if she had a lot on her mind. Jenny noted her head was down, and she held her hands crossed and down in front of her, as if telling herself she should not use them. She went right up to Tom, and she heard her talking to him but couldn't tell what she was saying. She saw him look carefully at her, and while her head was mostly down, she could see that Tom was watching her closely. He spoke too, but she had no idea what he said, especially as his voice was so soft and low.

Now, Clara was standing directly in front of him. She looked up into his eyes. Then, suddenly, she stepped toward him and planted a quick kiss on his cheek. She left immediately, walking fast, almost running back to the hall. Only once, did she look back at him before opening the door. Jenny had not seen that coming. She hurried back to her place, hoping that Clara had not seen her watching.

As usual with Tom, they had plenty to talk about on the way back. The incident with Clara being only one of them. Yet for Jenny, it was the most interesting part. Especially Tom's take on it. "She's been through a lot," he told her. "Yet she's not afraid to express something of her feelings."

Jenny listened intently, wondering what he was going to say next.

"I mean coming up against a guy, probably outweighing her by fifty pounds, and doing what she did took some courage for a woman. Not that I liked what she did, but to me there's no doubt that Clara's got heart. I admire that in her."

Jenny smiled, but she didn't let him see it. She began to have her own thoughts about the whole matter, thoughts that she didn't want to share. Thoughts maybe only a woman would understand. Her ride home with Tom was enjoyable. Her esteem for Captain Tom continued to grow.

* * *

It was Saturday, the day she had been waiting for. She hurried through everything she needed to do including getting a meal ready for her father and David. She prepared it for them early, not knowing exactly when Daniel was coming. She stayed to eat with them, but left long before they were finished. She tended to be a light eater, and she wanted to prepare herself for Daniel's coming.

That gave her time to bathe, to assemble what she was going to wear from her limited wardrobe and to add some extra touches. She even found time to weave a flower into her hair.

Then she heard a buggy coming down the road and, looking out, was pleased to see it was he.

She waited inside, not wanting to appear overanxious, though she certainly was. When he opened her front gate, then she came out the door to meet him.

"Wow," he said. "Don't you look like a dream!"

She noticed his limp, but paying no attention to that, took in his whole presence. The first time she had seen him in full daylight for a long time. He wore a brown vest, a white, long sleeved button down shirt, tight fitting dark pants and boots. His full head of dark brown hair was as usual tousled by the wind. Most of all, she saw his smile and eyes, always with that certain playfulness that spoke to her like nothing else could.

"I could say the same of you," she said, as they walked the short distance to his buggy. He helped her up, and looking at him again, she felt she was home, with him.

211

"I've got an idea. Let's go in to town. We can look around, see what's happening, and I'd like to get you something. A gift."

"I would love to," she said, sitting back as he turned the rig around and they headed off.

It was a lovely September day, and as they traveled, Jenny took note of the fields they passed, mostly all harvested, and the green grass and trees that grew everywhere along the way. She noted the houses too, now coming closer together as they reached the outskirts of the small town.

They didn't have a plan, and she liked that. They arrived in town and he hitched the buggy to a rail and helped her down. They both took note of the bustling variety of people walking on both sides of the street. Women, some dressed in high fashion, and men, some wearing business suits and bowler hats, and many others who likely came in from the country wearing a variety of loose fitting homespun clothes and hats. Jenny also saw soldiers, or former soldiers, a few missing an arm or leg, and others whose faces or necks bore witness to wounds inflicted by the enemy. She was saddened by their plight.

They heard music coming from up the street and started walking that way. Whoever it was played a sprightly tune which made them want to hear it up close. But just as they were arriving to join the others surrounding the musician, he said, "Thanks for your patronage folks. You have been a great crowd." With that he set down his fiddle and reached for his hat, into which people had pitched money.

"Too bad we missed him," said Daniel.

"Yeah, he sounded good. Why don't we go to the general store? There's always interesting things there, and I would buy us some candy."

Daniel smiled, liking the idea. He had something in mind he wanted to get for her, and thought he might find it there as well. They walked together the short distance, she noticing his limp.

It was a comfortable evening and three old men sat on the bench and on one of the chairs outside the store, talking loudly. Going inside, immediately their noses were assaulted by the huge variety of smells, part of what made the general store exciting. One could easily distinguish the odors of the pickle barrel, ripe cheese, animal feed, tanned leather, coffee, and of course, the ever present smell of tobacco.

There were a fair number of people inside, and the shop keeper was keeping busy talking to customers and wrapping purchases in paper and twine while his assistant scurried to different places to bring down goods from above or to locate other requested items.

Jenny and Daniel looked to their left and right as they walked, observing the huge variety of items available. Daniel spied the big candy jar. "Would you like some of these?" he asked, pointing to it on the counter.

"Oh, I'd love it," she answered.

"I've got a couple of things in mind," he said. "Don't know where they have them, but lost my pocketknife somewhere in the army and need to get a new one."

"You look around, and I'll go over toward the women's things."

Daniel soon found the knives, right across from where the proprietor took the money and wrapped the goods. He looked carefully at the wide variety for he wanted one not too big but large enough to cut tough things on the farm as well as to do his fingernails. Selecting one, he held it in his hand and looked to find where they kept the dime novels. He found a good number of them on a rack, and looked at them,

213

trying to decide on one that Jenny might like. Finally, selecting one, he went to where he saw Jenny.

She came toward him, carrying a small roll of pretty blue ribbon and holding a bar of soap. "Smell this," she said holding it out.

"Ah, that is nice. I picked out this book for you," he said, holding it up so she could see the cover and the title.

"For me? That's so nice of you, Daniel."

They made their purchases, had them wrapped, and walked out of the store. "It's still early, we should do something else before heading back," said Daniel. They walked together, reached where the buggy was parked and put some of their things there. Daniel put the knife in his pocket. Then, they heard music in the distance.

"Think that's coming from the tavern," said Daniel. "Maybe they have music on Saturday night." He looked at Jenny to see if she might be interested.

Jenny hesitated. She could tell that Daniel wanted to go, but felt that a tavern wasn't really a place a woman should enter. "I don't know, Daniel. I've always heard those places are for men."

Nevertheless, they continued slowly walking, getting closer to the music. "I know that song," said Daniel. "It was one we sang in the army." As they came closer, Jenny and Daniel could hear not only the fiddle, but people singing along with the music.

"I think I hear women's voices along with the men. Let's have a look, Jenny. We can come right back out if you don't like it."

Jenny was reluctant, but she trusted Daniel, and though her father might not approve, she took his arm as he escorted her inside.

Jenny had never been inside a tavern, and she looked around, still holding onto Daniel. It was fairly dark inside, and a man stood behind a small counter, pouring drinks. Behind him, hung a plethora of glasses and mugs. Everywhere there were tables, with people sitting at them, and toward the back a musician played and a number of men and a few women were gathered near him. He started a new song, and right away they joined in.

"We'll need to order a drink," Daniel whispered into her ear.

"I don't know what to get."

"You could try a lager. It's a German beer that's become popular. It's light and not as strong as most drinks."

"OK. Get me that." She began reaching into the pocket of her dress.

"Hey, I'm buying." He spoke to the man, handed him money, and soon had their drinks.

They sat down, listening to the music, and Jenny looked around at the crowd. Mostly men, of all ages, though a few women too, all who seemed to be accompanied by a man. Gradually, as she looked and listened, she became aware that some of the younger men were handicapped, missing part of an arm or leg. Two others bore big scars, one on his face and the other on his neck. She realized these were Confederates like Daniel, who came back from the war having given so much for the South.

In the low light of the tavern, she looked at Daniel who sat next to her at the small, round table. Their eyes met, and he seemed happy to be there with her.

"How is it?" he asked. "The drink?"

She had only sipped at it. "I thought it would be sweeter."

There had been a lull in the music, but now the man started again. Daniel recognized the song instantly, telling Jenny, "That one we sang in our regiment." Jenny watched as in a low voice Daniel began singing along with the melody. She knew the song too, though not the words. The crowd liked the music for after it ended there was applause. Then, he played another song popular with the Confederate soldiers.

Jenny watched and saw how Daniel seemed excited by the music. He sang it out loud as did many in the tavern. The crowd applauded again when it ended and someone with a loud voice asked for more of those kinds of melodies. She saw the excitement in Daniel's eyes, and when he suggested they go to the back toward the musician, she couldn't turn him down. She only knew some of the songs, but Daniel seemed to know them all and she watched, fascinated as not only he, but many others joined in. She saw that even those handicapped by the war were singing with obvious joy.

He played many more songs of the South, and some other melodies known to both the North and the South. Jenny kept her eyes on Daniel, and saw he knew almost all the words and sang with joy in his eyes, turning frequently to her as she also sang along. When the musician began playing the first notes of Dixie, the crowd roared their approval. One of the women there was so affected by the sprightly song, she took hold of her husband's hand and the two did a lively dance in front of them. Jenny could see that Daniel was enjoying it immensely.

He played two more songs before stopping. The beautiful Lorena, and Home Sweet Home by Stephen Foster. Those two evocative songs brought tears to the eyes of some. Jenny could tell that Daniel was affected by the music. Jenny herself was affected. When the music died and the man set down his bow, Daniel took her hand saying, "We probably should go now, Jenny."

The return ride in his buggy seemed special to her. They talked about many things, about the music, about those who didn't return home because of the war, about faith in a better future even if it had to be in the next life. Jenny learned that singing was a thing done by soldiers of both sides, and that if the armies were close enough, like across a river, the music played by a regimental band and sung was at times answered by soldiers on the other side. It was truly amazing to her that such a thing might happen of an evening and then the next day the two sides could resume killing each other.

Daniel too, had very much enjoyed their time together. The two were quiet as they came closer to where he would let her off. Daniel began to think of Jenny in a different way. Yes, it seemed she had always been his friend, but now? Was he reading too much into things just because they had a great time together? What about Jenny? He felt that she respected that they were only friends. That's what they had always been. Daniel knew that she was being seen by the former Union Captain. He was glad for her, wasn't he?

He thought about the man. He didn't know him, didn't have anything against him even though he fought for the wrong side. Daniel knew that he and his friend Hank might not have made it without help from Union civilians, and he knew the captain had received medical help from those whose hearts belonged to the South. Daniel could no longer get his mind around why Americans fought Americans. He just wanted to be left alone to live his own life. He wanted the long war to end.

It was dark when they pulled up to Jenny's front gate and he stopped the buggy. He jumped down and helped her off. Putting a hand on the gate to open it, they entered and walked together toward her front door. Everything was quiet.

217

She turned toward him on the porch. "Daniel, I had a wonderful time with you today," she said.

Daniel looked into her eyes, and the thought came to him that whoever wins this girl would be a fortunate man. "I did too, Jenny." Then, taking her in his arms, he kissed her.

For Jenny, it was over too soon. She didn't know what Daniel was thinking, but she knew her own mind. She hoped that he would come again for her, and soon. It didn't have to be anything special like today. Just to be with him was enough.

"I will see you," he said.

"Yes," she answered. "I will be here." She would have liked to say, "I will always be here for you, Daniel."

Chapter Twenty-One

Jenny had never enjoyed being with Daniel as much as she had that Saturday. She was cheerful Sunday, when she went with her father and brother in the buggy to church. Not that her menfolk always went, but she almost always did. She had time later, after dinner, to read from the new book that Daniel bought her. Monday was a busy day as usual, getting all her chores done, especially doing all the time consuming laundry.

Tuesday, was an easier day for her, and she couldn't wait to finish her chores so she could go to see Sarah. She felt herself bursting with things to talk about with her.

There was still some daylight left when she walked toward her house. She knocked, then went in and was greeted by both her parents. Sarah came in through the back door and then suggested they leave her parents and go to the backyard where they could talk. They sat down on the chair and short bench Sarah's father had made.

"Sarah, I had such a wonderful time with Daniel on Saturday. We actually went to the tavern."

"Really? Does your father know?"

"Oh, no! He knows I was with Daniel, but not that."

"Did you drink too?"

"Well, yes. Daniel ordered me something he called "lager." It was OK, but not something I would ask for again. At least it wasn't too strong. We had a wonderful time there because there was a musician and people were all joining in singing the songs. And Daniel knew most of them by heart. Said they sang them in the army."

"Wow! Who would have thought it? Though I've heard they have lots of down time between marching and fighting. I've got news too, Jenny. Guess who came over to visit Sunday afternoon?"

"No idea. Not the boy you liked in school. Was it Clem?"

"No, Hank. Daniel's friend."

"Really? That's interesting. I guess Daniel could have told him where you live since you're the next house down the road from me."

"Well, you know we met at the dance last year. He remembered me from then."

"You've got to tell me more, Sarah."

"I was pretty surprised he would remember me, not having seen him for over a year. Of course, I recognized him when he came to the door. Mom and Dad were home, and he spoke right nicely to them for a while. Seeing his war injury got them started on Gettysburg and the war and all that. Hank didn't talk a whole lot, but he could tell them what things were like from a soldier's point of view."

"Oh, I know how the folks like to go on about all the political things relating to the war."

"For sure. Mom served up some cookies and tea while we talked. That was nice of her. After that, we came out here so the two of us could be alone. I wanted to see his hand, or what is left of it, but he told me it's too ugly and kept it inside that long glove he wears."

"Yeah. Daniel told me about that. So sad. When he and I were in town we saw a number of men back from the war, some with missing arms or part of their legs. I just can't stand what this war is doing to them!"

Sarah reached over to put a hand on Jenny's arm, seeing all the empathy she felt for the soldiers. They looked at each other, and Jenny brushed away a tear, saying, "Go on, Sarah. I just get feeling so bad for them."

"Well, we talked and after a while I got feeling comfortable with him. I guess you could say we kind of hit it off. I told him I wanted to move that heavy pot when my Dad got around to it. That one there with the herbs." He said, where do you want it moved?" I told him there." Sarah pointed to the pot near the side of the house.

"So he grabbed it, bad hand and all, and moved it for me. To tell you the truth, I was surprised."

"Yeah. He's big, and Daniel mentioned that he's strong. I guess he still is." She got up to go over to the pot. Taking the rim of it with both hands, she tried to pull up one side. Turning to Sarah she said, "What else do you have in here besides dirt, Sarah?"

"Dirt, with stones on the bottom for drainage. I keep it watered; that adds weight."

Jenny came back to sit with her. By now the evening sky was darkening and if either looked up they could have

221

seen a few bright stars appearing. The girls talked for a while longer, and Jenny learned that Hank asked to see Sarah again. She noted that Sarah smiled when telling her that bit of news.

* * *

The next day and the day after, Jenny looked forward to when Daniel would come again. He hadn't said when he would, and that was a bit of a problem, for there was no way he could tell her in advance when he was coming. Same with the captain. She thought he would come to visit her as well. There was no doubt in Jenny's mind whom she wanted to see more. Still, she did like Tom, and if Daniel just couldn't see things clearly, maybe she could settle for him. That is, if he was thinking of her in a serious way.

She wondered. Did she have the courage to tell Daniel that she wanted more, much more, than friendship with him? She felt that Samantha was now with Rex, and their relationship had lasted long enough already that maybe Rex would actually stay with one girl. Jenny didn't know exactly how men thought, but if she were Daniel, she would no longer have any interest in Samantha even if Rex were to leave her. Surely, Daniel wasn't hoping that would happen. In Jenny's mind it all came down to what it had been for her forever. Why couldn't he see that she was the one for him?

Jenny was not surprised when Wednesday evening Captain Tom came to see her. By this time, her father had resigned himself to the man, and could even talk civilly to him even though for him he still represented the enemy. Jenny admired Tom's ability to understand her father's side of things and also his ability to skirt things that could easily lead to arguments. She looked up to him for that. Then, the two of them left the house together. Jenny still had no idea what he wanted to do other than be together with her.

"Thought you might enjoy a ride," he said. "I discovered a lake in the woods. It's pretty there and I brought some dessert and apple cider. We could watch the sun go down. Do you know of it?"

"Yes, I did go there once." Jenny didn't tell him it was with Daniel. "I'd like that, Tom."

They went there, and found a nice spot overlooking the lake. Tom even brought a tablecloth to put the sweetened cupcakes he had brought for them. For Jenny, the evening went well, and they talked about many things, even the book she was reading. Jenny learned the truth of what she had long suspected—that Tom was rather well off in having a large farm, cattle and even employees who helped him take care of it all. He also owned a dog, a black lab that he was quite fond of. One thing he talked about surprised her. Clara, the woman who yelled at him and then later apologized. Clara, who lost her husband, Eli, at Gettysburg.

Jenny was surprised that Clara was still on his mind. She looked at Tom as he reminisced about their two meetings, one violent and the other rather touching on Clara's part when she apologized to him. Jenny wondered that he would bring it up again. A man who had often faced enemy fire and who had been severely wounded by two minie balls. Yet, as she thought about it, he had probably never encountered a woman who physically attacked him, even though no harm was done. Maybe that made the difference. Or, another thought came to her. *Could it be that he likes her?* Though they talked about other things on the way home, that thought remained in her mind.

Arriving at her house, they said goodbye, and Jenny thanked him for a nice time. As she walked into her house, her thoughts went immediately to Daniel. She didn't know it, but Daniel was also thinking of her, in a way that was new to him.

Jenny was happy in the coming week as she went about her life. What made her glad was that Daniel would be coming Sunday to go to church with her and attend the social that would follow. One thing surprised her; Tom did not visit. Of course, she had no idea why as there was no way he could have told her. Even a letter would have been far too slow. She hoped he was all right.

But really, his not coming didn't matter that much anyway. Daniel was the one who brought excitement to her life. He was the one she had set her sights on. If only he could feel the same. Now that Samantha was practically taken by Rex, he should realize that she was the one he should be thinking about.

That was what was on her mind more than anything else whenever she had time to think. How could she get him to see it?

Finally, Sunday morning came. Of course, Jenny was wearing her Sunday best, a light blue gown trimmed with pink at the neck and wrists. With white lace above her breast and a rose belt emphasizing her narrow waist, she felt all decked out. Later, she would add the fashionable wide hat with the single large pink ribbon that circled the hat and fell in the back.

Putting on her yellow apron, she served breakfast to her father and David, sitting down herself to eat but keeping an ear out for when Daniel would come. Every time a carriage came down the road, she was up quickly to look out to see if it was he.

"Jenny, surely he will come to the door," her father said.

224

"I know, Daddy, I just want to greet him right away when he arrives."

"It's love," said her brother, speaking in his droll way to her father.

So what, thought Jenny. A girl feels how she feels.

Her menfolk finished, she tidied up after them, taking care not to get anything on her pretty sleeves. Done with that, she resumed waiting for Daniel. Then, looking out the front window, she caught sight of him coming up the road. She ran to get her pretty hat and was there at the gate when he stopped.

"Whoa," he said to the horse, though he hardly needed to as the horse was by now used to stopping there. "Wow! Aren't you the prettiest sight to lay eyes on!" he said, even before he stepped down from the buggy.

Jenny couldn't help but give him a wide smile at his words. She took him in as he approached her. Tan vest over a light colored, wide sleeved shirt, tight pants and nice looking boots. To her surprise, he was even wearing a hat, also tan with a medium wide brim. It looked so stylish on him. "You look mighty nice yourself," she answered. "Come with me into the house. Pa and David should be about dressed by now, and I have some things in a bag to take for the social."

They entered, and Jenny was glad to see her Pa dressed and almost ready to go.

"Good morning, Daniel," said her father to Daniel, extending his hand.

"Morning sir," he answered as they shook hands.

David came out of his room, looking ready to go. "Hi, Daniel."

225

He and Jenny's father left the house first, and Jenny went to get the large carrying bag she was taking. By the time Daniel and she got into his buggy the other one had left. As they were underway, Daniel reached back and picked up a ball. Holding it up, he said, "See this. I spent a heap of time working on it this week."

Jenny took it in her hand and tried squeezing it. She noted how its leather was bound together with heavy stitching. "You made this?" she asked. "Looks well done."

Daniel took it back from her. "Yeah, it's actually my second one 'cause the first wasn't tight enough. It's yarn wound around a walnut covered by hide. They call it a base ball."

"What do you do, play catch with it?"

"You can, but there's a whole game built up around it. Actually played it once in the army. I heard they've been playing it in the north for almost twenty years."

Jenny turned to look at Daniel with a question in her mind. "Well, if it's a northern game, don't know why you'd have anything to do with it."

He looked at her and smiled. "Jenny, it's a game. Got nothing to do with war. Someone said they play it at the Confederate prison in North Carolina. Union prisoners against the guards. What I like is that there's no pulling rank in the game. Doesn't matter if you're an officer or a private. All that matters is if you can hit and catch."

Jenny asked no more about "base ball." She wasn't surprised as they pulled up to the church that there were a great many carriages there. They parked, Daniel helped her down, and she left her baked goods in the hall. Then they joined others streaming into the church. She led him to their usual place, and as the organist played the opening melody, she was proud to be standing next to her father on the left and Daniel on her right. As the service continued, she saw so many that she knew. Sarah was there with her parents, Samantha was with Rex and her mother and father, she saw Clara with her daughter Emily, old Mrs. Peters, and so many more. Then, she spied Captain Tom. He appeared to be alone, standing with other parishioners. She had never before seen him at her church.

Two hours later, the service ended and the whole assembly joined the choir in song as the church bells rang out loudly. Everyone moved to the church hall where servers awaited them with chicken fixings, boiled ham, potatoes, and all kinds of vegetables plus a nice assortment of cookies, cakes and pies. They sat at long tables and enjoyed the food and conversation.

Wasn't long before the children hurriedly finished and went outside to play followed soon by the men. Only gradually did the women go out, Jenny as well, for in truth the women seemed to enjoy talking and catching up with each other more than the outdoor activities.

Jenny was surprised to see a large number of men all together outside all talking enthusiastically. Then she saw them begin stepping off distances on the church grounds and marking certain spots with short planks of wood. They formed two teams, and Jenny saw two of the men come back to their wives. She heard one say, "Come and watch. We're going to play base ball." She joined a number of other women, those who didn't have to watch small children, and went to where the men were just beginning to play their game. Her new friend, Clara, with her daughter Emily, came and stood beside her as they watched.

How interesting, she thought, as she looked from behind the "home base" where one of the men was just now coming up to "bat." He held a short fence post that looked like it had been whittled down to a narrower dimension where he held it with both hands. A man they called "the hurler" looked at him and then threw a quick underhanded ball toward him. Jenny was glad there was a man standing behind the "striker" to catch it. She had never seen the game before, but she was quickly learning the terminology from the almost constant chatter of the men. She watched as the striker let a couple balls go by, swung at two and missed, and then cracked the third high over the fielders and began running to "first base" and then making it to "second base" before the ball was thrown back from the left field. The men were applauding the hit, and she and many of the ladies joined in. Cheering especially loud was the woman whose husband had given the ball a good whack.

Another man came up to strike the ball, and when he hit it, the men got real excited because the first man rounded "third base" and quickly ran to the "home base." The men cheered and said he made an "ace."

The men were obviously enjoying the game, but as time passed Jenny was hoping it would soon be over. She had expected to share much more with Daniel, but that wasn't happening. Finally, the game ended, with much cheering on the winning team. But she noticed that even those losing seemed to be in good spirits, some of them saying to the winners, "We'll get you next time!"

At last Daniel came back to her, tossing his ball up a short distance with his hand and catching it. "We won! What did you think of the game, Jenny?" He stopped tossing the ball to look at her.

"Glad you men liked it. Seemed kind of long, but I could tell you were enjoying it. My father and brother seemed so excited when they belted the ball."

"Yeah, they did well. Glad we had Tom on our side. I think he hit it far every time he was a striker."

228

Jenny knew he meant the man she had always thought of as Captain Tom. "You hit some nice ones yourself, Daniel."

"Good thing, cause I was sure slow at running."

"That's just the way it is, Daniel. You, Tom, my brother and another man all weren't as good at that but you all could play well."

Jenny was glad because Daniel put an arm around her as they walked together talking. Some of the parishioners were getting into their carriages to go, but she wanted to stay with Daniel as long as she could. "Why don't we go back into the hall and get some dessert?" she said to him.

"Good idea. Hope they have some more of that delicious apple pie left."

The hall was much darker now for the sun was starting to go down, but some of the church ladies were putting things away and others were doing just as Jenny and Daniel, looking to get a last dessert before leaving for home.

Luckily, Daniel found his pie, and Jenny picked up a few cookies to take with her. Then, on the other side of the hall she made out her friend, Clara, and her daughter. She was about to raise her voice to speak to her when she noticed there was a man with her. At first, she couldn't make him out but then she realized it was Tom. Daniel was ready to leave, so she left with him, still wondering about Clara and Tom.

The trip home was great. She and Daniel had much to say, mostly about the very successful church social. She enjoyed getting his male viewpoint on things, not only the social but even going back to the minister's sermon. She was relaxed in the seat next to him listening to him talk. And when she was the one talking, he listened. She felt when she talked he took to heart what she was saying, like it really meant something to him. It made her feel warm inside, cared for, and she wanted more.

It was already dark by the time they arrived at her house. He helped her down, opened the gate and walked her to the front door. Then, he reached down the short distance to take her in his arms, to give her a kiss. She thought he would, and she was ready. Putting her arms around him she kissed him back with all that she felt for him. His lips were soft as they pressed deeply into hers and she heard a deep sigh as their lips parted. He looked at her, a question in his eyes, and then he bent down to take her again. She felt as if time stood still, that the only reality was his lips pressing hard on hers. When he lifted his head, his eyes smoldered and he said, "I will see you again. Soon."

"Yes," she answered breathlessly, feeling that whenever he came would not be soon enough. "Soon," she repeated.

* * *

The next day Daniel was out with his Pa on the farm helping to repair a fence that somehow their cow must have knocked down. They took spades, hammer and nails and posts with them as they went to the site. "Something must have scared her," Daniel's father was saying.

They reached the spot and Daniel took a look. "Yeah, completely broke off two of the posts. But I didn't see any claw marks or bites on her when I milked her."

They began digging out the broken posts so they could put in the new ones. "You seeing that Tilden girl now, son?" his father said, breathing hard from the digging.

"Yes I am, Dad." He stopped shoveling for a minute to look at his father.

"Don't mean to get into your business, son, but I've always had the feeling she likes you."

"We've been good friends for a long while."

"Well, I know that, just from seeing you with her enough. But I always felt that maybe with her there was more to it than friendship."

"Really?" Daniel stopped shoveling to look at his father. "What makes you think that, Dad?"

"Oh, nothing much. Just the look in her eyes I've seen on occasion when she was with you. And then you've told me she wrote more letters to you than anyone else while you were in the army."

Daniel thought for a minute about what his father had just said. Then, facing him he said with a smile. "You just might be right about that, Dad."

Daniel did a lot of thinking that day and the next about what his father had said. Could he be right? If so, he had been a bigger fool than he realized. Samantha had always been the one he had seen as his girl, but had he been seeing her for what she really was? She was always dressed so elegantly and her hair was always lovely. But that was because she had slaves to do things for her and rich parents who lived well because of the slaves they had to do most of the work. He thought of Jenny. She lost her mother years ago and she took on her duties. He knew it was hard work, caring for her men and Marcus before he ran away. Yet she never complained. He thought of all the times he had told her, "the second prettiest girl in the county."

Suddenly he felt bad for what he had said. Of course, Jenny couldn't always dress up like Samantha. She had work to do. A lot of work. Was he so impressed with Samantha because she affected the ways of the wealthy—always proper, always genteel? Or was he secretly hoping to be like her, living in prosperity? Already the slaves had been freed by Lincoln, at least in the territories controlled by the North. That fact didn't bother him in the least. He had fought for southern pride, against the incursion of military force into the South. Not for slavery. Slavery didn't matter to him at all. He expected he would make his living by hard work, not by slaves doing the work for him.

Why for years did he believe that Samantha was the one for him? She, rather than Jenny, who, like him, worked for a living? A girl who didn't dress in the style of a southern belle, but one who always spoke what was in her heart and not in some affected way. Suddenly, he was glad that Rex was now with Samantha, for it exposed a truth that he was until now too blind to see. It was Jenny he should have been seeing all along. She was the faithful one.

Thinking about her now, he amazed himself that he didn't see it before. As he thought about all the times he had seen Jenny, usually on the way to Samantha's, he became more and more aware that probably his father was right. She was the one who really did care for him. She was the one who corresponded regularly with him. Who sent him things in the mail. Things she had spent the time to make herself, like the warm scarf and stockings. Just now, Daniel felt himself to be a very foolish man. He hoped he could make things right. He looked forward to when he would see Jenny again.

Then, a very different thought came to his mind. One that could possibly fix all that he had failed to do before. An idea that he remembered from talking with a soldier in the army. He had noticed the man's ring, thinking it to be a wedding band, but then learned that instead it was an engagement ring. One that promised marriage when the war was over. Daniel had fairly well gotten over Samantha. Now, he suddenly felt the need to have someone he could count on in his life. He hoped it would be Jenny. Daniel had money left from his army pay. He would spend it on Jenny if she was willing. Suddenly excited, that same afternoon he made a trip into town to see about rings.

Chapter Twenty-Two

Jenny had her own thoughts about the wonderful Sunday she spent with Daniel. Any doubt in her mind between Daniel and the captain were completely erased. Besides, as they were ready to leave the darkened church hall, she had seen Tom with Clara. What a surprise that was! The man Clara was so angry with because to her he represented the Union side. One of those who had killed her husband. Jenny shook her head in disbelief just thinking about it.

She returned to thinking about Daniel. Maybe he was at last drawing closer to her. Maybe he was beginning to see that she could be much more than a friend. The way he had been acting lately when they were alone was giving her good feelings. He gave her good feelings. She hoped that she could gradually win him to seeing things her way-- that she was the only one for him. How she looked forward to his next visit.

Jenny was happy when Daniel came on Wednesday. Knowing he was coming, but not knowing when, she had tried each day to get her work done early and to be ready for him. Glad she was that supper was done and she had cleaned up the dishes and had time to remove her apron, clean up and fix her hair.

She let him in, and for a short time they talked with her father and her brother about ordinary things, the weather, their farms, etc. She was glad that Daniel seemed comfortable with her family as they did with him. After a while, they left the house and Daniel said, "Let's go into town. There's something I'd like to show you."

Jenny caught a note of something different in his voice. "What?" she said, looking at him with curiosity.

"A surprise," he answered.

Jenny had no idea what he might be thinking, but she looked forward to spending time with Daniel as well as the surprise. As they rode along, talking about most everything, she sometimes tried to get him to say what the surprise was, by asking leading questions, but after a while she gave up because he wasn't going to say and she would just have to wait.

They parked near the general store, and he helped her down and then hitched the horse to the wooden rail.

"Where?" she asked.

"Here, at the general store."

They walked up the one step to go inside and found, despite the late hour, several people inside. Daniel went right to the shopkeeper, who at the time was not busy assisting customers. "Oh, yes, I remember," he said, and walked away.

Jenny watched, wondering what was transpiring. Daniel came back to her and held her hand. "What is he going for?" she asked Daniel, looking straight into his face to see if there was any clue there.

"Wait," he answered.

The manager came back carrying a heavy case with lots of small drawers. He set it to one side of the counter from where he did business. "This is what we have," he said. At the moment, all the little drawers were still closed, but Jenny began to think what could be inside.

"I wanted to get you a ring," said Daniel, looking at her with utmost attention.

"Really?" she asked, as she faced him, having a hard time believing what was happening.

"Yes," he said, nodding toward the case. "For the most special girl I know."

The shopkeeper began opening the little drawers, and in each one was a ring, sitting within a miniature box. "Try one on," said the man. "We can see what your size is."

Jenny looked at Daniel, finding it hard to believe he was actually going to buy her a ring.

"Go ahead," he said. "I can pay for it."

At that point all kinds of thoughts were going through Jenny's mind. Especially, what did Daniel mean by buying her a ring? Her eyes fastened on all the rings in the drawers the proprietor had opened. She looked again at Daniel, uncertainty expressed on her face. "Daniel, nobody buys a woman a ring unless. . ." She found herself unable to finish her thought to him.

"Yes," he said. "It's because I want to marry you. Would you accept an injured Civil War veteran who loves you very much?"

Jenny turned to face him square on, her eyes fastened on his. Tears began to form in her eyes. Yes, this is what she wanted, this was what she had always hoped for, and yet she could scarcely believe it.

"Me?" she said. "You want to marry me?"

"I do," he answered, taking her in his arms.

"I do too," she uttered, her face inches from his.

He bent to kiss her, a long, sweet kiss.

A middle-aged woman and an older man noticed what was happening, and came closer, watching them. The store owner, said, "Ahem. Folks, about the ring."

* * *

Jenny had chosen a ring at last, making sure it fit snugly on her ring finger. As they drove away, she was happy, smiling, feeling coquettish, and holding her hand up so she could look at her ring in the last rays of the evening sunlight. She looked from time to time at Daniel, smiling, and he would glance at her too, but for the most part he needed to keep his eyes on the road ahead.

They came closer to her home as darkness set in. Jenny didn't want Daniel to have to leave soon, and she knew that arriving at home they would be obliged to talk with her father. Not that she minded that, but another thought came to her.

"Daniel," she said. "It's such a lovely evening. I don't want to go back right away."

Daniel turned to her. "What do you want to do, Jenny?"

"I want to kiss you."

Daniel leaned over and gave her a kiss. "Like that?"

"No. Not like that. Let's get off the road and find a quiet spot."

Daniel soon found a little used road leading into the woods and pulled off to one side, close to the trees and shrubs. The place was rather dark, covered with overhanging branches. For Jenny it was the perfect place. She turned to Daniel, seeing in the darkness not much more than the outline of his body and his eyes, glints of light turned toward her. "I'm so happy," she told him. "You don't know how long I've wanted you to be my beau."

"That's true," he answered. "Hope it hasn't been long."

"Oh, Daniel, it's been for ages," she said, feeling for his hand in the dark. She was glad when he enclosed her hand in his.

His head came closer to hers, "I truly didn't know. Maybe I should have."

"Doesn't matter now, Daniel, I really love that it seems like we have been friends forever. Now, we are going to be more than that, much more, but I still cherish our friendship."

"I do too, Jenny," he answered, his voice low and warm, his head inches from hers.

Jenny's lips moved the short distance to his. She was glad when his arms closed around her as his lips seemed to play with hers briefly until he pressed them down hard, pulling her tightly against him. Then he pulled back a little, his kiss moving to her neck as his hand caressed her bosom. She leaned into him, glad for his touch, glad he held her tight. Finally, she whispered to him, "We better go." She wanted to see her father, to have Daniel talk with him about his plans for the future with her. She wanted her father's OK. No, more than that, she wanted his blessing.

Jenny straightened up, as did Daniel. He turned the buggy around on the narrow road, as Jenny tried to straighten her clothes and hair. As they traveled the short distance to her house the thought came to her how prim she must look now as they traveled, how proper, when a short time before she had felt the heat of longing for the man who sat next to her.

The darkness was complete when they arrived at her house. Jenny was afraid her father had gone to bed. She hoped not, for she so much wanted to tell him the news. She wanted him to say yes.

Jenny and Daniel stood on her porch at the door and he said, "Jenny, if he's already in bed don't wake him. We can tell him another time."

"Let me check. Wait here just a moment." She opened the door and went to find her father. She found him in his bedroom, but still dressed with the wall candle lit. "Daddy, Daniel is here, outside."

"I'm going to bed, honey. Tell him I said goodnight."

"Daddy, there's something we need to tell you."

Her father looked at her. "Can't it wait?"

"No, Daddy. This can't wait at all," she said, telling him a little lie, but scarcely able to hold in what she had to tell him. "It's about Daniel and me." She saw that he looked at her with sudden interest.

"OK, honey. Let's go out to the sitting room." They did, he lit a wall candle there and she went to the door to get Daniel.

He came in, and standing, they both faced her father who had set himself down in his easy chair. "Sorry to bother you so late, Mr. Tilden," said Daniel.

239

"Jenny said there's news," he replied.

"Oh, yes, Daddy, big news."

"Well, what is it?"

"Mr. Tilden, I would like to ask for your daughter's hand in marriage."

Jenny saw her father look closely at Daniel, his appeal waiting for his answer, and then look at her. As for herself, she couldn't stop beaming.

"Jenny, this is what you want?"

"Oh, yes, Daddy."

"Fine by me, Daniel. I've known you long enough not to have any reservations about. . ."

His sentence was interrupted by Jenny fairly swooping down to where he sat on the chair, wrapping her arms around him, and kissing him on the cheek. "I love you, Daddy."

"Thank you, sir. I will love Jenny and take care of her all the days of my life." said Daniel, drawing closer to where he still sat in the chair. Her father rose from his chair, the two shook hands, and Jenny saw how they looked directly into each other's eyes.

"How soon?" he asked of Daniel.

Jenny had no idea what Daniel would answer, for they had not even talked about that important detail.

"In the spring," he answered. "When our house can be completed, at least on the outside."

"That's smart," her father answered. "Now, if you two don't mind, I'm going to bed. Oh, let me be the first to offer my congratulations to you both."

Jenny was elated, and she and Daniel talked in whispers about what had just happened, not wanting to disturb her father or brother who apparently had already gone to bed. After a while, Daniel left, after first giving her a right smart kiss on the porch. She felt tenderness for him, something she had not felt before. He was giving her his life, and she would give him hers. There was something very special about that. She turned to go to her bedroom, not knowing if she would be able to sleep. At last, she would have the man she always wanted.

Chapter Twenty-Three

Months passed. Winter gradually came on, with snows, increasing cold, winds and dark skies. Yet Jenny was happy. She so looked forward to the spring, when she would share her life with Daniel. In the meantime, she was taking time to make things for their future home.

One thing bothered her. She didn't see Daniel as much as she had hoped to. Why? He said he was busy, but didn't explain what kept him away. Oh, he gave little hints, making her wonder, but not really telling her anything. She was afraid it was going to be a long winter, waiting for spring, waiting for the day when she would become Daniel's bride. But Jenny kept busy, getting ready, embroidering pillow cases, sewing two tablecloths as well as napkins, making quilts and sewing clothes for herself so that she wouldn't have to wear the same thing every day except Sunday. She didn't want to have Daniel get tired of her always dressed in the same things. She was planning something for him as well, something that would be a surprise that he wouldn't see until on their wedding day. Two things really, and she was already excited about how he would react.

One cold, winter day he came over. He told her, "I know it's cold, but if you dress up warm, I'd like to show you something."

"You mean go for a ride? In this weather?" Jenny saw that there was about two inches of snow on the ground.

"We don't have to," he answered, "but I think it might be worthwhile for you to see."

"OK. I'll put on warm shawls, a hat and be ready to go with you." She looked at him. "Are you sure you're dressed warm enough to take another trip? I mean, you've already come this far through the cold. Want to warm up in the house first?"

"No, I'm fine. Let's go when you're ready."

He helped her into his buggy, where he had a thick mat on the seat, and she huddled near him, putting the blanket she had brought around both of their legs extending up to past their waists. Jenny never did like cold weather, but sitting close to Daniel she was content. She wondered where he was taking her.

"You really must have something to show me to take me out in this weather."

"I do," was all he answered in reply.

Jenny noted that they started in the direction of town, but then he veered to the left onto another road. The wind was fairly strong going that way and she huddled nearer to Daniel, comfortable enough to be next to him, but wondering where he might be taking her. She remembered taking the route a time or two before, but not recently. "Daniel, are you taking me to your house?"

"Not exactly, but you're close."

Jenny wondered to herself what he meant by that. "You are being awfully mysterious, Mr. Daniel."

He turned to give her a bright smile. "I love it when you're perplexed. You look so cute and I can almost see the wheels turning inside your head. Wait and see."

They continued on and now Jenny knew they were on the way to his father's house. She could almost see it already as soon as they turned the corner. But, to her surprise, she saw something else instead.

Daniel drove the carriage steadily toward it, and now Jenny was almost overcome by what she saw. "Daniel," she said. "Is that what I think it is?"

"Sure is, Jenny," he said, now looking at her eyes to see her reaction. "That's going to be our home." He stopped the buggy in front of the heavy timbered construction.

He helped her down, and now looking at it from ground level, she held onto his shoulder in the slippery snow. "Daniel, it's so big. I mean those heavy beams up there so high. How did you ever do that?"

"I had help, for sure. Once I cut the timber and planed it into shape, I got Hank and sometimes my Dad to help get them into place. Especially for the crossbeams. They are all mortise and tenon joints."

Jenny stood looking up at the construction, and then she turned to Daniel with admiration. "You are amazing." She gave him a kiss on the cheek.

Daniel fastened his eyes on hers, saying nothing, but giving her a big smile. Together, they walked up to their house to be, and Jenny ran her hands on one of the thick timbers that rose to the second floor of the house. "Sure looks strong."

"Oh, yes, and it goes deep into the ground. No wind is going to blow this house down. Let's go in, and I can show you how it's laid out inside."

They stepped through the open framework of the door. Daniel waved his arm across the space before them. "This will be our parlor where we'll greet our friends and guests."

Jenny looked around at the open space, bounded by construction timbers. "It's nice and large."

Daniel led them further into the house. "And this will be our sitting room."

Jenny looked with wonder at the large room, imagining where in the future there would be a comfortable chair or two, where there would be a light on the wall near one of them for reading, and maybe a deacons bench across, thinking how they could have their friends come and visit them. Turning to Daniel she said, "Oh, Daniel, this is all so grand and wonderful."

"Going to take a lot of work to get it all finished, but I'm glad you can kind of visualize what it will look like, Jenny." He led her further into the house. "Over here will be the kitchen. You can see there'll be a window looking out back so they'll be plenty of light for you during the day. I'm thinking of digging out a root cellar over here," he pointed out a place to the right toward the side of the room. "We'll have it covered with a lift up door and steps leading down into it. Should help keep things like carrots, onions and potatoes cool so they'll keep better."

Jenny stepped to where he had pointed and walked to stand there. "Right here, you think? We'll definitely need one, though with so much else to do could get by without it for a while."

They left the kitchen, and Daniel raised his hand toward the second floor. "Not sure where we should put the stairs up. We'll need the space for a bedroom or two when the children are older."

Jenny looked to where he showed her. His words about children affected her in a way that went to her heart, but she only said, "Yes, we'll have to think about that."

Daniel turned and said, "over there will be a small bedroom for when they are small, and here, in the larger space here," he went toward it, "this will be our own bedroom. I'm hoping we can afford a nice big bed where we can be comfortable together."

Jenny looked at the area he showed her and in her head she imagined the bed and also the two of them in the bed. Thoughts came to her such that she turned away from Daniel, but only for a moment. She turned back, looking him full in the face and saying, "I will be happy to sleep with you, Daniel."

This time it was Daniel's turn to look away from her direct gaze. Then he turned back to her, and taking her in his arms he said, "Yes."

It was a tender moment, one they both felt. He held her, and she was glad to be held. It was an adventure, they both realized. One they would take together.

She stepped out of his embrace, thinking. "When do you think we can get the house framed in?"

"I got plans for that too, Jenny. I've saved up most of my discharge money, and Pa's going to help too, so I'm thinking we can get the siding delivered early May. Then, we can invite everyone we know, anyone willing to help, have food, drinks and maybe even dancing at night if we can get it framed in. Then, we can get married."

Jenny looked at Daniel with pride. "You sure do have it all figured out. Hope it will work out for us just as you say."

He put an arm around her waist as they stood looking together at their future home. "Jenny, I feel like with you at my side we can do anything."

* * *

Jenny felt as if she were floating on air. Everything had gone so wonderfully. So many had come for the house raising that now the outside was done. She was proud of Daniel, though scared at the time, for he, Hank, and Nate had spent much time doing the up high work that needed to be done. Her father and brother had come as well, and everyone pitched in. Even Clara came with her daughter, Emily, accompanied by Tom, the former Union Captain. Jenny was so glad that no one said anything to him about fighting for the wrong side.

The women pitched in as well, holding on to the long boards while the men sawed them to size. They supplied the food, making sure there was more than enough for everyone. They also brought desserts and coffee, water, and juice. The men worked hard the whole day and needed plenty to eat and drink. As the sun began to set in the west, Daniel went up to the top of their good sized home for what he hoped would be his last time that day on the ladder. From there, he surveyed the roof and top of the house and then proclaimed, "We did it!" while lifting his hammer high in the air.

That's when the party started. Everyone went inside, someone brought candles, and they were lit and put in bottles. Two men, one a neighbor who knew how to fiddle, provided the music. Oh, what a grand time they had! To dance with Daniel, to see their friends dancing together, and everyone feeling good about what they had done. It was wonderful. The whole thing didn't last far into the night as usual, but that was to be expected. After working all day, people were tired. Jenny herself was exhausted and so happy when everyone left and Daniel took her home in his carriage to her father's house. How tenderly she kissed him on the porch. Soon, they would be moving into their own house, once it was provisioned. But the best part was yet to come. Their wedding!

Of course, there was still much to be done inside their house, but that she looked forward to doing together with Daniel. Doing it in the homey way she had envisioned. Already, since the house raising, Daniel had supplied wood for their stove and some basic food, like beans, potatoes, cornmeal, cow peas and honey. He was working on making a chicken coop, and when it was finished, they would have birds, courtesy of his father and her father. Then, they could have fresh, home bred chicken meat to eat. Daniel told her he could also supply fresh fish from a nearby stream to supplement their diet. Yes, they would have a lot to do to become a fully functioning farm, but thanks to the help of their parents, they looked forward to having almost everything they needed, other than what they would get from the general store, especially when cold weather set in.

A week later, it was the night before her wedding and Jenny was nervous. She and her bridesmaid, Sarah, had spent much time talking of every possible thing about the wedding, but as Jenny went on her way again to Sarah's house, there was something else on her mind.

It was the evening before her wedding day, and Jenny had been to Sarah's house so often that sometimes her parents barely greeted her before continuing to do what they had been doing. Today, however, Sarah's mother said, "Jenny, tomorrow's the day. Are you excited?"

"Yes, Mrs. Foster," she said before going to join Sarah in her room.

Sarah looked up when she entered, "Hi, Jenny. I think we have just about everything in readiness now, don't you think?"

"Yes," Jenny answered. "Everything except me."

Sarah came to her, looked at her in the brightness of daylight that still came through her upstairs window, and put an arm around her shoulder. "You look fine, Jenny. What do you mean?"

"Suddenly, I feel so nervous. I mean I've never done anything like this in my life and I just hope everything goes well."

"You mean about the wedding? The minister has done it so many times before. Even if you forget what you're supposed to say, he will know just what to do. Don't worry."

"It's not about that, Sarah. It's how it will be later with me and Daniel."

Sarah backed away from her friend to take a good look at her. "Jenny, don't worry about that. Believe me, from all I've heard, men know what to do. All you have to do is go with what they're thinking."

"Oh, I've heard that too. Why can't I let myself be at ease? I'm just too nervous."

Sarah came back to her, putting a hand on her shoulder. Looking intently at her she said, "Jenny, you worry too much. They say it's all quite natural. I mean, look at us. We're here thanks to our parents. It can't be all that complicated. I mean we've both seen animals do it, and you know we're much smarter than they are. Besides, the way humans do it is much nicer. Much more personal. You love Daniel and he loves you. Don't worry. It will be fine."

249

They talked about many other things, all having to do with her wedding tomorrow. Late that night Jenny went home, feeling better about everything. Tomorrow, their friends would come to celebrate the very special day in their life together. Even if everything wasn't quite perfect, what did it really matter? She and Daniel would be married, hopefully the start of a long life together. After talking with Sarah, who was so practical about many things, Jenny found that she was able to go to sleep that night feeling good that she would enjoy the next day.

* * *

Jenny awakened to a surprise. Her father had made breakfast for her. "Daddy, that was so nice of you," she said, giving him a hug. "Bacon, eggs, and even pancakes."

"It's you're special day, darling."

After they finished eating, there was another surprise. David got up from the table and went right out to bring in the tub. He set it down in the semiprivate place where they always put it. Then, to Jenny's surprise, as she looked at what he was doing, he picked up a bucket, went outside to pump water, and started a fire in the stove. "What are you doing, David?" she asked, when he came in from outside.

"I know you're going to want to bathe, so I'm getting up the water for you."

"Really? You're doing that for me?" She went to stand next to him.

"Well, it's not every day a girl gets married," he drawled.

"Sometimes you can be so sweet," she said, giving him a peck on the cheek.

"Ah, Jenny, you don't need to go on about doing that," he said, wiping his cheek where she had kissed him. She saw him take a good, long look at her. "Pa and I are going to miss you when you're gone. When I get this water heated up you go first for a change."

She looked at him, touched by his kindness. "I'll miss you and Pa too, but you're hardly going to see the last of me. Daniel and I won't be that far." She left him to go to her room, to put on her gown for when she would step into the warm tub of water. Once bathed, she knew Sarah was coming over sometime after noon to help with her hair and wedding dress. She could hardly wait until later that day when she would meet Daniel and their friends at the church.

* * *

Jenny sat crowded between her father and brother as he drove her to the church. The trip itself was sentimental for her, for she knew it might be the last time he would be taking her in his buggy. After the ceremony, she would ride home with Daniel. To their own home! How proud and how grateful she felt that they would have a home of their own.

As they approached the church, she saw many other carriages and she waved to friends who were also just arriving. Actually, she felt she was a bit late, and before her father parked, she let herself down and went into the church. Right away, Sarah grabbed her. "Jenny, finally you're here! Let's go to the side room so we can get you all ready."

A short time later, Jenny and Sarah emerged from the room. Now, Jenny felt like a bride. Every hair of her head

251

was in place, her cheeks glowed with the blush Sarah had lightly applied, and her sheer white veil covered her face, which didn't prevent her from seeing that apparently all the guests had arrived.

Her father was there in the back waiting for her, and though usually a stoic kind of man, she sensed something more in his demeanor, especially when she came beside him and he told her, "Jenny, you are a beautiful bride."

The three of them stood at the back of the church, ready to go up the aisle at the start of the music. Half the little congregation craned their necks to look at them. Jenny's eyes were looking further to the front where Daniel, his best man, Hank, and the minister were standing, ready to receive her.

Daniel and she exchanged glances from across the church. Jenny could hardly believe how handsome he looked wearing his open tan buckskin vest over a blazing white shirt, dark pants and a crimson cravat. His full head of warm brown hair was trimmed and, so unlike him, every strand was in place. She couldn't wait to stand next to him.

Softly, the fiddler began the wedding song, and Sarah, carrying her bouquet of beautiful yellow flowers walked in time with the music to the front. Jenny and her father walked a few steps behind, his arm enclosing hers. As they moved forward, Jenny felt the solemnity of the occasion, and kept her eyes straight ahead. When she reached the front where the minister stood, she handed Sarah her bouquet, and looked to the right at Daniel, standing ready.

"Who gives this woman in marriage?" asked the minister.

"I do," said her father.

Daniel immediately came to her side. She watched his eyes, and saw his great smile as her father gave her to him. They joined hands, and following the minister's direction, sat down next to each other on the two cushioned chairs set near the front of the altar.

Jenny felt joy to be in this special position, next to Daniel. Everyone in attendance saw that it was now her and Daniel, today, tonight and forever. She turned to look directly at him, and he turned to her. He tightened his grip on her hand. She knew the feeling between them was mutual.

* * *

Afterwards, as she went on her way with Daniel toward their house, much of the readings and even the words spoken by the minister were a blur for her. Except the solemn words they spoke to each other which she would never forget.

"I Daniel Jenkins, take you, Jenny Tilden, to be my wife, to have and to hold from this day forward, for better, for worse, for richer, for poorer, in sickness and health, until death do us part."

And her own words:

"I, Jenny Tilden, take you, Daniel Jenkins, to be my husband, to have and to hold from this day forward, for better, for worse, for richer, for poorer, in sickness and health, until death do us part."

Now they were a pair. For life. Making one of their first trips together to their own house. For that is where their party would begin. And why not? It was big enough, and though lacking in furniture, it provided a large open space where their friends could enjoy refreshments and dancing.

Glad she was that she had insisted that Daniel quickly add a bedroom door. For that was her concern. What if their guests didn't leave? She knew that sometimes happened. At least she and Daniel would have their own private room.

By the time they arrived, already many of their friends were there waiting for them. A great shout arose as they entered their house. People had brought an extra table and set it next to their own and others had brought in extra chairs.

Now, the women were piling up big pans and bowls of chicken, turkey, bread, rolls, jellies, coleslaw, strawberries, Indian pudding, and two dark fruit cakes which appeared to be cherry. To drink there was cider, corn liquor, eggnog, and whiskey.

Jenny looked at all those she knew, a big smile on her face. "Kiss! Kiss!" shouted some of the guests, and she turned to Daniel and they did, smiling at each other.

Jenny stood with Daniel, and she turned to look at all their guests. Besides her father and brother, there were old school friends, women from the Ladies Aid Society, including Clara and Tom, Daniel's father, mother and sister and several neighbors including one who was going to play the fiddle for dancing. Right away, they wanted the wedding party to sit down at the table, to start the food first and then everyone could join in.

Jenny, Daniel, Sarah, and Hank sat down as the crowd milled about them offering congratulations to Daniel and best wishes to her. Jenny wished they had more chairs for the guests, but those would come in time. Their lack of furniture opened their house for dancing which would begin after everyone had dined.

The next few hours passed in a blur for Jenny. She and Daniel talked with each of their guests, they danced and they drank as did everyone, some having cider, others eggnog and many of the men drinking corn liquor and whiskey. Jenny was beginning to notice some of them were getting tipsy.

At last, people started to leave. Jenny had had a wonderful time, but she wanted to be with Daniel. Only with

Daniel. She and he said goodbye to the last of their friends, but two men had passed out, one leaning against a wall and the other lying flat on the floor. Daniel tried to wake them to no avail. Jenny didn't feel it was right to try to push them out of the house. Unfortunately, they would have to stay.

At last, time with Daniel alone. As they went into the bedroom where a single candle burned, they locked the door, and Daniel looked at her so dreamy eyed she hardly knew what to think. Had he had too much to drink? She was apprehensive enough already on this her wedding night. "How do you feel," she asked him, looking into his eyes.

"Good."

Her apprehension deepened at what she knew was coming. "Daniel, you know. . ." She couldn't quite get out what she was going to say about having no experience.

"Let's just hold. You and me in the bed."

"Should I take off my wedding dress?"

"I would like that."

"Don't look."

Daniel obligingly turned the other way. "If you don't mind, I'll remove most of my clothes too."

Jenny thought about that as she began undoing her dress. Of course, he would remove his clothes. It took her more time than usual to get out of her wedding dress, but maybe it was because she was nervous.

She turned and looked at Daniel. He was stripped down, except for his drawers. She had seen his chest before, so masculine, it held no surprise for her. He lay down on the bed, waiting for her. Then she saw his foot. "Oh, Daniel, I had no idea!" she said, taking a place on the bed where she could look more closely at it. "My poor baby. Does it hurt?"

255

"No, only if I walk too much."

"I don't see how you can walk at all." She moved her face to his foot and began kissing it. "My darling, I didn't know how bad."

Daniel was looking at her as she ministered to his bad foot. "I use a thin, flat board underneath it to help fill out my shoe. It helps with walking. But Jenny, let's leave my foot alone. How about coming up to be close to me?"

Jenny looked up at his face, saw his smile, and something else. Was it anticipation?

She moved to be next to him, and gave him a smile. "Do what you want to, Daniel. I'm all yours."

Chapter Twenty-Four

Early April, 1865. It already had been a late winter and hard spring for Jenny, for she had seen her father weaken and then die. Toward the end, she went to see him every day. It was so sad to see him so sick, for he had always been a strong rock for her, especially after her mother's death. At the very end she was glad that she, her brother and Daniel had all been there in his final moments. More than ever, she was glad she had Daniel. Now he would be her rock.

In the days that followed she thought of her brother David who would now be alone. She wondered how he would be able to do all that needed to be done on the farm. She suspected that a lot would not get taken care of. She loved David dearly, but she saw him for what he was, kind of a loner who would likely never marry. And yet, like everyone, he needed to have some contact with other people. Since he didn't take it upon himself to do much visiting, she planned that she would make the effort to stop by and see him at least once a week.

Yet foremost on her mind was the baby growing within her. She was already big with child, and the midwife thought that her weeks were numbered. In fact, that very day she and Daniel were going to take the buggy into town to get some supplies in preparation for that forthcoming happy day. She hoped not so much that her delivery would be easy, no one could expect that, but ordinary and safe. Every mother knew that some women died in labor, along with the baby. Jenny took some solace in realizing that her hips were of a womanly width, wide enough so that she didn't think that would be a problem as it could be for some.

As they rode along into town, Jenny appreciated that Daniel went slower than usual, and made an effort to avoid any ruts in the road. She knew without asking that he was doing it for her and their baby. When they arrived, there was great commotion in town, and they soon learned its cause. The war was over! The South had surrendered at Appomattox the day before, and now the telegraph lines, the newspaper, and the people on the street told the story. And yet, judging from what they saw, it was not despair for the defeated South, but rejoicing that the long war was finally over. Now, young men who had long been away fighting would at last be coming home!

Jenny felt as if a breath of fresh air had come to her town and likely to her nation, and she hoped that soon things between the North and the South would return to normal.

Daniel turned to her. "I'm so glad, Jenny, that the fighting and killing is over."

"Me too, Daniel," she answered, her gaze lingering on his in sharing the thought they both felt deeply.

He pulled up to the rail, tied the horse and helped her down. They went into the general store, Daniel looking around while Jenny went to get baby powder, diaper pins, and soft cotton to make into baby clothing. Jenny had already made what she thought would be enough diapers. She and he met toward the middle of the store, Jenny with what she wanted to buy and Daniel, holding something behind his back. Jenny laid her things on the counter for the man to add up and wrap. "What did you get?" asked Jenny.

He held it in front so she could see.

"A book! For me?"

"Yes. I figure you'll be laid up for a while with the baby and might like something new to read."

"Daniel, that is so thoughtful of you," she said, putting her arms around him. He held her and they kissed, the sweet kiss of friends who happened to be married.

* * *

Jenny was each day at their house doing what needed to be done. She realized she was slower than before in going about her work. The main thing she wanted to do every day was to make sure that Daniel had a delicious supper. He praised her cooking so much, and she was happy when he ate up her food with gusto. Hard for her to believe he could eat so much and still not show any fat. Of course, she knew he worked long hours on their farm, especially now that planting season was almost upon them.

Then came two surprises. The first was a letter from her brother, Jeb. Jenny rued that he wrote so seldom. As she read, she learned that he had left the army at the end of the war, and had settled down with a farm girl he met while he was still in the army in Pennsylvania. He was sorry not to invite her to the wedding but explained that everything had happened so fast for them. In fact their wedding date was moved up so there was no time to send out invitations. He wished them all the best and expressed the hope that someday they would all be able to meet. The letter was signed

259

by both him and Abbie. *Obviously, his wife*, thought Jenny. She began thinking about what was in the letter and smiled. How glad she was to receive it and to know that Jeb was alright. Yet the fact that the wedding had been moved up suddenly made her wonder. Was a baby coming too soon? Someday, she hoped they would all get together. She wondered, did Jeb even know that their father had died? She would write to him.

A second surprise. Marcus appeared at her doorstep. Marcus and Angela. Jenny remembered that Marcus had been seeing Angela when she was a slave in Samantha's household. Marcus was wearing the blue pants of a Union soldier, but his overhanging shirt was of a homespun gray fabric.

"What a surprise!" said Jenny. "Come in."

"Thank you. Jenny," he said. Jenny sensed he felt uncertain on how he would be received. "I wanted to see you. You know, Jenny, I'm not a slave anymore."

Jenny looked at him and the woman with him. "I know, Marcus, and I'm glad for you."

Marcus flashed her a smile. "Do you remember Angela?"

Jenny's smile took in Angela. "She's the one you were seeing. You told me she was teaching you to read as I remember."

"Yes, she's the one," he said, looking at Angela with pride. Angela raised her eyes to Marcus. "She's going to be my bride," he added, his smile growing even larger.

Jenny looked at Angela, who was also wearing a smile, though she kept her head down. *A rather shy bride to be,* thought Jenny.

"I'm happy for you both," she said. "Come in, sit down. Let me get you something to drink."

"I've already been to your farm, and talked with your brother," said Marcus. "He told me you were married and how to find you. I'm sorry about your father."

Jenny looked at Marcus, brushing away a tear at the mention of her father. "Thank you, Marcus. He was too young to die, but God knows when our time is over."

"He was a good man. Jenny, there's more news. David is going to let me stay on with him, and we can work together like before, doing everything it takes to run the farm."

"Oh, Marcus, that is so wonderful! I know David could sure use the help."

"Angela and I will live in the shack for now, but I've already got plans for how I can enlarge it. Maybe someday we can have a real fine house. A place to raise our children."

Jenny's feelings were somehow strongly affected by what Marcus was saying. She could see that he too, like anyone, former slave or free man wanted the best for his family. Yet she didn't know just what to say to Marcus. In the back of her mind was the thought that Daniel might be able to help them when the time came to build a bigger house. She would talk to him. Finally, she said, "I'm so happy for you both."

Two years later

Jenny was so excited. At last, they were going to have what she wanted to have for the longest time. But the birth of two children, not one, had put everything off. Two was so much more work than one, and nursing them had left her tired. But now they were two years old and able to walk and even run. Oh, how she loved them, Abbie and Bryan. They were old enough to do some things on their own and yet they loved to be cuddled. Abbie in particular loved to follow her mother around, even trying to "help" when she was working in her nice sized vegetable garden. Jenny smiled thinking of her. In two or three years she really would be able to be helpful.

Putting down the dishcloth, she thought of the coming evening. They would be having a party, and she wanted everything to be right for it. She had already baked two apple pies, courtesy of her husband's parents' trees. Their own trees were still too small for fruit. She had also made sweetened apple cider which she thought most of the women would prefer. Daniel had bought a large bottle of whiskey from the store. She knew her friend Sarah was bringing something sweet and delicious, something right from her mother's stock of recipes.

Her brother was bringing an extra chair, and Daniel had already borrowed two from his parents' house. She wanted everyone to be able to sit down and enjoy each other's company. She was so glad Daniel had made their sitting room large, and though she had never had a large group over before, except for their wedding, she was hoping there would be room enough for all. Of course, she expected the men would end up going outside, where some of them would do their spitting. She didn't have a spittoon, and hoped never to have one in her house. She was glad Daniel had never taken up the nasty habit of tobacco chewing like so many men.

Jenny looked out and saw that the sun was starting its downward curve to the horizon. Plenty of daylight left, and she knew Daniel planned to return to the house early to clean up and to help with anything she needed done before their guests arrived.

* * *

Evening came, and now their house party was in full swing. She and her best friend Sarah were in the kitchen, preparing to bring out the apple pie to serve to all those who were mostly seated in the sitting room, talking and sometimes laughing. After they served the pie, Jenny went to light the wall candles, as it was beginning to get dark. Then she walked around the room, offering her friends Sarah's cookies. She smiled at each, truly glad that they had come.

Their friend Hank, who had married her best friend, Sarah, held their little girl on his lap with his good hand. Her other best friend, Clara, also was holding a small child while her daughter Emily stood beside her and her husband Tom looked on. Even Samantha was there with Rex, the banker. She had moved to the city with him, and Jenny heard they had a great house built near the edge of town. No children yet, though they had been married for almost three years.

Marcus was there as well, with his wife Angela, and they too had an infant child that Angela held close. With so many little ones, Jenny was glad that none at the moment were crying. Lastly, there was her brother, David, who Jenny was glad seemed more relaxed than usual. He was sitting next to Marcus, eyeing their little girl, Cammy. David hadn't married, and Jenny thought he probably never would. But he seemed to have formed a fine friendship with Marcus, their former slave, who was now his partner in working the farm.

As she was serving the cookies and listening to all the talk, Jenny's heart was lifted by all the warmth she felt with all those she knew and loved. The war years had been truly difficult, but now it was long over and peace reigned over the land. She thought to herself, we are a most wonderful group of people. A former Yankee captain who fell in love with a confederate girl, sitting down with those he fought against, and a former slave and his wife sharing and enjoying the company of those for whom he had previously toiled. A well off banker and his wife coming in from town to sit down with country folk. How wonderful, she thought to herself, that all could come to her and Daniel's house and enjoy each other's company. She hoped that from now on America could be that way, all living together in peace and harmony.

Jenny had returned to the kitchen to set her tray down, but she heard Daniel's voice above all the talk. "Rex, why don't you play for us? I think everyone would love to listen to your music." Jenny heard others second the motion, and when she came back into the sitting room, she was glad to see Rex, with Samantha at his side, taking his instrument out of its case.

He stood up and said, "I'm sure you all know this one. This is for Jenny. The title is, I dream of Jeannie with the light brown hair."

Jenny sat down to listen, and she was touched that his first song was for her. Nice of him to show appreciation to his host. Jenny smiled as he played.

"I dream of Jeanie with the light brown hair,
Borne, like a vapor, on the summer air;
I see her tripping where the bright streams play,
Happy as the daisies that dance on her way.
Many were the wild notes her merry voice would pour.
Many were the blithe birds that warbled them o'er:
Oh! I dream of Jeanie with the light brown hair,
Floating, like a vapor, on the soft summer air."

Next, he played the always loved and beautiful "Lorena." Jenny knew the history of the song. She recollected that it was composed by a poor preacher who was prevented from marrying his love because her wealthy relatives refused to allow her to marry below her station. A sad song, though it ended with the couple finally being together in the afterlife. All listened closely to the cloying words of the song, which Daniel had told her was a favorite tune played by military bands on both sides of the civil war.

After taking a short break to have a drink of whiskey, Rex began with a much sprightlier melody, the always loved favorite, "Dixie Land," which had a melody that seemed to invite dancing. Jenny took a quick look at Tom, the only Union man there, and was glad when he stood up to dance. She remembered seeing in a newspaper that even President Lincoln before his tragic death had said it was one of his favorite songs. Jenny looked up as Daniel came to her. She glanced down at Abbie and Byron at her knees, and was glad when her brother David quickly came and took them with him back to where he was seated.

"Love this song," said Daniel facing Jenny. "The best song ever played when we were marching and also a great song for dancing." He looked closely at his wife before taking her in his arms. "You look so pretty tonight."

"Really? With all the rushing around getting ready?"

"Especially. I know we were busy with everything, but now you look so sweet and just plain beautiful."

Jenny pulled closer to Daniel. He always seemed to know the words that went straight to her heart.

"I love you," she whispered into his ear.

He stopped dancing a moment to face her directly and kissed her, a kiss that wasn't long enough for Jenny. Sensing she wanted more, he whispered into her ear, "Later, when everyone is gone and the children are asleep."

Jenny smiled broadly at him, knowing by his expression just what he had in mind. Then she again said, tenderly. "I love you, Daniel."

Daniel smiled back at her and pulled her close, saying, "I'm thinking we are a special couple."

"Yes," she breathed. "I believe we are."

The true story

This novel is loosely based on the true experience of a young man and woman during the American Civil War. The girl's actual name is Hannah Cone, and she had eyes for Newton Scott ever since they were classmates in the one room school house. They were friends, but Newton didn't realize Hannah wanted to be more than just a friend. He had his heart set on another girl, Hattie. In the story, and in real life Hannah wrote to Newton faithfully the years that he was in the war. She very much feared for his life. Not until near the end of his service did she tell him that Hattie didn't wait until his discharge and had married another. When Newton came back from the army, Hannah was there for him. Hannah and Newton then courted, married, and lived together for 44 years, raising their five daughters and four sons. Of course, they also had many grandchildren. Hannah died in 1911 and Newton lived on until 1925 when he died at the age of 83.

I am impressed that in the modern age of so many changes, people fall in love, marry and live happily together for 30, 40, 50 and more years. Not that there aren't problems, for no two people will always see eye to eye. Yet long term couples deal with their situations and solve them. A tribute to those older couples who find and keep lasting love.

Check out Tom's other books on Amazon. Most are available in both paperback and eBook editions. To find them, look for **Tom Molnar** in books. Scroll down if Amazon has sponsored titles listed first. If you really enjoyed one, your thoughts in a short Amazon review would be greatly appreciated.